Adam could not recall seeing anything quite as grand as Cristiane MacDhiubh

enjoying her first sunrise on Bitterlee. Her eyes were wide, framed by gold-tipped lashes. Her lips were full and moist, and entirely too alluring.

His heart began to pound. The rushing surf was naught compared to the roaring in his own ears.

In the growing light he saw that she was covered from neck to toe by a thin linen kirtle, yet her enticing form would never be hidden from him again, no matter how well covered it might be. Burned into his memory was the way she'd looked in the firelight the morning he'd seen her undressed.

'Twould take only the slightest movement of his hand to pull her close, a trifling tip of his head to bring his lips into contact with hers.

And every fiber of his being demanded that he do so…!

MARGO MAGUIRE

Bride of the Isle

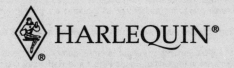

HARLEQUIN®

TORONTO • NEW YORK • LONDON
AMSTERDAM • PARIS • SYDNEY • HAMBURG
STOCKHOLM • ATHENS • TOKYO • MILAN • MADRID
PRAGUE • WARSAW • BUDAPEST • AUCKLAND

ISBN 0-373-29209-0

BRIDE OF THE ISLE

Copyright © 2002 by Margo Wider

This edition published by arrangement with Harlequin Books S.A.

Visit us at www.eHarlequin.com

Printed in U.S.A.

Available from Harlequin Historicals and
MARGO MAGUIRE

The Bride of Windermere #453
Dryden's Bride #529
Celtic Bride #572
His Lady Fair #596
Bride of the Isle #609

Please address questions and book requests to:
Harlequin Reader Service
U.S.: 3010 Walden Ave., P.O. Box 1325, Buffalo, NY 14269
Canadian: P.O. Box 609, Fort Erie, Ont. L2A 5X3

This book is dedicated to Amy Ho,
enthusiastic backpacker, avid reader,
daring volunteer and student extraordinaire.
May all your dreams and wishes come true.

Prologue

Isle of Bitterlee, in the North Sea
Autumn, 1299

"**N**ay, Penyngton," said Adam Sutton as he restlessly paced the length of the tower room. "I'll not marry again. And certainly not a Scot."

"But, my lord," Sir Charles Penyngton protested. He had license to speak to his lord in this manner, only because of his long term as seneschal here at Bitterlee. "You are still a young man. Merely one and thirty. And you have no heir. As Earl of Bitterlee, 'tis your duty to provide…"

Distractedly, Adam stopped at one of the long arrow loops in the wall of his solar and gazed out at the sea beyond. Bitterlee was a bleak, isolated place. According to legend, it had been named the "Isle of Bitter Life" by one of his ancient ancestors after his wife had ended her life here. 'Twas said that the name had changed over the years—been corrupted—to Bitterlee.

"*This* Scotswoman is perfect," Charles said. "Cristiane of St. Oln. She is accustomed to a harsh climate such as ours, and is said to be a hearty lass."

"Unlike Rosamund," Adam said starkly. He knew what Charles and the others assumed. That he still mourned the death of his wife, Rosamund. And that was true, to a point.

What they did not understand was that he had never cared for Rosamund the way he should have, nor did he mourn her loss. Oh, true enough, he mourned her death, as he would have mourned anyone in his household.

But Rosamund had never been part of his heart or his being. Adam did not care to think how he would feel if she had been more to him than she was.

Even now he did not understand how Rosamund's father could have given her to him in marriage. Surely the man had known Bitterlee's characteristics, its isolation, its harsh winters…its fierce beauty. Rosamund had been a delicate young lady who should have married a southern lord. She'd have fared so much better wed to a man with connections in London, a man with aspirations at court.

Instead, she'd come to this godforsaken isle. And languished here for nearly five years. She had despised it.

"My lord," Charles began again, but his words were cut off by a spate of coughing. When Adam would have seen to him, the seneschal waved him off, insisting he needed no help. "There are other considerations," he said, once he'd caught his breath. "Your daughter, my lord…she is in need of…"

Adam frowned and speared Charles with his steely gray gaze.

"Er…that is, Margaret needs… I mean to say Lady Margaret does not seem to—to *adjust,* my lord."

Adam had to admit that much was true. Though

everyone at Bitterlee had kept secret Rosamund's cause of death, Margaret was clearly traumatized by the loss of her mother. The child was a wraith. She looked nothing at all like a Sutton, and was as frail and wispy as her mother had been. Since Rosamund's death, Margaret had closed herself off. She never spoke, and she showed little interest in anything that would normally hold a child's attention.

And if Adam did not do something about Margaret's impassivity, she would not survive the year.

But marry a Scotswoman?

"Tell me more of this…Cristiane of St. Oln," he said, his words and attitude without hope. He'd recently suffered bitter losses at the hands of the Scots, and could not imagine bringing one of their kind to the isle. "But do not assume that I will go along with your plan."

Chapter One

The Village of St. Oln, Scotland
1300

Cristiane *inghean* Domhnall, the half-English daughter of Domhnall Mac Dhiubh, sat on a rocky promontory overlooking the crashing black waves of the North Sea. The wind had kicked up, and the clouds overhead were thick with moisture. Cristiane knew there would soon be a downpour.

'Twas no matter. There was a cave nearby if she needed to find shelter. She would not return to the village by choice. Lord knew she was barely tolerated in St. Oln since the death of her parents.

Cristiane stretched one arm out and opened her hand, letting it rest quietly beside her. Soon enough, a pair of soft gray kittiwakes approached, one more shyly than the other. The bold one stood looking at Cristiane, then hopped closer, eyeing the outstretched hand, tilting his head this way and that, viewing from all angles the bit of bread she held.

Cristiane smiled wistfully. 'Twas a game she'd played

for years, with the guillemots, the shags and the puffins that inhabited this place. The birds were unafraid of her. Wary, of course. She expected nothing less of them.

But soon she would see them no more. For her mother had arranged for her to be escorted to York, to the estate of her uncle. Elizabeth of York had known that Cristiane had no future here in St. Oln. When the lass's father, the Mac Dhiubh, had been killed in a skirmish with a neighboring clan, Elizabeth had begun to seek a new home for Cristiane.

She wondered if a likely husband existed in York. There was no one in St. Oln who'd have her, especially now that her father was gone. No Scotsman would willingly take a half-English wife.

Again, 'twas no matter. There was no one Cristiane was interested in having, either, though she did yearn for a man of her own, and a family. By the age of two and twenty, all the village lasses were well and truly wed, and some already had babes and wee children playing at their feet. It hurt Cristiane deeply to know that she was never to have the same pleasure.

She knew she was different from them. Besides being half-English, she had been reared separate from the other village children. Her father had tutored her in French and Latin, and she could read. She'd also had hours of leisure to explore the cliffs, and to learn the ways of the creatures that lived here.

'Twas no wonder none of the men of St. Oln would have her.

The brazen kittiwake approached, and with its long, sharp beak, quickly snatched the bit of bread from Cristiane's hand. Then it hopped away to pick at its food and argue with the shy one over it. Cristiane closed her hand. She pulled her knees up to her chest and wrapped her arms around them.

She knew she had only a day or two left at St. Oln before the earl's men came for her. 'Twas her mother's dearest desire that Cristiane leave this poor, unfriendly land where Elizabeth had been banished by her own father so many years before. Now that her mother was dead and buried, Cristiane was compelled to carry out her last wish.

'Twas a bittersweet promise. Cristiane had no regrets over leaving the village of St. Oln, but when she traveled to the strange land to the south, she would lose the comforting presence of the familiar birds and the wee creatures that nested on her beloved cliffs.

But she had no choice in the matter. Her English-bred mother had been wife to the Mac Dhiubh, and therefore tolerated as long as there was peace in the land, and the laird was alive. But the once-prosperous St. Oln had fallen on hard times. War with the English king and with neighboring clans had made the people suspicious of all outsiders, including Lady Elizabeth and even Cristiane *inghean* Domhnall. Her father's influence was no longer a force to be reckoned with.

Cristiane had always known she had ties in England. Her mother's elder brother was the Earl of Learick, away south in the land of York, and it had been her mother's last wish that Cristiane remove to his estates there. On her deathbed, Elizabeth had made her daughter promise to go with the earl's men when they came for her.

Cristiane had no idea what her mother's connection was to the Earl of Bitterlee, or why 'twas Bitterlee's men who would come for her. By the time her mother had spoken of these plans, she had been too ill to be questioned. It still seemed strange to Cristiane that it was not her uncle who was coming for her, to take her directly to York.

Ah, well...'twas too late now to learn any more from her mother. Elizabeth had rarely spoken of her family until the very end, so Cristiane knew little of them. Only that her mother had been disowned by her father all those years before, and sent away to St. Oln to marry Domhnall Mac Dhiubh. Domhnall had been chosen because her Yorkish uncle had known him in Paris years before.

Cristiane sighed as the first drops of rain touched her face. 'Twas spring and the weather was fine, but the rain was cold and biting. She gathered up her thin, ragged skirt and climbed to her shallow cave, where a few of her precious belongings were stored. Since no one ever came up here, Cristiane knew they were safe.

'Twas a strange provision, Adam thought, that the Mac Dhiubh girl be allowed to adjust to Bitterlee before he made her his wife. Still, he'd allowed Sir Charles to agree to it when he wrote to Elizabeth Mac Dhiubh. After all, it suited Adam's own purposes perfectly. This way, he would not be compelled to wed the girl if she were unsatisfactory.

Nay, 'twas lucky for him that her mother had insisted she be given time to adjust to Bitterlee before he even suggested they wed. 'Twould give him time to evaluate and adjust, as well.

Adam doubted the girl would be suitable, anyway. Even if she *were* half-English, she'd been raised here among the lowland Scots, barbaric people who had a decided mistrust of all things English. Clan Mac Dhiubh might even be responsible for harrying English border estates.

Adam did not need a bloodthirsty Scot for a wife.

The village of St. Oln was a poor one, he thought, as he and his escort dismounted in front of its ramshackle stone church. His leg, horribly butchered during the clash at Falkirk, pained him from sitting so long in the saddle. The cold rain hadn't helped, either. He stood still a moment as his two knights flanked him, then he limped to the church steps, glancing around him at the village.

Here lived the true victims of the wars, he thought, the people who remained after the battles, ragged and hungry and disillusioned. The villagers gathered their children and scampered into their huts in order to avoid the three hauberk-clad English knights who rode in, just as bold as could be.

"Be ye the Sassenach lord, then?" a deep masculine voice intoned from the open door at the top of the stairs.

Adam glanced up to find a grizzled old village priest looking down at him. He gave a quick nod and started up the steps.

"I thought ye'd have been here 'afore now," the old man said, turning to move out of the rain.

"If you would tell my men where to find Lady Elizabeth," Adam said, grateful to step into the relative warmth of the church, "they will fetch her and her daughter here."

They'd ridden past a broken-down, stone-and-timber keep that was clearly no habitable abode for anyone. Not even a Scot. So Lady Elizabeth must be housed in one of the hovels that lined the narrow lane. Adam hoped she was not too frail to travel, thus delaying their departure from this unpleasant town.

"Nay need fer that," the priest replied. "Everyone in St. Oln saw ye comin'—it willna be long before the lass arrives."

"And her mother?" Adam asked.

"Passed on a fortnight ago, God rest her soul," the priest replied, crossing himself as he spoke. "The lass is alone...*truly* alone now."

The cleric's words added a sharp chill to the cold Adam already felt clear to his bones. What now? The agreement was for Adam to escort Lady Elizabeth and her daughter to Bitterlee, where they would spend the summer. Then, if all was favorable, the lass would become his bride. If not, he would see that the two women were transported to York.

Now that she was alone, would Adam still be expected to take Lady Cristiane to Bitterlee? Did the agreement still hold?

"Come," the priest said, dodging the trickle of rain that dripped through the leaky roof. "Warm yer bones a bit." He led the three men to a brazier near the altar and held his own hands out to warm them. Adam and his two men did the same. "Cristiane canna remain here at St. Oln any longer. Now that both her father *and* her mother are gone, 'tis only a matter of time afore somethin' happens to the lass.

"I promised her dyin' mother I'd see that yer end of the bargain was met. Take her to yer island home, my Sassenach lord. For the lass's own good, and safety, take her to Bitterlee with ye."

Adam considered the priest's words in silence. He wondered what dire consequences would occur if Lady Cristiane remained here at St. Oln. Surely they would be minor, considering that the girl had been raised here. Her father had been head of the clan. The fact that she was half-English would be forgotten now that her mother was dead.

Harsh voices outside distracted Adam from his

thoughts, and he limped to the entrance of the church to
see what was afoot. The rain had let up, though there
was still a salty mist in the air. The people, mostly
women, had come out of their dwellings and were shout-
ing angrily at a pair of ragged people walking through
their midst, the man pulling the woman by the arm.

"Ah, 'tis Cristiane," the clergyman said, poking his
head out the door.

Adam's brows came together. The young woman
wore a dingy brown kirtle that even the lowliest peasant
would have shunned. She carried a small sack in one
hand and moved along quickly through the hostile
crowd. They shouted at her in their Scots tongue, and
although Adam did not understand what they were saying, there was no mistaking the intent.

Apparently they had not forgotten the lady was half-
English.

Through it all, Lady Cristiane held her head high, her
back straight, her bright eyes focused ahead. Her hair
was a glorious mass of shining red curls and her skin as
pale as a winter moon, with the exception of the bright
flush of color that bloomed on each cheek. Not one of
her features was particularly remarkable, but taken together, Cristiane Mac Dhiubh was a strikingly beautiful
woman.

She was not at all what he had imagined. He had not
expected to be so...susceptible to the woman and her
plight.

"Why are they so angry with her?" he asked, his
male instincts on full alert. 'Twas all he could do to keep
from rushing down into the crowd to rescue her.

The priest shrugged. "Who can really say?" he replied. "For bein' half-English? For bein' daughter of the

laird who failed to protect us from the raidin', blood-happy Armstrong clan?''

Someone pitched something—a stone, perhaps—that struck Cristiane. Suddenly a bright streak appeared on her high cheekbone, though she faltered only slightly and continued on her way in spite of the blow.

Adam could not stand still. Anger simmered as he descended the steps, moving more quickly than he had in months. When he pushed through the crowd and arrived at the lady's side, taking her arm possessively in his own, the jeering stopped and the villagers backed off. His fierce visage dared them to throw anything else.

He gave a quick glance to the lady, and watched as one sparkling tear spilled over thick, auburn lashes. Her chin trembled almost imperceptibly, but Adam sensed fierce pride in her, a solid wall that would not allow her to show any more vulnerability than this.

He closed his right hand over hers, tucking her arm close to his waist, and proceeded to the church.

Under other circumstances, Cristiane's knees would have gone weak at the sight of the stunning knight who came to her rescue in front of One-eye Mòrag's cottage. The mere touch of his bare hand on her own was enough to make her tremble in awe. As it was, however, she refused to buckle in the face of the overt hostility of her father's people.

In truth, she could not blame them for their malice. For it had been English raiders who had damaged the clan, making the Mac Dhiubhs vulnerable to the Armstrong attack that had killed so many more men, along with her father. The people of St. Oln had no reason to be sympathetic to the daughter of a Sassenach woman.

Cristiane might wish for things to be different, for

acceptance and respect, but that was not to be. She was the daughter of an Englishwoman, and the people of St. Oln would never accept her. She reminded herself again that she was fortunate, indeed, to have the freedom to leave.

'Twas not until she began to climb the steps with her knight rescuer that she noticed his limp. A sidelong glance revealed his strong jaw clamped tightly against the discomfort of each step. They made it up to the church doors without mishap, and the knight ushered her inside.

"Cristy," Father Walter said familiarly, taking her hand when the knight released her. "Are ye injured, lass?"

"Nay, Father," she replied quietly, touching her cheek with two fingers. "Merely bruised, I think."

With his hands devoid of gauntlets, Cristiane's knight—for that was how she thought of him—took a cloth and wiped gently at her cheek, removing the dirt and a small speck of blood that oozed from the scrape.

Cristiane stood still and searched the man's eyes. Dark gray they were, as stormy as the sky above the thrashing sea. His brows were even darker, caught together. in a frown as he dabbed at her tiny wound. His nose was straight and his lips full but well-defined. A cruel scar marred the perfection of his jaw, and Cristiane wondered what battle, what terrible wound, had caused such frightful damage to his otherwise perfect face.

If her Yorkish uncle ever found her a husband, Cristiane hoped he would be something like this man who stood, so tall and broad shouldered, before her. Many were the times she had dreamed of someone like him, with strong, but gentle hands, intense, fascinating eyes.

Someone who had the prowess to keep her safe…. Cristiane had never thought her dream could be real.

Until now.

"My lady," Father Walter said more formally, "these gentlemen are here to escort ye to Bitterlee, as your mother wished."

"Aye, Father," Cristiane replied, uncomfortable with the turn her thoughts had taken. "So I gathered."

When the priest addressed Cristiane's knight, her surprised eyes flew to the stranger. "M'lord Bitterlee," Father Walter said. "This is Lady Cristiane Mac Dhiubh."

This was the lord? This man, for whom she felt an attraction unlike anything she'd ever experienced before? Cristiane swallowed against the sudden dryness in her throat.

She reined in her wayward thoughts and realized she did not know whether to be flattered or distressed that the English lord had come for her himself. She had never met a high chief before. She'd met no one, in fact, who had more power or influence than her own father. And Domhnall had merely been the Mac Dhiubh, chieftain of this small clan. He'd been more a scholar than a leader, and certainly not a warrior, though he'd done his best to defend her, as well as the clan.

Cristiane cringed as she considered her appearance. Her hair was unbound and uncovered, her feet bare and her kirtle a mere scrap of poor homespun that her mother had received in trade, along with food and a meager shelter, for their own finer garments.

She remembered the fine clothes her mother had worn years before, when Cristiane was still a small child. And she recalled the snippets of information Elizabeth had told about her home in York and her one visit to the English court.

Cristiane knew with certainty that she looked nothing like the "lady" Lord Bitterlee must have expected to find.

To his credit, he showed no disdain—although Cristiane could well imagine what he must think of her. She curled her toes and tried to hide her cut and bruised feet under her hem.

"Lady Cristiane," Bitterlee said, tipping his head slightly. "We will depart St. Oln within the hour. Please make ready to leave."

"Aye, m'lord," she said. "I'm ready now."

She kept her chin up as she replied, knowing how foolish a barefoot noblewoman who carried all her possessions in one small sack would appear to him. She could not allow his opinion to matter, however. She had said her farewells to her beloved cliffs, and now 'twas time to move on.

She could not bring herself to ask any of the questions that burned the back of her throat, either. Cristiane was too ashamed to draw any more of his attention to herself.

"What're yer plans, m'lord?" Father Walter asked.

"We should cross the Tweed by nightfall, then we'll camp just south of it."

The old priest nodded. "Aye, 'tis a good idea to get yerselves to English soil," he said. "But how will Cristiane travel? Ye might have noticed we have no horses here in St. Oln."

Chapter Two

He'd thought he could do it, but 'twas not possible. He could not take an uncouth, butchering Scot to wife. His experience at Falkirk, coupled with Cristiane's utter unsuitability—her hair, her dress, her speech—nay, he had no choice but to find himself an English wife.

Still, Adam was not about to let Lady Cristiane ride with either of his men. So she sat before him on his destrier, her hips pressed to his loins, her back colliding with his chest at every bump in the road.

They rode for hours this way, and kept near the coast whenever possible, though the terrain sometimes made it necessary to move inland.

After a few hours, Cristiane's posture began to slip, and she leaned into him. Without thinking, Adam closed his arms around her more securely, to keep her from falling. He had no objection to her sleeping as they rode, but he did object mightily to the possibility of her falling.

She was warm and soft, and her scent made him think of the outdoors and the sea. A few light freckles dusted her nose and cheeks, but they seemed to make her flawless complexion even more perfect. If that were possible.

The structure of her bones and the fine veins of her graceful neck enticed him, while the steady pulse beating there fascinated him more than it should.

Her mouth was slightly parted in slumber, her generous lips moving a bit with each breath. Her unruly hair brushed across his face, eliciting a response he had not experienced since before Falkirk. He wanted her.

'Twas impossible. She was as far from being an acceptable wife as a barbaric infidel woman from the east. Cristiane Mac Dhiubh did not even vaguely resemble a gentle English lady, though she was of noble birth. Adam would carry her to Bitterlee, see that she was outfitted more appropriately to her station, then send her with an escort to her uncle in York.

'Twas unfortunate that Cristiane was so damnably Scottish, or he might have considered marrying her. But her fiery red hair and freckled skin were only the most visible aspects of her Scottishness. Even though she spoke with more gentle a burr than the other inhabitants of St. Oln, she dressed like a savage, with feet as bare as the poorest villein in the village.

Nor did Cristiane seem at all a meek or pious sort of woman. He had to admire the fortitude and courage she'd shown amidst the hostile crowd at St. Oln, but those attributes were neither highly desirable nor necessary in a wife. He could not imagine that she'd been tutored in any of the finer womanly arts, so what kind of mother would she make to his little daughter? What kind of example?

A poor one, without a doubt.

In her favor, she did not seem dull or ignorant. She was well-spoken and held herself with the proud bearing of the noblest Englishman. Her blue eyes were bright with intelligence and interest, though tinged with sadness at leaving her home. Or even more likely, she suffered a lingering sadness at the recent loss of her parents.

Cristiane muttered in her sleep, and as he looked down at her, she licked her lips and spoke softly. Though he could not quite hear what she said, he caught the final muttered words, "...*in vacuo.*"

Latin?

He shook his head to clear it. Surely no untutored Scotswoman spoke Latin in her sleep. He must have been mistaken.

Yet he considered the translation of those words: alone. Isolated. Lady Cristiane was probably more alone than she'd ever been in her life, with her father's death and her mother's more recent demise.

"The river, m'lord," Sir Elwin called from his position up ahead. He slowed his pace to allow Adam to catch up. "Would we be crossing now, or waiting until morning?"

Adam looked ahead and saw that the River Tweed was in sight. 'Twas nearly dusk and he felt a strong urge to set his feet on English soil as soon as possible. There were no towns or villages nearby on either side, so they ought to be safe in the sheltered forest on the other side of the river. Adam decided they would camp near the river tonight, then move on in the morning.

"We cross."

Sir Elwin spurred his horse and rode ahead with Sir Raynauld, leaving Adam alone with Cristiane, who remained soundly asleep. He indulged himself with her softness for another moment more, cradling her, going so far as to span her waist with both his hands, spreading his thumbs to the forbidden territory at the base of her rib cage.

She made a low, unconscious sound that made Adam

think of intimate pleasures. He shuddered with a hunger he knew he would never appease with this woman, then spurred his horse toward the river's edge.

Cristiane knew she must have been dreaming. Surely she had not felt Lord Bitterlee's hands caressing her body as if he had the right to do so. 'Twas only the aftereffect of her foolish ruminations when she'd first seen him in St. Oln that made her imagine how it would feel to be possessed by such a man.

Since the river crossing, Lord Bitterlee had been nothing but solicitous and respectful of her, seeing to her comfort, helping his men set up a tent for her use. And he kept his distance. Clearly, she was not at all what he expected of a high-born Englishwoman.

She could not blame him. She felt more like the commonest of peasants than a true noblewoman. Less, even. In St. Oln, even the lowliest of women owned shoes.

Life had changed drastically after the death of her father. He had never had the kind of wealth possessed by some chieftains, but Cristiane and her mother had been comfortable, if not entirely accepted by the townspeople. They were tolerated, but not much more.

'Twas no wonder Elizabeth had sickened and died within months after losing Domhnall's protection.

Cristiane looked around her. She was sorry she had slept through so much of the journey so far, and promised herself to do better on the morrow. After all, she would never travel this way again, and she wanted to see and savor all of the country through which she traveled. Once she reached York, and the home of her uncle, 'twas doubtful she would ever leave.

While the knights went fishing to catch their evening meal, Cristiane walked down to the river's edge and waded into the shallows to wash. Then she found a quiet place to sit and watch the waterfowl as the sun set over her shoulder. She saw plenty of familiar birds—the proud razorbills sticking out their fat white chests, a few guillemots and some squawking herring gulls.

But the birds that most fascinated her were of a breed she had never seen before. They were huge white waterfowl, with long, graceful necks. A pair of full-grown birds swam before a line of smaller ones. 'Twas a family, or at least it seemed that way to Cristiane. The king and queen of the river. Closing her mind to the uncertainty of her future, she sat back and observed the majestic birds as they made their way downriver.

"You should not stray so far from camp, Lady Cristiane," said Lord Bitterlee, startling her from her thoughts. He had removed his chain hauberk and wore a plain blue tunic over dark chausses. His casual mode of dress did not make him any less appealing, though his tone of voice betrayed irritation with her.

Cristiane pulled the hem of her kirtle over her naked feet and looked out at the river. The feelings he aroused in her made her restless, even when he wasn't nearby.

"Aye, m'lord," she said contritely, "I'll not do it again, if 'tis bothersome to you."

"'Tis for your own safety," he said gruffly, "not for any particular convenience to me. Sir Raynauld is back at camp. He and Sir Elwin are cooking the trout they caught."

"Then I'd best go back with you," Cristiane said as she began to rise, keeping her bare feet out of sight. Lord Bitterlee gave her a hand and helped her to stand. The heat of his flesh on her own nearly made her jump, but she did her best to ignore the unwelcome quivering that came over her when he touched her.

"M'lord," she said, intent on distracting herself from the foolish thoughts crossing her mind. She took her hand away from his and pointed downstream. "Do you know what those bonny white birds are called?"

He turned and glanced at the birds she wondered about, then looked back with an expression that reminded her of her father's, when she'd said something incredibly foolish. "Why, they're swans," Lord Bitterlee said, as if he were stating the obvious. "Two parents and their brood following."

"Parents?" Cristiane asked. They began walking through a thick stand of woods, toward the campsite. "You mean, these birds rear their young? Together?"

"I believe so." He shrugged. "I've never really thought much on it."

"Ah," she said, glancing back at the swans. She would have to remember everything about them, for she doubted such birds were very common.

Cristiane realized how hungry she was when the delectable aroma of cooked trout assailed her nose. She hurried up the path toward their camp, but stepped on a sharp stone that threw her off balance. Lord Bitterlee kept her from falling by quickly throwing an arm about her waist.

"Are you all right?" he asked, his voice deep and caring.

"Aye," she replied, more breathlessly than she liked. She pulled away once again, and nearly ran up the path.

Adam could not imagine that the woman had never heard of swans till now. Her life must have been even more parochial than he'd first thought. Which would account for her coarse clothing and bare feet, as well as the unkempt mop of her hair—glorious though it was.

He watched Cristiane as she ate with her fingers, pulling tender meat away from the bones adroitly, delicately licking the juice from her fingers. She tipped her mug and drank slowly, the muscles of her throat working as she swallowed. Adam lowered his eyes against her unconsciously arousing display and tried to ignore the tightening of his body in response. He concentrated on his own meal before him.

These intemperate reactions would have to stop. They had at least two more days of travel before they arrived at Bitterlee, and they would be sharing close quarters until then. Very close quarters. He'd made a solemn promise to Cristiane's mother either to wed her or to see her safely escorted to her uncle in York. Since he'd already decided he would not wed her, lust had no part in this.

When he looked at Cristiane Mac Dhiubh again, she was standing. She had taken the tin plates from Raynauld and Elwin, and was coming toward him.

The stride of her legs, and their movement against the coarse cloth of her kirtle, aroused him in ways he refused to consider. She was just a young girl, he told himself. Inexperienced, untried. His masculine appetites may have suddenly returned unbidden, but Adam knew he had no business centering them on Cristiane Mac Dhiubh. She was not at all the kind of wife he needed or wanted. Nor was she some cheap strumpet....

He would set Charles Penyngton the task of finding a more appropriate wife—an English lady—as soon as he returned to Bitterlee.

"Your plate, m'lord?" Cristiane asked quietly. "I'll rinse it with the others in the stream."

The setting sun was at his back, and it illuminated her eyes as she spoke. Her lashes were thick, dark near the roots and sun-kissed gold at the ends. Though her gaze was direct, she looked at him almost shyly, as if she knew how unsatisfactory he considered her, while she waited for him to reply.

He stood and handed her the plate, then stalked away with his ungainly gait into the woods. He had more important things to consider than the length of Cristiane's eyelashes or the berry-red softness of her lips.

As Penyngton had repeatedly said over the last few weeks, Bitterlee needed a mistress. Little Margaret needed a mother. Adam knew that no one could replace his wife in that respect, even though Rosamund had never been very attentive to their daughter.

However, common sense told him that the little girl needed someone who would care for her in the manner of a mother—accepting her faults, disciplining her with kindness and tolerance. And until he found the right person, Adam intended to become more of a parent to his child.

He knew that Margaret's life depended upon it.

She had become little more than a silent skeleton since Rosamund's death, with wide, hollow eyes. Her nurse, Mathilde, could not seem to draw the child out of her cocoon of grief. Little Margaret scarcely left her chamber, except to venture into the castle chapel to spend excessive amounts of time in prayer.

Adam did not need to know much about children to understand that this was not typical behavior for a five-year-old child. He would do something about all that when he returned to Bitterlee.

Preoccupied, Adam limped back to camp, where the men were setting out their bedrolls near the fire.

"Has Lady Cristiane returned from the river?"

"Nay, my lord," Sir Raynauld replied. "I was just thinking of going down there to see if all is well."

"Never mind," Adam said. "I'll go."

He walked quietly down the path toward the river, caught up in his thoughts about his daughter and his unwelcome attraction for Cristiane Mac Dhiubh, until he caught sight of Cristiane near the water. She stood perfectly still, facing the sunset, the skirt of her kirtle rippling slightly in the breeze. One hand held back her hair; the other was outstretched.

And at the end of that hand stood a red deer, touching Cristiane's fingers with its nose.

Chapter Three

Adam did not move.

Stunned by the sight before him, he stood stock-still and watched as the doe sniffed Cristiane's hand and then licked it. Cristiane said nothing that Adam could hear, but soon turned her hand and gave the deer a gentle rub on the underside of its chin.

The animal suddenly looked up and saw Adam. He watched as panic spread through the doe's body and it dashed away.

He let out the breath he hadn't realized he'd been holding.

"Ah, m'lord," she said, turning to see what had frightened the deer. "I was just about to—"

"Lady Cristiane," he said, flustered, "that was a deer just now. A—a deer standing next to you, touching your…"

"Aye." Cristiane nodded as she crouched down to wash her hands in the stream. "Too young to know any better, though she's a bonny one."

Adam was thunderstruck. The doe had known well enough to flee when it had seen Adam. Besides, young or old, he'd never heard of a wild deer approaching a person in this manner. How had Cristiane done it?

"My lady," he said. But then she stood and looked at him with those clear blue eyes and he forgot what he was going to say. Or ask.

'Twas ever so pleasant to have a man—a handsome, well-bred man—come to escort her back to camp. The knights had set up a lovely, spacious tent for her, and Lord Bitterlee explained that they had expected to be escorting both her and her mother to Bitterlee, then to York.

And so it was that Cristiane Mac Dhiubh settled down for the night, comfortably, with thoughts of her mother and better times running through her mind.

Morning dawned bright and sunny. They rode again as they had the day before, with Cristiane seated sidesaddle ahead of Lord Bitterlee. She was certain that every time he looked down, he noticed her bare feet protruding from the edge of her kirtle. At least they were clean now, she thought, still embarrassed to be without shoes.

They'd been taken from her in St. Oln, along with most of her other meager possessions. Cristiane would not have cared, except that now she would arrive in Bitterlee looking no better than the poorest villein. She had never thought of herself as overly proud, but this lack of shoes was one thing she could not abide. Yet there was no way to remedy it.

The day passed uneventfully, though rain threatened as they traveled farther south. Part of the time they rode along the cliffs above the sea. Sometimes the track took them through wooded lands, where Cristiane made note of the new green growth everywhere, and the small animals that darted and scurried to hide from the human intruders.

When dusk approached, she wondered if they would soon stop to camp, for she was weary and it had begun to drizzle. Her back and legs ached from the long hours on horseback. Eventually they came upon a village of sorts. Nay, she amended, 'twas not quite a village, but merely an inn with a few cottages nearby.

She hoped Lord Bitterlee intended to spend the night here. They rode into the yard and saw that a number of horses were already tethered there. Voices carried from the inn, and by the sound of it, the place was crowded. Lord Bitterlee dismounted, then turned to help Cristiane down.

"Shall I go inquire about rooms, my lord?" Sir Elwin asked as he tied his horse to a post.

Lord Bitterlee nodded. "Stay close to me," he said to Cristiane. "While we're so near the border, there are risks. Especially for you, but for us as well."

Cristiane nodded. Hostilities ran hot along the Scottish border, and though they were actually on English soil, she assumed that strangers would not be trusted. She almost wished they'd stopped somewhere along the road, where she could spend the night in the tent they'd brought along for her. She would have felt a great deal safer.

Resigned to staying here, where raucous voices disturbed the peace of the day's end, she drew close to Lord Bitterlee and waited for his knight to return.

There was a chill in the air, and Cristiane shivered. Then she felt Bitterlee's arm go around her shoulders, and he pulled her closer. The fine mail of his hauberk should have been cold, but Cristiane could feel his heat radiating through the steel.

'Twas a long time since she'd felt so protected. Not since the sudden and violent death of her father had anyone helped her with life's difficulties. She'd been so alone since her mother's illness...Cristiane blinked away the sudden moisture in her eyes, brought on by the kindness of Adam Sutton and the strength of his arm around her.

"M'lord," Sir Elwin said, "the men here are a rough lot. I don't know that it would be wise to take Lady Cristiane inside."

"Are there any rooms?" he asked as he glanced quickly at Cristiane. She was wet and shivering.

"Only one," he said with a sigh. "I told the landlord to hold it."

Lord Bitterlee nodded. "Is there a back entrance?"

"Through the kitchen, m'lord," he said. "We might be able to get her ladyship in with no one the wiser."

She felt the lord's hand at her lower back as he urged her to follow Sir Elwin. He followed close behind, while Sir Raynauld remained to deal with the horses.

There was a haze of smoke in the kitchen, and a multitude of aromas hit her at once. Mingled with the smell of smoke were the strong odors of food, grease and ale. A raucous crowd had taken over the common room. Men's voices were raised with excitement and lust over an upcoming raid.

"We'll have to climb a staircase adjacent to the main hall, m'lord," Elwin said, keeping his voice low. "'Tis the only place where her ladyship might be exposed to view. But there is no other way up the stairs."

"We'll flank her on the way up, and guard her from sight," Bitterlee said. "Move quickly, my lady."

He shielded her from the crowd below, but someone managed to catch sight of her and called out that there was a woman on the stair. Cristiane cringed with fear as Adam propelled her up the remaining steps. Then, along with Elwin, he turned and drew his sword.

Four men rushed them, drawing their own weapons, but Adam planted a booted foot on one man's chest and shoved, knocking him back down the stairs, and two others with him. Adam turned to climb the stairs again, but more of the revelers closed in on them.

Quickly, Adam and Elwin engaged in battle. Swords clanged. Men grunted and cursed. Blood flowed.

And Cristiane's limbs were paralyzed. She could move neither forward nor back, for she saw before her eyes the battle in which her father had been killed. She felt dizzy and weak. Her ears buzzed and hummed, shutting out the sounds of aggression just below her.

She went numb.

Then, as now, she had watched from a dark corner in the main staircase of the keep as her father had fought to save her from the Armstrong enemy. She had seen Domhnall speared through his chest, and had watched his life's blood flow from him, spreading a dark stain on the landing and down the steps.

"Cristiane!"

Her father had managed to wound his killer, so the man had retreated. He'd left Cristiane alone, but she had cowered there in her dark refuge until all had gone quiet around her. The acrid scents of burning buildings and burned animal flesh filled her nose, her mind. The sight of her father's blood dripping down the steps—

"*Cristiane!*"

Lord Bitterlee's commanding voice finally penetrated her hazy consciousness and she shook her head. She blinked her eyes in confusion and tried to turn her attention to him.

But she still felt bound by the same sluggishness that had plagued her for weeks after her father's death. Cristiane knew she should be moving, following Lord Bitterlee's directions, getting to safety. Yet her legs would not obey his commands, nor would her body allow her to turn away from the battle being waged before her.

"Cristiane! Move! There must be a room—ugh!" One of the men butted Adam's midsection with his head, and Adam slammed the flat of his sword down on him, throwing him off.

Raynauld arrived and fought his way to Adam's side. Adam turned quickly, took two steps at once and gathered Cristiane in his arms. Seemingly without effort, he threw her over one shoulder and shoved his way into a room, slamming and barring the door behind him.

A pathetic little fire in the grate gave sufficient illumination to keep Adam from falling over anything. Quickly, he set Cristiane on the bed in the corner of the room.

"Are you all right?" he asked.

She did not respond to his question, so he knelt in front of her and took both her hands. They were like ice, and she was shaking, but Adam knew better than to think Cristiane was not as barbaric as every bloody Scot he'd encountered at Falkirk. She might be half-English, but she'd been raised among them.

Cristiane's silence perplexed him, however, and he started to rub her hands between his own as he kept one ear attuned to the noises on the stairs and below. He did not think any of the attackers had been killed, but blood had flowed. And Cristiane's reaction had been one of horror. Looking at her colorless visage, he could no longer deny it.

God's cross! Why had they stayed here, knowing

what was brewing within? They could very well have spent another night out-of-doors, with Cristiane safely lodged in the canvas tent. What difference was a bit of rain? Adam and his knights had lived through worse.

"'Tis over now, Cristiane," he said gently. "You're safe now."

"Aye," she said quietly, looking up at him blankly. The red scrape on her cheek stood out in sharp contrast to the paleness of her skin. "I know."

"You'll sleep here, and my men and I will keep watch."

"All right."

"Can you...er, your clothes are wet," he said. "They'll need to come off. I'll just step out for a mo—"

Cristiane grabbed his hand. "Dinna go!" she whispered, sounding more Scottish than he'd noted till now. "Please. I..."

Adam ran a hand through his damp hair and tried to think of a way to calm her.

"I'll be here...just inside the door," he finally said as he extricated his hand from her grasp. "I'll turn my back and you can get undressed."

He heard her swallow. Adam had not been told what had happened in Cristiane's village, but he'd seen the ravages of recent battle. Judging by her reaction just now, Cristiane Mac Dhiubh may have been in the thick of it. Mayhap even a half-Scot would be unable to witness that kind of butchery without being affected by it.

He stood in front of the grate and faced the fire, listening as she pulled out laces and slipped her kirtle from her body. As articles of clothes continued dropping to the floor, his body reacted swiftly, shocking him with its intensity. He had not felt such a wave of pure lust since... He could not remember.

He wondered again if this had been such a good idea. "M'lord?" she said. "'Tis safe to turn now."

She appeared small and vulnerable in the bed, under a thick layer of blankets. At the moment, it was difficult to think of her as a Scot. Or even as the woman who had walked so proudly through the hostile villagers in St. Oln.

She was just a woman now, frightened and vulnerable.

Against all rational thought, he wanted to gather her up in his arms to reassure and comfort her.

Instead, he picked up the clothing next to the bed and spread it out before the fire to dry. He hoped the raiders below stairs did not decide to pursue the woman they knew was here, rather than go on their intended raid.

Still, Lady Elizabeth of York had been correct when she'd written that her daughter was a hearty lass. Lady Cristiane had lost both her mother and father in a short span of time. Her village had showed naught but hostility toward her when she'd left, and she'd been forced into the company of three strange, foreign men who had carried her far away from all that she'd ever known. She was holding up remarkably well.

Adam walked to the other side of the room and sat down with his back against the door. He lay his sword on the floor next to him and tried to relax. The forced intimacy they'd shared during the journey so far had been difficult. Sharing a horse, holding her body close to his during the long daylight hours, breathing in her fresh, womanly scent, having his nose and chin constantly caressed by wisps of her hair…Adam hadn't thought it could get any worse.

Yet as he sat gazing at her clothing, Adam knew that every stitch she possessed was drying by the fire. And he wished the thought hadn't occurred to him. The last thing he wanted was to begin imagining beautiful Cristiane Mac Dhiubh naked.

Sometime during the night, Cristiane heard a light tap at the door. 'Twas Raynauld, informing Adam that all was quiet down below, and the raiders had either left or were passed out from drink in the great room of the inn.

Adam must have been awake all night, she thought as she watched him pick up his saddle pack. He stayed as quiet as possible, taking a blanket from the pack and spreading it out near the fire.

He added a few bits of wood, then stood and untied the leather laces of his hauberk. He pulled it over his head, keeping only his light linen shirt on. Then Lord Bitterlee wrapped himself in his blanket and settled down to sleep.

He'd looked weary. And with good reason, Cristiane thought. He'd stayed on guard most of the night, sitting by the door with his legs outstretched. His hair was disheveled and there was a dark shadow of beard on his jaw. He was as handsome a man as she'd ever seen, even tousled as he was.

Cristiane's heart fluttered. She'd been completely defenseless—overcome by the stark memories of her father's death—when Lord Bitterlee had rescued her and carried her to safety. Then he'd kept a vigil all night to see that she stayed safe.

Not only was he heroic, he was also a man of honor. He could easily have taken advantage of her vulnerable state. But he hadn't. He had calmed and reassured her when she was caught deep in the memories of the past, then he'd gallantly turned his back so that she could undress. What other man would have done so much for her?

She knew so little of men. Her father had kept her far removed from his warriors, and the people of St. Oln had had no fondness for her, so she'd spent little time among them. She did know, however, that 'twas the rare warrior who had the patience to deal with her so carefully. Most would likely have stashed her in this little room and returned to the thick of battle.

She preferred Adam's way.

'Twas difficult to think of him as Lord Bitterlee now. The sound of his title was too imposing, too harsh. Nay, Adam was a kind and considerate man, a chivalrous knight, a noble warrior. Whether she would ever be impertinent enough to call him Adam, she did not know. But in her mind, he would never be the lord of Bitterlee to her again.

Chapter Four

It had to be close to dawn, by the sound of the birdsong outside. Adam didn't think it was the birds that woke him, but soft whispery sounds in the room itself. He was too tired to move, and his leg was stiff and aching. He managed to open one eye, however, and caught sight of Cristiane Mac Dhiubh.

His mouth went dry at the sight of her.

She had gathered up her clothes and was in the process of dressing, but she had not gotten far enough to impede his view of her soft, feminine curves.

She was lovely. Her hair cascaded in gentle curls over her shoulders, teasing the naked tips of her breasts, but leaving enough bare flesh for Adam to appreciate their soft fullness. Her legs were well-shaped and strong, and the feminine V where they met was shielded by an enticing russet shadow.

It made him ache to look at her this way, to know what lay concealed under her ugly brown kirtle.

As he watched, she pulled on a ragged underkirtle that reached only her hipbones, leaving that most intriguing part of her delightfully, seductively bare. The laces were open, so most of her torso was exposed, as well. He must have groaned inadvertently, for she gasped and moved to cover herself.

Slowly, he dragged his eyes up the length of her gloriously blushing body and caught her own heavy-lidded gaze. He had no doubt that she was as aroused as he, but painfully embarrassed by her nakedness. Neither the tattered underkirtle nor her arms managed to cover her sufficiently.

"Your pardon, my lady," he said as he stood. His grimace was due only in part to the stiffness of his wounded leg. "I will leave you to your privacy."

Cristiane stood rooted to the floor as Adam retreated through the door, then she threw on her clothes as fast as she could. She was not going to be caught unawares again!

Yet as she tied the laces of her kirtle, she realized that she had not disliked having Adam look at her. In reality, she had enjoyed the look of appreciation in his eyes. Still, it was terribly embarrassing to have her most private parts exposed to his view.

She wondered if it would have seemed so embarrassing if Adam had also been unclothed. He was broad shouldered and lean hipped, though he had the powerful legs of a horseman. She wondered how 'twould feel to be naked with a man. Unconsciously, Cristiane moistened her lips and speculated that this was one of the pleasures husbands and wives shared. She knew so little of such things. Her parents had been respectful of each other, but Cristiane had never witnessed any special intimacy between them.

Voices in the inn yard below distracted her from these intriguing thoughts, and Cristiane quickly finished lacing her kirtle. She rolled up Adam's blanket and stuffed it into his saddle pack, then opened the door to leave.

She drew up short when she considered what had happened on the stair the previous night. Would it be safe to go downstairs? Unwilling to suffer a repeat of that incident, she turned back and sat down on the bed to wait for Adam to return. Then she heard footsteps approaching.

"Lady Cristiane."

"Aye, Sir Raynauld," she said, sagging with relief as she recognized the friendly voice. She opened the door to Adam's knight and he took the pack from her. She could not help but wonder where Adam was.

"The landlord's wife has prepared a meal for us," he told her. "If you're ready, I'll take you down and you can break your fast."

"Thank you."

They walked into the common room, where the landlord was setting bowls on the table. Cristiane glanced around in search of Adam, but he was not in sight.

With a sigh, she sat down at the table and began to eat.

Adam returned to the inn, pleased with his purchases. The villagers had been happy to take his coin for their goods, and he'd found a few small novelties to take home to Margaret. He'd also found a woman willing to part with her shoes, since her husband was a tanner skilled in shoe craft.

These he intended to give to Cristiane before they left for the last stretch of their journey to Bitterlee. He had seen how her lack of shoes humbled her, and when the opportunity to acquire a pair had presented itself, he'd not hesitated.

He'd kept his mind thoroughly occupied since his hasty departure from Cristiane's chamber, fully aware that he had to do all in his power to avoid any more intimacies with her. This morning's interlude had clearly demonstrated how susceptible he was to her charms, and he knew he had no business fostering any further attraction between them.

For Lady Cristiane had not been oblivious to the heat of the moment, either. He'd seen confusion in her eyes, and embarrassment as well. But underneath it all was the subtle excitement of arousal. And knowing that she felt the same surge of lust made him nearly groan aloud.

Adam did not think he could endure riding several hours more on horseback with Cristiane's hips wedged between his legs and her back pressed against his chest. And though it cost a pretty penny, he convinced the landlord to part with an ancient mule in his stable. Cristiane would ride separately the rest of the way to Bitterlee.

"Good morn, my lord," Sir Elwin said as Adam strode into the inn yard.

Adam nodded. "Has Lady Cristiane broken her fast yet?"

"She has, my lord," Elwin replied as he continued saddling his horse. "She's still inside."

Adam continued on into the inn, where he found Cristiane alone in the common room. One glance told him it was a mistake to look at her.

She looked almost ethereal with the morning sunshine glancing off the bright highlights of her hair. She had just stood up from the table and gathered her oddly shaped satchel against her breasts when she looked up and met his eyes. Her lips were parted, her nostrils slightly flared. Neither of them moved for a moment, though Cristiane blushed delightfully.

She was remembering.

Even now that she was shabbily, but decently, dressed, Adam could not keep his eyes from roving over the length of her, or forget the alluring picture she'd made that morning in their room. At the time, her Scottish blood had not mattered in the least.

He cleared his throat and set his package on the table.

"I found these for you," he said.

Cristiane looked down at the bundle, then back at Adam with questions in her eyes. "What...?"

"Just a..." he began, then shrugged. "Open it."

She bit her lip and unwrapped the string from the package, then pulled the burlap apart. "Shoes," she whispered, gazing up at him. Her eyes grew suspiciously bright, and though she blinked quickly, there was no mistaking the sheen of moisture there.

Not one tear fell, though—for which Adam would be eternally grateful. Yet her humble gratitude made his belly clench with some strange emotion.

"The tanner is a shoemaker of some skill," Adam said as he watched Cristiane lift one of the shoes to admire it.

"I...I had shoes at home..." she said. Her voice was soft and wistful, and she sounded more English than Scottish. "Gylys the Bald took them from me the day my mother died. He said his w-wife had greater need of them than I..."

Adam controlled his reaction to her revelation. He was appalled to think that a mere villager would presume to confiscate the belongings of the laird's daughter, and he was dismayed to consider how alone and defenseless Cristiane had been in St. Oln.

He made a silent vow to see that she suffered no further abuse or humiliation while under his protection.

Cristiane sat down on the bench, and before she could

put on the shoe, Adam crouched in front of her, taking it from her hand. He lifted her foot and carefully slipped the shoe on, past delicate toes, over the heel and arch.

"It fits," she said, her voice thick with emotion.

Not daring to look at her face, he laced the shoe, then reached for the other, repeating the process.

After her feet were clad, Cristiane put one hand on Adam's shoulder and leaned forward. He looked up, and as he felt her move closer, he anticipated the touch of her lips on his. He could imagine how soft they'd feel, how enticing the intimate contact would be. He could not take his eyes from those lips, full and inviting, moving toward his own.

Then she shifted slightly and kissed his cheek.

Before Adam could react, Cristiane stood and dashed out of the inn.

"'Twill be a much more comfortable ride for you," Sir Elwin said as he introduced Cristiane to the notion of riding the mule that stood before her. "Lord Bitterlee acquired him for you earlier this morn."

Cristiane felt a pang in the pit of her stomach. She had never been on horseback in her life, except for the hours she'd spent on Adam's horse—with Adam.

And now he expected her to ride this mule—this animal whose back was higher than Adam's destrier—the rest of the way to Bitterlee.

While she knew he'd been wise to put some distance between them, she did not know if she'd be able to handle this beast all the way to Bitterlee.

She did not know if she'd be able to handle it to the end of the lane.

With Elwin's help, she mounted. Adam was nowhere in sight, but that did not delay Elwin and Raynauld, who

flanked her as they rode out of the inn yard. Though
Cristiane felt more than a little insecure perched alone
atop the mule, she could not resist breaking her concen-
tration to look down and admire the lovely leather shoes
Adam had gotten for her.

Adam rode ahead all day. He'd traveled this route two
years before, riding in the back of a wagon, wounded
and out of his head with fever. He couldn't remember
much of that journey.

Then he'd arrived home on the isle and learned of
Rosamund's death only a few days before. Even through
his fog of pain and fever, the shock of that terrible news
was something he'd never forget.

Adam wondered if he could have prevented her sui-
cide had he remained at home rather than answering
King Edward's call and joining the English army in
Scotland. He also wondered if his impending return had
driven her to seek her own death. 'Twas a question that
would forever haunt him.

Beyond her maladjustment to marriage, Rosamund
had not adjusted to life on Bitterlee, either. Everything
about the isle had been too harsh, too stark, too unforgiving. After Margaret's birth, Rosamund's spirits had
sunk ever lower.

Yet for the first three years of Margaret's life, the
child had doted on Rosamund. She'd worried and fretted
whenever her mama was unwell—which was often—and
wanted naught more than to be allowed to play quietly
in her chamber. It seemed an unlikely way to rear a
child, though Adam knew little of these matters.

A sense of bitter sadness took hold of him, as it always did whenever he thought of Rosamund. She'd been

so distant and fragile. He'd never quite known what to do with her, or about her, from the time they'd met and wed. He'd been paired with her through the efforts of her sire and his own, with nary a thought to how satisfactory a match was being made, or how well Rosamund was suited to the place *or* the man who would become her husband.

Adam presumed his own father had decided that any young woman of noble birth would suffice, as long as she was capable of bearing his heirs. Adam's father could not have been more wrong, but the earl had not lived long after the marriage had taken place. He hadn't witnessed Rosamund's growing despondency and subsequent withdrawal.

By the time Adam returned home from Falkirk, life at Bitterlee had changed dramatically. Rosamund was gone. Mathilde, the stern old nurse who had come to Bitterlee with Rosamund, had taken Margaret in hand, and seen to her care. Adam's uncle, Gerard, had taken charge in a harsh and incompetent manner, looking after matters on the isle. Luckily, Penyngton had been there to see that his excesses caused no harm.

Unfortunately, a great number of Bitterlee men had gone to Falkirk with Adam—and not returned home. Too many fields lay fallow now, for lack of farmers. And too few fishermen plied the seas with their nets.

Upon Adam's return from Falkirk and the carnage there, he'd had a difficult time mustering the strength to reclaim his demesne and his daughter. He knew he'd left Gerard too long in charge. And little Margaret shrank away from the stranger who was her father—the man with the terrible scar across his jaw, and the ungainly limp.

He knew he must seem a monster to her now.

It had taken Charles Penyngton's persistence to show Adam that things must change. The seneschal had helped Adam reclaim his rightful place as lord of Bitterlee, gently relegating Uncle Gerard to his favorite pastime—overimbibing the castle ale and wandering the isle at will. Gerard sometimes stayed for days in one or another of his many secret places on the island.

Penyngton had also managed to convince Adam of the need for a wife. A new lady of Bitterlee.

Adam would find one. Soon. 'Twas quite unfortunate that Cristiane Mac Dhiubh would not do—that her Scottish side overbalanced the English blood that must run in her veins. But he was determined not to err again in his marital duty. Though the woman managed to stir him in ways he'd all but forgotten, she was wholly unsuitable for Bitterlee. Naught less than a gently bred, *English* lady would do.

Still, he would not shirk his responsibility toward Lady Cristiane. On Bitterlee, he would see that she was clothed properly, then assign an escort to take her to her uncle in York. 'Twould be no hardship for two or three of his knights to make the journey. Spring was upon them, and travel would be easy.

As for this short journey to Bitterlee, Adam knew Elwin and Raynauld were entirely capable of protecting Lady Cristiane, so he felt no qualms about keeping his distance from her. Now, if only he could keep his mind as far from removed from her as his body was…

'Twas no use trying to keep his thoughts on Bitterlee. She had an untamed beauty that enthralled him, but a vulnerability that was frightening. He did not want another sensitive female under his care. Certainly not a bloody Scottish one.

* * *

The day continued fair and sunny, and Cristiane grew accustomed to the rhythm of the mule's gait. They did not travel fast over the woodland path, but made good progress south. She could smell the sea to her left as they rode, and she wondered if they would camp near water as they had on their first night out.

She also wondered if they would meet up with Adam before nightfall.

Though Elwin and Raynauld were good company, Cristiane found herself wishing for Adam's presence. She sighed quietly as she thought of his strong, capable hands, lacing the shoes he'd acquired for her. She'd never noticed any other man's hands before, but something about Adam's caught her eye.

They were large, but well formed, with dark hair on the backs and thick blue veins prominent under smooth skin. His clean nails were neatly trimmed. Cristiane would feel safe in those hands, if he ever chose to touch her again.

Which he would not. She was certain of that.

She'd seen something in his eyes that morning while she dressed, something that even now brought a blush to her cheeks. But he'd withdrawn from her. He'd made a point of staying away—other than during those few short moments when he'd fastened the shoes on her feet. Clearly, he had not experienced the same rush of heat she had. Whatever had been in his eyes, it had not been a wave of lust.

More likely embarrassment.

'Twas foolish to ruminate over it now. Adam's lack of interest was of no consequence to her. She would not tarry long at Bitterlee. 'Twould be a mere fortnight or less, she guessed, before she continued her southward journey to her uncle in York.

She felt fortunate that she at least had shoes for her arrival in York, but wished she owned something to trade for better clothes. Her belongings were meager, and of them, the only possessions of value were her two books, which she'd managed to hide away in her cave. Cristiane did not think she could part with them, even for the finest of kirtles. For they'd belonged to her father and she'd learned so much from them.

Nay, she would just have to arrive looking a pauper…as she truly was.

"Not much farther to go, yer ladyship," Sir Elwin said. "We'll meet Lord Bitterlee just over that rise."

Cristiane was surprised by that news. She'd had no idea where Lord Bitterlee had gone off to, but her heart beat a bit faster, knowing she'd soon see him again.

"He stayed ahead of us all day," Raynauld remarked.

"Why?" she wondered aloud.

"For safety's sake," Elwin replied. "After our encounter with last night's raiders, he did not want us to be riding headlong into another ugly situation."

Cristiane had not thought of that, but she was glad Adam had. The idea of running into those English marauders again made her blood run cold. She did not care to repeat her reaction to the violence on the stair the previous night. She'd been incapacitated, and her mind had taken her back to the battle in which her father had been killed.

Prior to this, she'd only seen his violent death in her worst nightmares. Never while she was awake.

"We've kept up a good pace," Sir Elwin said, turning her mind from the possibility of danger, "so we'll be reaching the Isle of Bitterlee before nightfall on the morrow.''

"The isle?"

"Aye," Raynauld replied. "Bitterlee is an island in the North Sea."

"Oh!" Cristiane said with wonder. "No one told me that Bitterlee was an isle." She could hardly imagine standing in a place where she would be surrounded by water. What a wonderful thought. There would be birds, and tide pools and wee sea creatures…

"Aye," the knight continued. "With Lord Bitterlee's castle perched high on the cliffs overlooking the sea."

"'Tis a fair wondrous place in summer," Sir Elwin added. Then he frowned. "But our winters are harsh. 'Tis not a clime for the fainthearted."

Cristiane thought Elwin would have said more, but he stopped himself, and Raynauld took up the discussion.

"Besides our lovely summers," he said, "we've always got food to spare, even when the grain harvest is sparse…."

"Aye, Bitterlee's fishermen are England's best."

"We feast on codfish and whitynge year-round!"

"'Tis how we fare in St. Oln, too," Cristiane said, though many fishermen had died recently on battlefields. So had farmers. Food was now scarce in her village. 'Twas one more reason they wanted her gone.

She did not notice the look that passed between the two knights, but rode on, wondering when they would meet with Adam and stop for the night. Every now and then the sun broke through the trees, but they could see that it rode low over the horizon. Night would soon be upon them.

Cristiane was weary. The day's ride had taken its toll.

She was more than ready to lay her head down for the
night and rest her sorely tested muscles.

They'd been riding through a dense forest for several
hours, but when they reached the crest of the hill that
Elwin mentioned, the land below was clear. From their
perch, the sea was visible in the distance.

"Lord Bitterlee will be in the dell alongside the
river," Elwin said.

They made their way down the hillside and soon
reached a stream that Cristiane considered more a wee
burn than a river. But she did not contradict her escort.
She was just glad to know she'd be able to dismount
soon. Her legs were sore, and her back ached from holding it so stiffly all day.

They rode three abreast, following the burn. When
they smelled the welcoming aroma of a wood fire, and
of cooking meat, they knew they were close. They followed the curve of the little stream and soon came upon
Lord Bitterlee, who had just stepped out of the frigid
water.

To Cristiane's shock, Adam was shirtless. She'd never
seen a man of St. Oln so unclothed. Always, for mod-
esty's sake, the men kept on at least an undergarment,
even while performing the hottest, most arduous tasks.

But Cristiane could not find fault with Adam's near
nakedness. His chest and arms were well formed, and
his belly...something about the way those hard muscles
moved made Cristiane's insides flutter.

Dark hair furred his chest in a swirling pattern that
trailed to a point below his waist, where his chausses
and braes rode low on his hips. The chausses themselves
were damp, and Cristiane could make out the firm lines
of the muscles of his legs, though she could discern no
indication of the reason for his limp.

What had caused it? A battle wound?

She suddenly realized that she was sitting motionless atop her mount. Raynauld and Elwin had ridden well ahead of her as she'd sat staring at Adam, and she flushed with heat. 'Twas embarrassing to be caught with her jaw agape.

Chapter Five

Adam threw on his undertunic quickly. The icy bite of the river had no effect on him now. If anything, he felt too warm. Lady Cristiane's unabashed appraisal of his naked form was surprisingly arousing. Suddenly, all he could think of was the way her lips had felt on his cheek after he'd placed the shoes on her feet. All he could smell was her scent, soft and musky. Intriguing.

He'd never known a noblewoman to be so appreciative of the male form. Rosamund had certainly never been. If anything, she had abhorred his superior size and strength. In their four years of marriage, Rosamund had never been at ease with him. She had given excuses to keep him from sharing her bed, and certainly had not enjoyed the few times he'd gotten past her defenses.

'Twas a miracle she'd ever conceived Margaret.

"Looks like the weather will stay clear, my lord," Raynauld said, dismounting and leading his horse away. "An easy night for sleeping out-of-doors."

Adam nodded and stepped over to the campfire, where he'd left his mail hauberk. He assumed, *hoped*, Elwin had assisted Cristiane from the mule.

But Elwin led his horse past him, asking, "Your ride was uneventful, my lord?"

"Aye, not a..." He turned and caught sight of Cristiane. She was attempting to dismount alone, but the distance to the ground was too great. Raynauld was out of sight and Elwin was heading in the opposite direction.

Adam muttered a reply and rubbed the lower half of his face with one hand. The last thing he wanted was to touch her again. He'd made his decision regarding Lady Cristiane, and it was a sound one. She would never do as a proper English wife, but he knew his body would betray him again if he did not avoid touching her.

She could dismount without assistance, he told himself. She was robust and hearty, and he was certain she had no need of his help.

Yet, in spite of all this, he stepped over to her. "Allow me," he said, holding his hand out to her.

She took it without hesitation and slid down the mule's side. Adam caught her waist to steady her as she slipped down the length of his body. He gritted his teeth and refused to acknowledge the sparks set off by the contact, and she seemed to do the same. But her legs were unsteady and she faltered as she tried to step away.

Adam took hold of her again and led her to a likely seat—the trunk of an uprooted tree. As he held her, he was almost painfully aware of how flimsy were the layers of her clothes, and his hand learned the supple curves of her waist and hip the way his eyes had already been tutored.

"Thank you, Lord Bitterlee," she said as she sat. "I'm sure I'll be fine in a moment."

He knew she could not have been accustomed to riding, with no horses in St. Oln. He should have anticipated how difficult it would be for her to ride that mule all day.

Would she be able to ride again on the morrow? They had only a half day's journey ahead of them, and he wanted to make it back to Bitterlee. These days, he did not like being away from home too long, not with Margaret so frail and Gerard so ready to take control of the isle.

Adam wished Penyngton had known how unsuitable Cristiane Mac Dhiubh would be. He'd have saved himself the trip.

He limped back over to the fire and picked up his water skin. Returning to Cristiane, he handed it to her. "The food will be ready shortly," he said, watching her lips close around the opening of the skin. A thin trail of water splashed down her chin and onto the cloth of her kirtle, pasting it to her skin.

He swallowed thickly and looked away. "'Tis nearly dark. If you need, er, if you care to wash, there's a secluded place downstream, 'round that curve."

He'd never had occasion to speak to Rosamund about such private matters, and he did not care to dwell on them now, with Cristiane. "Do you think you can walk?"

"Oh, aye," she said, handing his water skin back to him. She wiped the droplets from her chin, then pushed her hair back. For the first time, he noticed how delicate her hands and wrists were. She was not as tiny as Rosamund had been, but Lady Cristiane was still distinctly feminine.

She walked away, following the edge of the brook, and he could not help but notice her unsteady gait. Stepping toward her to give assistance, he stopped himself.

Determined to stay clear of her, he decided that if she stumbled, one of his men could bloody well help her.

Cristiane managed. Her legs were not exactly sore, but wobbly. It made no difference; the end result was the same. She was unsteady as she walked around the curve of the burn.

Puzzled by Adam's attitude toward her, she washed in the stream and tried to understand why he should seem annoyed with her, even as he showed her kindness. It made no sense.

Pushing aside her confusion, she thought about the island she was about to visit. She'd never been beyond the boundaries of St. Oln, but she'd heard of islands in the North Sea, and knew they were occupied by a multitude of birds and other wildlife. She wondered if Bitterlee would be the same.

'Twas merely a half day's ride to Adam's isle. Cristiane was doubtful about making it alone on the back of the mule for that length of time, and wished Adam would take her up with him on his mount.

Besides, she wanted to feel his arms around her once more. She'd never before known the kind of heart-pounding reaction he caused in her, and wanted to experience it again. She craved his touch in a way that was wholly unfamiliar. She wanted to see his naked form again, even though she supposed 'twas sinful to have such a blatant desire of the flesh.

A bit stunned by her strange feelings, she wiped her face on the skirt of her kirtle and turned back to join the men in camp. Their low voices carried and she could hear them talking comfortably together. She found Elwin turning the hares that were cooking over the fire, and Raynauld was looking over some colorful bits of cloth with Adam.

"These will look well in Margaret's hair," Adam said.

"Oh aye, my lord," Raynauld said, holding up several lengths of ribbon. "No doubt she will love them."

Margaret.

The name was repeated a thousand times in Cristiane's mind as she tried to sleep, and another thousand times as she rode the damnable mule the rest of the way to Bitterlee. Adam rode far ahead, out of sight.

She should have realized he had a wife. 'Twas the reason he'd kept his distance. Sure enough, there'd been heat between them, but Adam—*Lord Bitterlee,* she amended—had done the honorable thing and stayed away from her.

She could not help but feel disappointment. He'd been her hero, her savior, on the stair of the inn. He'd taken gentle care of her and seen that she was protected through the night. Was it so strange that she would feel some attachment to him? Was it odd that she should want to believe there was more than basic chivalry in his concern for her?

Cristiane sighed. She was just an inexperienced lass from a small village too far north of anywhere that mattered. However, she was intelligent enough to realize that she would have to guard her heart as she traveled, and not succumb to every attraction she felt. Just because a man paid her a kindness did not mean he intended to commit his life to her.

Yet it hurt to know that she was naught more than a responsibility to Adam. 'Twas likely he owed a debt to her father, or mayhap to her uncle, and that was why he'd been compelled to escort her from St. Oln.

She was merely the means for payment of that debt.

'Twas fortunate for Cristiane's peace of mind that the scenery changed. It intrigued her. As they rode closer to the sea, on high embankments and across wide beaches, she drank in and savored all the sights.

Her beloved guillemots and fulmars, puffins and razorbills, all nested and fed here in huge numbers. She watched as they circled over the water, screeching, then diving, and resurfacing with their catch.

"Are there many birds on the island?" she asked.

"Aye," replied Elwin. "All along the cliffs south of the castle."

"And does…does Lady Margaret walk along the cliffs?"

"Oh, ye know of Lady Margaret, then?" Elwin asked.

Cristiane nodded.

"Well, nay, she does not," he answered. "The lord would be afeared of her slipping and falling."

Though Cristiane had skipped among the rocky cliffs above St. Oln all her life and knew there was little danger for the surefooted, she wished that some likely lad might have had a care for *her* safety. 'Twas clear that Lord Bitterlee held his lady in high regard.

Cristiane put those thoughts from her mind. She had many miles to cover before she met her uncle in York, and it would not do at all for her to pine over what could not be.

"Look!" Raynauld said. He extended one arm to the left and pointed. "Bitterlee!"

In the afternoon sun, Cristiane could see a dark mass rising out of the glittering sea in the distance. It was impossible to make out any detail from so far away, but it was comforting—nay, exciting—to have her destination finally within sight.

* * *

The Bitterlee lords kept a tiny village on the mainland, where a perfect harbor was well situated for launching boats to the island. Adam tied his horse to the post in front of the wineshop that also served as an inn, and went inside to wait for his men to arrive with Lady Cristiane.

The weather was fair enough now, so the crossing should pose no problems. The only difficulty would be once they reached the isle. He had not yet figured out how to avoid Lady Cristiane.

The castle was large, but only a small part was inhabited by the family. There was only one appropriate place to lodge Cristiane, being a guest, and that was near his own chambers, not far from Margaret's. As usual, meals would be served in the great hall, and he could see no possible way to stay away from them. Or her.

He could turn her over to his uncle, but Gerard was a decidedly unfriendly, inhospitable fellow. He was a mere decade older than Adam, and for many years he'd resented Adam's inheritance of the Bitterlee title and demesne. His actions of late indicated that he still resented him for it.

Gerard Sutton had spent the greater part of his youth as a knight in King Edward's employ, only returning to Bitterlee upon the death of Adam's father. Mayhap at that time, Gerard had hoped he would somehow inherit Bitterlee. Adam knew 'twas entirely possible his uncle had petitioned the king in this matter, too.

But King Edward was not fool enough to make exception to the laws of inheritance. 'Twould start a precedent that would cause chaos in the kingdom.

Nay, Adam was lord of Bitterlee, and he would be until the title passed to his own son.

If ever he had one.

"Rain in the air, m'lord," the innkeeper said, drawing ale from a barrel.

"Aye," Adam replied. "I smell it, too. But not for a few hours."

"Right you are," the man said as he set Adam's ale before him.

"Lookin' fer some refreshment, m'lord?" the innkeeper's wife asked. "A meal or—?"

"Only if you've something prepared," Adam said, noticing the woman for the first time. She was redheaded, like Cristiane, but her hair color was dull, uninteresting. Her features were unremarkable, too, without the vividness of Cristiane's bright blue eyes, or the delicacy of her nose and jaw. This woman did not have full, soft lips like Cristiane's, lips that could…

In frustration at his wayward thoughts, he turned and prowled back to the open door. He'd managed to avoid thinking of her all day, and now this. The image of her face came to mind, as well as all the attributes below her neck.

"When my men arrive," he said, turning, "we won't tarry. I want to cross before the rain comes." He would get Cristiane situated somewhere in the castle and forget about her. Soon he'd meet with Penyngton and have him draft a letter to all the lords of the realm. One of them had to have a daughter of marriageable age. Adam would have a marriage contract drawn up, and wed a proper Englishwoman.

Then he'd be able to get on with his life.

"Aye, m'lord," the innkeeper said. "Wise. There's some cold chicken, and mayhap a bit of mutton left."

"Whatever you have will do, Edwin," Adam said.

The innkeepers left him to his own devices as they

went to the kitchen to prepare the meal. Adam walked back to a table, sat down and lifted his drink.

He knew what his problem was, and it had naught to do with Cristiane Mac Dhiubh. Any woman that pleased the eye could solve it. Mayhap he should send Elwin and Raynauld ahead with Cristiane to Bitterlee. Then he could ride inland to Watersby, a good-size village at a crossroads, where the tavern women were pretty. *And* willing to take care of a man's needs.

If he rode hard, he would make it there before dark. He could spend a couple of days slaking a need that had not troubled him for eons, then return to Bitterlee, refreshed and immune to Lady Cristiane's allure.

He had almost convinced himself that it would be best to head out for Watersby when he reminded himself it had been a week since he'd seen his daughter. Little Margaret was frail and sickly, and he could not stay away for as low a reason as he'd just considered. Nay, he was not so depraved as that.

He would return to the isle and see to his daughter, just as he should.

A gust of wind caught one of the shutters and slammed it against the wall of the inn, forcing Adam's attention back to the elements. Mayhap the storm would come sooner than he expected. He went outside and glanced down at the harbor, then looked at the sky.

The clouds were still far in the distance, but he hoped Elwin and Raynauld would ride into the village soon. They would have time for a quick meal, then make the crossing before the rain came. Judging by the cold bite of the wind, this storm was going to be more than a gentle shower.

Impatiently, he paced outside near the door, anxious for his men to arrive with Cristiane. When he finally spotted them on the road, still a fair distance away, he felt both relieved *and* on edge.

Some of the villagers began to approach him cordially, glad to pass the time of day with the lord. Many followed him back inside the wineshop, where Adam gulped another cup of ale, listening to their news. He learned who'd died in recent weeks, and who had birthed new babes.

Still holding a great deal of animosity toward the Scots for their losses at Falkirk, the people complained of the shortage of men to tend sheep and till the fields. Adam promised to send his knights to help, as they had done the previous spring. He knew there was too much work for the men who remained here. It would be years before the population returned to what it had been before so many had gone with him to answer King Edward's call.

Raynauld finally entered the wineshop, with Elwin and Cristiane following. By degrees, the people became quiet as the strange woman proceeded deeper into their midst. They recognized Lord Bitterlee's knights, but the young woman with the flaming red hair was strange to them.

Cristiane kept her eyes down and remained behind Raynauld as he pushed through to Adam's table. Adam stood and pulled out one of the rough chairs for her, and watched as she sat.

The villagers knew better than to question the lord, but he could see they were full of unfriendly curiosity regarding the stranger he'd brought into their midst. He resisted the preposterous urge to gather her into his arms and protect her from what he was sure would be a hostile reaction to a Scottish woman audacious enough to step upon English soil. Adam wished to spare Cristiane that.

She'd had enough difficulty in past weeks—from her *own* people.

The innkeeper's wife brought a platter of food to the table, and as Adam and his party began to eat, the people slowly dispersed, leaving Adam uncomfortably close to Cristiane.

"'Twill be good to get home," Elwin said, cutting a leg from the cold roast fowl that had been put before them.

"Aye," Raynauld agreed, "before the storm hits."

"Looks like a good 'un about to start."

"We'll make it," Adam interjected.

"How do we cross to the isle?" Cristiane asked quietly.

"A galley will carry us over," Adam replied. "The crossing takes a quarter hour, mayhap a bit more."

Cristiane nodded.

"Have you ever been on the sea, my lady?" Raynauld asked.

Adam watched as Cristiane bit her lower lip, and he knew her answer before she spoke. "Nay," she finally replied. "I havena."

Her burr was thick suddenly, and Adam remembered how that had happened before, when she was nervous. "'Tis a very easy crossing, Lady Cristiane," he said.

"Aye, 'tis true, milady," Elwin added. "Naught to worry about."

"Ach," she said, with a shrug that caused her shoulder to brush Adam's arm. Her body was warm, welcoming. He clamped down on his inappropriate reaction to her touch. "I'm na worrit."

Elwin laughed. "Tell me that when your color comes back."

She lowered her eyes and blushed, feeling the heat.

She had to know that the color was back in her cheeks, if only from embarrassment, but she did not say more.

"Did you send a boy to the ship with the horses?" Adam asked his men.

"Aye, m'lord," Sir Elwin replied. "All will be ready when we arrive on the wharf."

"And oarsmen?"

"Aye," said Raynauld. "They'll be there."

Cristiane ate little, but Adam did not remark on it. He would not urge her to eat, then board the galley. It could very well become a difficult crossing if the winds continued, and then they'd all be glad her stomach was empty.

He remembered that Rosamund had never had an easy time with the crossing. She did not usually become acutely ill, but her complexion would grow sallow, and she'd lose all color in her lips. After she reached dry land again, 'twould take an hour or more before she returned to normal.

'Twas a quick, but windy walk to the wharf, and Cristiane held on to her skirts with one hand to try to keep them from blowing up to her knees. With the other hand, she captured her loose hair and held it tight.

Adam forced his eyes away from her lissome form.

The horses and Cristiane's mule had been sent ahead on another ship to the island, so Adam and his party boarded a lightly burdened galley. Hopefully, 'twould make their passage all the faster.

The wind took on a bitter bite as they found their seats in the open ship. The galley was manned by eight oarsmen, and Raynauld and Elwin added their strength to the rowing, too. They would use no sail, for the wind was too sharp, but Adam had faith that they would make good speed to the isle.

For the first time in days, Adam felt a lightening of his spirit. Soon he would be home, where he belonged. His promise to Cristiane's mother had been partially fulfilled, and he was now free to undertake the responsibilities he'd neglected far too long at Bitterlee.

The men rowed the ship out of the harbor on rough seas. The bow reared up and crashed over the waves as they made their way toward the land mass that rose up ahead of them. Adam stood at the bow with the ship's master, exhilarated by the ferocity of the elements, and kept watch as they rowed farther out.

The wind took his breath away, whipped his hair to a tangled mess and pasted his clothes to his long, muscular frame.

"That's a Scotswoman you brought with ye, eh, m'lord?" the master asked.

Adam raised an eyebrow at the question, but did not begrudge the man an answer. He'd been the skilled master of the harbor for many years, always loyal and reliable. "She is," he replied simply.

The man pursed his lips and thought a moment before speaking again. "D'ye think the island people will take to her, m'lord?"

"'Tis no matter. The lady is my guest," Adam said, raising his voice to carry over the wind. "She will be up at the castle for the length of her visit. I don't expect the island people will be bothered by her."

Adam thought the master made a sound deep in his throat, but could not be sure, because the man turned away just then and began to shout orders to his oarsmen. Adam dreaded turning to look at Cristiane, certain that he would find her cowering in the hull of the ship, green to her gills.

Instead, he watched the sky as several large brown

skuas rode the wind, impervious to the impending storm. They screeched as they flew, then dived into the waves or at the smaller gulls, each one securing a meal. Adam watched them for a long moment, putting off the time when he'd have to go and see to Lady Cristiane.

An unfamiliar, musical sound made him turn to the hull of the ship, and he discovered Cristiane standing at the port side, pointing up at the flying birds. She laughed as she watched them dance across the sky, and the color in her fair cheeks was good.

The wind blew her skirts up above her ankles, and she absently pushed them down with one hand. Adam was painfully aware of what lay beneath those skirts, and he desperately hoped that the wind became no fiercer. Otherwise, Cristiane would most certainly be embarrassed.

And Adam would have to throw each and every man who saw her overboard.

He crossed to her and gripped her arm more fiercely than he intended. "The seas are rough, Lady Cristiane," he said. "'Tis best if you take a seat."

"Ach, but—"

"'Tis true, m'lady," the master shouted from his post at the bow. "Can't have no accidents on m' ship, now!"

Cristiane complied with both men's wishes, finding a seat away from the oarsmen. Adam sat down beside her, oddly disturbed by her ease in the circumstances. He should have been relieved that she was not puking over the side, yet her exhilaration in the face of the wind and high seas was confusing. Never had he known a woman so comfortable with the elements.

"'Tis wonderful, is it na, my lord?"

"What? The storm?"

"Aye! And the bonniest great skuas I've ever seen." Cristiane laughed again. "They're like the ruddy kings of the sky—diving for food, but stealing the prey from smaller birds!''

Adam had to smile at her likening the big gulls to a king. She was more accurate than she knew.

''I'm glad 'tis so...so alive for the crossing,'' she said, spreading her arms wide. ''Aught else, and 'twould have been a dull ride!''

Something inside Adam made him want to shake some sense into her. Didn't the foolish girl understand there was danger here? That the weather could turn frightful in an instant, with dangerous lightning and torrents of rain?

'Twas clear he'd have to look out for her while she remained on Bitterlee. She didn't have the sense God gave a...a skua.

Chapter Six

The town lay at the southernmost point of the isle, slightly east, at the mouth of the harbor.

Adam's family had long been popular with the people, for Bitterlee was a prosperous holding, and well administered. Bitterlee's sympathies became even more fully engaged when Adam returned from Scotland nearly two years before, a grievously wounded hero, only to discover that his young wife had died.

Little Lady Margaret became one of their own. Prayers and indulgences doubled on behalf of Lord Bitterlee and his poor, motherless child. Adam was revered as their tragic young lord, and their hearts went out to him.

And they blamed the Scots for all the troubles that had befallen them.

Cristiane fell in love with the isle the moment the ship pulled into harbor. It called St. Oln to her mind, but Bitterlee was so much more. The town that nestled 'round the harbor was pretty, with neat cottages near the water and on the hillsides, along well-tended lanes. A multitude of fishing boats lined the harbor, all tied securely against the growing gale.

The lush aromas of freshly tilled earth and salty air filled her nose, but 'twas the high ridges and cliffs that drew Cristiane's attention. As the wind battered the trees high above them, she could see rough peaks in the distance, black, rocky crags enshrouded in a heavy mist. The castle wall was white against the gray haze, and behind the wall rose gleaming turrets and towers. Cristiane's breath caught in her throat at the sight. She had never seen so magnificent a place.

Townspeople came out in spite of the weather and welcomed Lord Bitterlee and his men back to the island. Children, along with barking dogs, ran up and down the planks of the dock as the men and women gathered, creating a festive atmosphere.

Uncomfortable with the thought of joining this mass of people, Cristiane remained onboard the galley with Raynauld and Elwin until they were ready to disembark. There was no doubt that the people on the mainland had realized she was Scottish, mayhap because of her red hair, and had shunned her. She did not doubt that she'd be greeted with suspicion and hostility here as well.

She crossed her arms over her chest, then rubbed her hands over her upper arms to warm herself against the sudden chill. She'd faced a number of difficulties since the death of her father, the very least of which had been the unkindness of the people of St. Oln.

She would survive them again.

After all, as wondrous a place as the Isle of Bitterlee was, she would not be staying long. A week, mayhap a fortnight, and she would make the crossing back to the mainland, and leave this intriguing place. She promised herself she would explore every ledge of the cliffs before she left. She wanted to discover all the nesting creatures in the rocks so high above the sea.

The wind lashed at Cristiane's hair and she struggled to gather it in one fist. She caught sight of Adam at the center of the crowd at the base of a hill as he made his way to a shelter where the horses and her mule were tethered. 'Twas clear he'd forgotten her.

Cristiane tamped down a wave of alarm. She was being ridiculous. He hadn't abandoned her yet, and she doubted he would do so now, even though his people would surely scorn her.

"Come, m'lady," Elwin said. "Best we be getting home before the clouds burst."

She nearly had to run to catch up to the knights as they walked ahead of her, shielding her from the worst of the wind. Still, she could see Adam up ahead, continuing to walk toward the animals' shelter, yet speaking to all who would have his ear. She stopped herself from wishing he'd give her half as much attention. 'Twas quite an improper thought, knowing as she did that the man had a wife awaiting him.

Turning her attention to the high cliffs where the castle stood, remote and protected, she said, "How will we climb up there? The rocks—"

"There's a good path along the escarpment, though you can't see it from here," Sir Raynauld said. "We'll ride the horses."

"Would it not be wise to stay in the village until the storm passes?" she asked.

Elwin and Raynauld exchanged a glance. "Nay," said Raynauld.

"But we must move quickly now," Elwin said, mindful of the coming storm. "We cannot tarry!"

With that, he took Cristiane's arm and propelled her forward. The crowd parted as they headed toward Adam, and silence followed in their wake, just as it had in the

tavern on the mainland. Cristiane wished she had a shawl
to cover her offending hair. She felt utterly conspicuous,
penetrating their midst, looking so much the stranger,
and a Scotswoman at that.

Voices whispered around her, then became rude mut-
terings. Cristiane heard the words and girded herself
against the hurt they caused. She knew *she* was not responsible for the deaths of their men or the wounding
of their lord. *She* was not the one who'd raided their
borders or taken up arms at Falkirk.

She was just like any of them, having watched the
knights and soldiers of St. Oln leave for battle, some
never to return. Yet in Scotland, some had stayed to fight
on home turf. Her father had been one of those.

And he had died defending her.

Before she had even a moment to reflect on that, she
was thrown off balance by a nasty tug on her hair. Then
someone shoved her. Soon the voices became louder,
more hostile, and Cristiane was knocked to the ground.

"Hold!"

Anger seethed. Adam had never been so incensed in
his life. He had never seen these people behave cruelly,
yet their treatment of Cristiane was unmerciful and
would have become even more brutal if he had not intervened.

Pushing through the crowd to where his men were
helping her up, Adam realized he should have sensed
they'd take one look at her and know she was Scottish.
And by the way she was dressed, Cristiane looked no
better than any of them. They did not know she was the
granddaughter of an English earl, or the daughter of her
clan's laird.

If only Adam had been able to find more suitable attire

for her, they'd never have dared to treat her so, Scot or not.

Feeling fiercely protective now, Adam took Cristiane's hand and placed it in the crook of his arm. "Lady Cristiane is a guest of Bitterlee," he said sternly as he studiously avoided looking into her overbright eyes. Even so, he could not help but feel her trembling. "'Tis true she is of Scots blood, but she was no less harmed by the war than all of you."

Subdued but not cowed by Adam's words, the crowd made way as he escorted Cristiane to the horses. Raynauld and Elwin followed close behind, as the wind grew even worse. Adam would normally have considered staying in town until the storm blew itself out, but he would not subject Cristiane to that. He knew that his words had not quelled the people's hostility.

Quickly glancing at the sky, he judged that if they hurried, they would have time to make it to the castle. Just barely.

The path was difficult, and Adam did not want to waste time guiding Cristiane and her mule. So he hoisted her onto his own horse, then mounted behind her to ride as they had together early in their journey from St. Oln.

"My lord?" she asked after she'd caught her breath. Her voice was unsteady and her body trembled against his, but he tightened his muscles and swung his horse out of the shelter without answering.

'Twas necessary to travel single file, for the path was narrow and sometimes followed the edge of the escarpment. Dangerous as it was, Adam felt it necessary to hold Cristiane close. She leaned into him as if she belonged there, as if they had not spent more than a full day apart.

Her head fit just under his chin, and her back rested

against his chest. He could not help but slip his hands around her waist and pull her even closer. Her breath caught in her throat, and Adam felt himself becoming aroused.

He knew he had to pay close attention to the ride. One misstep had the potential of sending them over the cliff. But even as the wind battered them and the rain threatened, he knew a fierce desire to tip his head down and taste the tender skin at her nape. He would have liked naught more than to raise his hands and fill them with her breasts.

"Best close yer eyes now, as we come up to these peaks!" Elwin called, turning to speak to Cristiane from his position in the lead.

"Why?" Cristiane called back to him, as if she were unaware of Adam's pulsing need. "You would have me miss the most glorious views I've ever seen?"

Elwin barked out a laugh, then turned to mind his own way along the path. Adam knew Cristiane would not think Bitterlee quite so glorious once she'd lived through the full ferocity of an island storm.

He'd heard tales of his own mother's frequent absences from Bitterlee; evidently, she had not been able to bear the fierce weather or the isolation of the place. And there was the legend of the ancient lord whose wife had poisoned herself in despair at having to remain on the isle.

And Rosamund. Adam's poor, timorous wife had preferred death to life on Bitterlee. With him.

Who was to say Cristiane Mac Dhiubh would be any different?

Adam had more than enough reason to steel his thoughts away from her. He had to keep his attention on the narrow horse path. He ought to be considering the tack he would take with little Margaret to bring her out of her grief. He should give due attention to the changes that were necessary on the isle and the mainland to get the rest of the spring crop in.

Instead, all Adam could think of was the rampant protectiveness that had surged through him when he'd seen Cristiane manhandled by the crowd in town. He could not remember ever feeling so outraged or helpless as when she had been pushed to the ground.

He could not get to her fast enough.

Riding together, with nature about to give her most powerful display, Adam found Cristiane's scent filling his senses. Her hair tickled his nose, and his hands itched to do more than hold her steady against him.

Yet he could not pursue this untenable attraction. The reaction of the Bitterlee townspeople had shown him beyond a doubt that she would never fit in here. She was not for him, and 'twas his duty to see that she arrived untouched at the home of her uncle, just as he'd promised.

Cristiane's attention was torn between the wonder of the isle and the intense sensations caused by the man whose heat warmed her as they rode through the mist toward the castle. The hard muscles of his chest buttressed her back, and she felt like curling against his body like a kitten.

Yet she could not. 'Twas sinful to lust after another woman's husband, and Cristiane would not stoop so low. She straightened up and pulled slightly away from Adam. A husband would be found for her in York, and Cristiane would go to him as a chaste bride.

"Be still, Cristiane." Adam's voice rumbled close to her ear. In spite of her resolve to remain detached, she could not prevent the flare of heat caused by his breath, or the tightening of his grasp on her.

"Sorry, m'lord," she said, realizing she'd been squirming. "D-do you often have such fierce weather?"

She turned slightly, and her head bumped his chin. He gave a curt nod and swallowed.

"And is there m-much damage?" she asked. "Trees down? Cottages wrecked?"

"Occasionally," he replied gruffly. *Especially in spring,* he thought, looking at the sky. "We are accustomed to the elements here on Bitterlee."

She did not remark on that, but looked over the edge of the cliff to the sea, and its dark waves crashing on rocks far below. She truly hoped there would be an opportunity to explore these cliffs before she had to leave.

Before long, the castle was in sight. 'Twas an impregnable fortress, rising high above the cliff and surrounded by tall, crenelated walls made from gleaming white limestone. It had not seemed so massive from down below, and Cristiane had to crane her neck to see the towers that rose high above the wall.

She heard voices calling over the howling wind, and soon the gates were open and they were riding through them into a grassy yard. Adam took them to a broad stone stair that led up to the main doors of the keep. Bitterlee grooms, wearing russet and black, surrounded them, taking hold of the reins of the horses and pulling down the packs. Adam dismounted, then helped Cristiane down. He guided her up the steps and inside.

In the great hall, servants scurried about, lighting tapers as well as the candles of a huge chandelier that hung over a long wooden table. Cristiane had never seen such a spacious or well-tended room.

A fire crackled welcomingly in a huge fireplace at one

end, and a comfortable settle along with two stuffed chairs were situated nearby. Cristiane thought it made a cozy place for the lord and his lady to spend an evening together.

Two big dogs were lounging by the fire, but they jumped up and crossed the rushes to greet their master, whining happily and wagging their tails frantically when they saw Adam.

"Down, Ren!" he said sharply to the wolfhound that jumped up on him. "Good girl, Gray," he said as he petted the other wolfhound—the one that had behaved.

The dogs were curious about Cristiane, and she held her hands out for them to sniff.

"They're quite gentle," Adam said, "otherwise I would not keep them, not with Margaret…"

"I understand," Cristiane said. She'd never known a man to be so solicitous of his wife. 'Twas not a common attitude in St. Oln. Not even her father had taken such care of her mother, and he'd loved her dearly. With a pang of regret that she did not care to pursue, Cristiane petted the dogs.

A servant came into the hall, carrying Adam's saddle pack and Cristiane's belongings. "A chamber has been made ready in the east tower, my lord," he said. His manner was cold and unfriendly, but Cristiane thought naught of it. She'd been subjected to much worse, of late. "Would you care to follow me now?"

Cristiane looked up at Adam, who nodded. She turned then and followed the servant, with Adam right behind. "Where is Lady Margaret, Stephan?" Adam asked.

"In the nursery, I believe, my lord," the man replied. "With Mathilde."

Cristiane kept her eyes on the floor as she crossed the hall, shocked by her reaction to what she'd heard. A wife *and a child?* She was truly damned for coveting this man. Yet her heart did not feel damned.

It merely felt shattered.

The rain came with a vengeance as they climbed the steps to the second level and walked down a long gallery. A crash of thunder rattled the walls, and Cristiane knew that if they'd been anywhere near a window, she would have seen the flash of lightning.

At the far end of the gallery was another set of stone steps, a spiral staircase in a circular tower. Fortunately, Stephan held a lamp to light the way, and Adam carried another behind her, else Cristiane would not have been able to see at all.

'Twas not surprising that Lady Margaret had not met them in the great hall. After all, the castle was huge, and they'd started up the stairs before a servant would have had an opportunity to summon Adam's wife.

Cristiane could not bring herself to regret the delay in meeting Lady Margaret. In fact, the longer 'twas put off, the better she felt about it. Truly, she needed some time to settle in and put on her most gracious demeanor.

She could not help but wish she had something more suitable to wear when she met Adam's countess.

A door swung out at the top of the stairs, and they filed into another dark corridor, with a multitude of closed doors on each side. Cristiane did not know if she would ever be able to find her way back here without an escort. "This way, my…lady," Stephan said as he led her to a large, open chamber.

Cristiane pressed her lips tightly together and followed. She would not allow a servant's attitude to rattle her.

'Twas dark within the chamber, even though there were two windows. While Stephan lit the candle of a large iron lamp that sat on a table between the two windows, Cristiane opened the latch of one window, pulling the heavy framed glass inside. She laughed when the rain sprayed her, then turned to see Stephan and Adam gaping at her. Quickly, she closed the window and wiped her wet hands on her kirtle.

"'Tis fortunate we reached the castle in time, is it not, my lord?'' she asked, embarrassed to appear so foolish. Cristiane loved rainstorms, even when they came with terrible thunder and fierce lightning, but she knew full well that her passion for the weather was not shared by many.

Stephan went out of the chamber and disappeared, while Adam lingered. "Aye. 'Tis indeed fortunate," he said. "Lady Cristiane…" he said, reverting to the formality he'd shown when he'd first met her, "have you any skill with a needle?"

Cristiane quirked her brows. "Some, my lord."

"I am quite sure that my wife left some good cloth hereabouts," he said. "If I were to find it, would you be able to sew—"

A clap of thunder drowned out his words.

"Sew, my lord?"

The lamp in his hand cast a flickering light on his face. The fine stubble of a beard darkened his jaw, but did naught to detract from his fierce good looks. Cristiane forced herself to think of needlework and thunder and cool rain on her face…

"Yes," he said. "You're in need of some new gowns before you go to York. There is a woman in the village who can help you tailor them."

"But, m'lord," Cristiane said, "your wife…she must have her own purpose for the cloth."

In the wavering light, Cristiane could not be sure, but

she thought a muscle clenched in his jaw before he
spoke. "My wife has been dead nearly two years, Lady
Cristiane," he said. "She has no further use of any
earthly goods."

Then he turned and left her.

Chapter Seven

Cristiane knew she should not feel the kind of elation that filled her heart now. The man's wife was dead, and she could only feel glad of it.

Ashamed, she turned to look at the room that would be her home for the next few days. 'Twas nicer than any she'd ever had before, even in her father's keep. A large bed, heavily curtained, lay against the wall opposite the windows. An empty wooden trunk sat at the foot, and a small table, wrought of oak and iron, stood next to the head of the bed. A small lamp was there, and Cristiane lit it. Then she sat down in a chair next to the fireplace and wondered who Lady Margaret might be.

Adam bypassed his own chamber on his way to the nursery. He would not allow his thoughts to linger on the forlorn look in Cristiane's eyes as he'd turned and left her. He clasped his hands into fists. He had spent more time than was prudent, thinking of pulling her into his arms and offering the protection of his body.

Nay. He would not consider touching her. He was determined not to let the vulnerability in those deep blue eyes ensnare him, nor those luscious curves tempt him.

Margaret needed his attention now, as did Bitterlee, and he would train all his attention to setting matters to rights.

He opened the nursery door to find his little daughter kneeling on the floor before a crucifix hanging on the wall. Her pale gray eyes were closed, and her lips moved slightly in prayers. Her beautiful, angel-blond hair was covered—too severely, he thought—by a pristine, white wimple that also covered her ears and her neck.

She was the mirror image of her nurse, Mathilde, who knelt beside her in fervent prayer. He remembered seeing Rosamund kneeling in just the same way with Mathilde, deeply immersed in devotions.

"My lord!" Mathilde exclaimed when she noticed Adam.

Margaret said naught, but looked shyly up at him, from under pale lashes.

Adam approached. His little daughter had always seemed so fragile, so delicate. She was just like her mother, and he knew 'twas necessary to treat her with care.

At least, that was what Mathilde advised. The old nurse knew Margaret better than anyone, but Adam had begun to wonder if her way—so coldly ascetic—was the best way for Margaret.

The child still grieved for her mother, and prayed often for her soul. He'd not heard her speak a single word aloud since his return from Falkirk, and Mathilde said 'twas not unusual for a child to manifest its grief for a time, then return to normal.

Yet he wondered how long her grief would continue.

"Margaret is well?" he asked.

"Yes, my lord," Mathilde responded, coming to her feet to face him. "Devout and dutiful as always."

Adam nodded as Margaret lowered her eyes again and resumed her prayers. He did not think it normal for a child to spend so much time on her knees, but what did he know of child rearing? *Not much,* he answered himself. *And even less when it came to little girls.*

The rain continued to beat against the heavy glass panes in Cristiane's windows.

She laid a fire to take the damp chill from the room, then opened her satchel, removing the two books that were her most prized possessions. In truth, they were her only possessions, other than a few pretty shells and a colorful stone she'd once found on the beach. She set everything in the trunk, taking care not to damage the finely tooled leather that covered her books. She took her comb, worked the tangles out of her hair and braided it neatly. Then she sat down to wait.

Surely a servant would soon arrive with a basin and ewer of water. At the very least, someone would come and show her where to find what she'd need in order to wash after her journey.

After waiting the better part of an hour, Cristiane stood and began to pace. She bolstered the fire, then opened her window in spite of the rain.

Many were the times she'd been caught in her cave during a raging storm, and she had never felt any fear. Nay, she'd loved those fierce demonstrations of nature's power. She would like naught more than to go out in *this* storm, and see how the wind tore at the cliffs, how the waves crashed against the shore.

But she knew better than to begin her explorations during a raging storm. Better to wait until all was calm.

Becoming even more restless, and hungry now, she saw that she had no choice but to find her way back to

the great hall. Evidently, with the excitement of the
lord's return to the castle, she'd been forgotten, and
would have to fend for herself.

'Twas no matter. No reason to take offense. Certainly
her isolation was merely an oversight. She picked up a
lamp and descended the two sets of stairs, then made
her way to the great hall.

From her position on the stair, she saw servants
spreading a large white cloth on the big table and moving chairs and benches to it. Others were putting various
silver and clay pieces on the table, along with knives
and empty bowls.

Adam was seated by the fire, near a child who sat
quietly on the rushes. The dogs were not in sight.

Sir Raynauld stood nearby, along with an older
woman wearing a dark gray kirtle and the most severe
wimple Cristiane had ever seen. The stiff material cut
into the woman's forehead and chin, and had to be terribly uncomfortable.

The child also wore a wimple and a dark gown. Cristiane stood still, watching as Adam spoke quietly to her.
The child kept her eyes down, not responding to anything he said.

A deep voice behind Cristiane startled her. She gasped
and lost her footing, shocked that the intruder had come
upon her so soundlessly.

"My great-niece never speaks," said the man. "And
even if she did, this family has no love for the Scots.
She would have naught to say to you." His face was in
shadows, but Cristiane detected a decidedly unfriendly
gleam in his eyes. His hair was long and unkempt, and
he wore a full, bushy beard that was frosted with strands
of silver. "Shall we go down and join the others?" he
asked, his breath thick with old ale.

"Aye," she said, her voice a mere croak. She cleared it and led the way down the rest of the steps.

"Lady Cristiane!" Sir Raynauld said when he caught sight of her. "Sir Gerard."

Adam stood, then drew his brows together as he watched Cristiane approach with his uncle. She was still wearing the ugly brown kirtle that she'd worn for the duration of their journey, and she looked disheveled and dusty. Yet she'd done something to her hair—confined it somehow, making it appear slightly more tame than usual.

He had specifically instructed the servants to see to Cristiane's comfort, yet 'twas clear she'd received no hospitality from Bitterlee as yet.

"Mathilde," he said to Margaret's nurse, as he restrained his anger, "find Sibilla and fetch her here." Normally, Sir Charles Penyngton would have charge of the servants, but Penyngton had fallen ill during Adam's absence and was still abed.

Adam had visited the seneschal only briefly and had been concerned by his friend's sickly appearance. He promised to see him later, and to send Bitterlee's healer, Sara Cole, to him as soon as possible.

Mathilde went to do Adam's bidding, and he drew Cristiane into the chair he'd just vacated. "You've met my uncle then, Sir Gerard Sutton…"

"In a m-manner of speaking, my lord," she replied. She seemed shaken, out of sorts. Who could blame her? She'd been deposited in a strange dwelling in the midst of a torrential storm. He was certain she'd been given no water with which to wash, nor ale to drink. He'd told Sibilla to find a suitable set of clothes for Lady Cristiane, yet that had not been done, either.

He was more angry now than he'd ever been with the

Bitterlee servants. Though her ragged clothes—and what they had barely concealed—would forever hold a cherished place in his memory, 'twas not appropriate for the granddaughter of an earl to be so poorly attired. And with the way the servants had ig—

"My lord?" said a short woman in a russet gown and white wimple. She wore a chain around her waist, with keys dangling from it. Her head was high, her lips pinched, and she appeared ready for a dressing-down.

"There seems to have been a misunderstanding, Sibilla," Adam said, concealing his anger. "Apparently, the maids are not clear on the duties I set forth with regard to Lady Cristiane."

Sibilla shuffled nervously. This was the woman who directed the other household servants' activities. Adam intended to make Sibilla understand that he would brook no disrespect for Cristiane, no matter her native land. He would give the housekeeper one opportunity to rectify matters, but there would be serious consequences if his orders were not carried out.

"Y-yes, my lord," Sibilla said. "I will see to matters immediately."

She scurried away without asking for specifics, and Adam felt sure there would be no further difficulty from the servants. He had not anticipated they'd be so hostile toward Cristiane, but it did not matter. If they wished to remain in his employ, they would treat her with the respect and courtesy due any guest, especially one of her rank.

When he turned back to Cristiane, he found that Raynauld was keeping her distracted with light conversation. Adam's uncle Gerard remained standing at one side of the fireplace, taciturn and dour, observing all that was taking place, but not joining in.

But the most surprising thing of all was Margaret. Left alone by Mathilde, she was gazing up at Cristiane with eyes that showed more interest than Adam had seen since his return from Falkirk.

And 'twas Cristiane Mac Dhiubh that had caused it.

Adam swallowed the lump that suddenly developed in his throat, and reached over to touch his daughter's head. He crouched down to be closer to her, placing himself near Cristiane's knee. "Margaret," he said quietly, "this is Lady Cristiane. Cristiane, my daughter."

"I'm very glad to make your acquaintance, wee Margaret," Cristiane said, reaching to take the child's hand. "And I thank you for the loan of your papa."

An odd spark lit Margaret's eye, but she lowered her lashes quickly, tipping her head down so that her chin nearly touched her chest.

"Aye…he traveled all the way to my home, away north in Scotland," Cristiane said quietly, seeming to sense something amiss with the child, "and brought me here to Bitterlee. But he's yours again, see?"

Her voice was oddly breathless, but there was hardly a hint of the burr. Adam thought 'twas well that she kept her speech from reminding his people of Scotland. Though he did not doubt that the servants would cooperate now, matters were likely to be strained until her departure.

He watched as Cristiane gently caressed his little daughter's fingers before letting go. If she were offended by Margaret's silence, or by the slight shown her by the servants, she did not show it. She merely looked up at Raynauld when he remarked that the servants were about to serve the meal.

"Shall we be seated at table, Lady Cristiane?" Adam asked, reaching for her hand. Though he sensed that she was ill at ease, her hand was warm, and she clasped his as she stood. He did not dare look at her face, for fear of seeing that streak of vulnerability in her eyes.

"Will Elwin join us, Raynauld?" Adam asked as they walked to the table.

Raynauld shook his head. "Nay, my lord. His wife…" The knight paused uncomfortably and blushed. "She, ah, requires his presence for now."

Adam read the subtle message in Raynauld's words. The occasional references to lusty wives dumbfounded him. He'd never experienced such a thing, and could not imagine Elwin's wife behaving in a bawdy manner.

Mathilde took Margaret's hand and began to lead her away, but Adam stopped her. "Hold, Mathilde," he said. "I would have my daughter join us this eve."

Though she tried to conceal her disapproval, 'twas clear that the nurse believed the child's place was not at table with the adults. Adam wondered if she was right. Children were usually relegated to their nurseries and their nurses. 'Twas not a parent's business to see to the care and nurturing of them, other than to assure that servants provided what was needed.

Still, something was wrong. He remembered his sparkling child, playing on the floor of Rosamund's chamber, so full of questions and comments. Though Rosamund most often lay listlessly upon her bed, Margaret never seemed to mind, as long as she was allowed to stay with her mother. Mathilde was always there, too, keeping a watchful eye on the child *and* Rosamund as she plied her needle.

Here it was, two years later, and Adam thought Margaret's grief went beyond natural and normal. She was silent. She was torpid and drawn. Her skin was transparent, and she was not growing as she should.

Yet he had no idea what to do. He was nearly without hope that he could effect any change in her. Mayhap finding her a new mother was not the best thing, but he'd tried all else he could think of. He'd worked at getting her to eat more, but with little success. He'd had music added to her lessons, only to discover she had no talent for it. Same for sewing. Margaret just didn't have the knack, or the interest.

Adam glanced at Cristiane. Her profile was a strong one, with her straight nose and prominent cheekbones. Her chin was slightly cleft, and her ears small and well formed. He knew she had recently come through a great deal of tragedy. How did she cope? Could she somehow show him a way to help Margaret past her grief?

The first course of the meal was served in awkward silence. Cristiane knew she was not welcome here, although Raynauld and Adam made a valiant attempt to disguise that fact. They conversed together as if naught were amiss, as if they had not returned to Bitterlee with a daughter of their Scots foe.

"When the rain lets up, you must visit Bitterlee's garden," Raynauld said, turning to Cristiane. He was a fair knight, young and handsome, and Cristiane knew it could not be long before he chose some young woman for his wife. "'Tis always a favorite spot of the ladies."

"Aye," Cristiane replied quietly. "I'd like that. Is there a path I might follow to get to the seashore?"

"The seashore?" Raynauld asked.

"Aye," she said with amusement. "It must be all around us."

"You are right in that, Lady Cristiane," Adam said. "But 'tis a dangerous coastline here at Bitterlee. Only one short mile is sandy beach, and that's down near the town. The rest is all high cliffs, and rocky escarpments."

"I...I see," she said, masking her disappointment.

All were silent for a moment, then Adam cleared his throat. He looked as if he might speak, but changed his mind.

"We have a fine waterfall," Raynauld remarked weakly, "on the far side of the castle wall..."

Cristiane gave a slight nod and wondered when she would be able to take her leave. Even among these people at table, she had never felt so alone. She wanted naught more than to escape to her chamber, as cold and unwelcoming as it was.

"There are many worthwhile sights on Bitterlee. I will show you myself," Adam said, though he looked as if he might choke on his words.

Cristiane knew he had not intended to say them, but had only tried to fill the void left by her obvious disappointment. "Thank you, my lord," she said in a small voice. "'Twill not be necessary. You have been away many days and must attend to—"

"Nay, Lady Cristiane," he said. "I am at leisure to do as I please."

She did not know how that was possible, but did not argue. However, she caught sight of Margaret at that moment, showing a great deal of interest in the conversation between Adam and herself. She knew naught of children and the things they liked, but said anyway, "Mayhap Margaret would like to join our tour?"

Adam hesitated, then a smile touched one side of his mouth. "Aye. Mayhap she would."

Chapter Eight

Bright flashes of lightning awoke Cristiane sometime in the night. Thunder crashed so violently that she wondered if the isle had been rent in two. Alarmed by the intensity of the storm, she tossed off her blanket and threw on the long-sleeved underkirtle that, along with a tub of bathwater, had miraculously appeared in her chamber after last night's supper.

A high-pitched wail pierced the night, and Cristiane stumbled to her chamber door in the dark, wondering what the sound could have been.

Another door in the gallery opened, and Adam stepped out, holding an iron lamp. In the dim light, Cristiane saw that he was still fully clothed as he walked in the direction opposite her. Cristiane followed, doubting he even knew she was there.

He opened the door to another chamber farther down, and went in. With bare feet, Cristiane stepped into the doorway and watched as Adam approached his daughter, who cowered in terror in the center of her bed. She was silent, but her eyes were wide with fear, her mouth trembling.

Another crash of thunder propelled her into her father's arms.

He held Margaret close, rocking her, murmuring reassuring words to her. Cristiane looked behind her, but the nurse did not appear. 'Twas just as well, she thought. Adam's loving embrace was likely to be of more comfort to the bairn than anything the stern old woman might do.

Cristiane felt a sharp pang of loss as she watched Adam with Margaret, and missed her father more than ever. She recalled the times he'd held and comforted her as a child, and wished for just a moment that she could share those times once again.

Returning her thoughts to the present, she saw that Adam clearly had no need of assistance, so Cristiane returned to her chamber.

But 'twas a long time before she was able to return to sleep.

Shortly before dawn, the rain stopped battering Cristiane's window. The quiet woke her. She hoped wee Margaret had been able to settle down for the night and allow her father to get some sleep.

Clad in the thin undertunic she'd put on during the night, Cristiane climbed out of bed and went to the window, then opened the casement. Leaning out across the thick wall, she looked down.

'Twas still too dark to see much, but Cristiane had the impression that this chamber overlooked the sea. She sensed it from the sounds of the roaring waves and the distinctive salty scent.

Cristiane leaned farther and breathed deeply. The smell of the air was heavenly. The clean, pure scent of the rain mingled with the strong odors of the sea and the rich, dark earth of Bitterlee. By the sound of it, the waves were crashing majestically, and Cristiane suddenly had an urge to see it all with her own two eyes when the sun rose.

Leaving her window open, she picked up a lamp and left the chamber. Quietly, she went to the end of the gallery, where the stairs continued on above her, and began to climb.

Castle Bitterlee was huge. It had many towers, and even more stairs and strange passageways. Cristiane was unsure where this stair would lead her, but from the conversation of the previous night, she thought it possible that it would lead to the top of the castle, mayhap to a parapet that looked out over the cliffs.

Without further thought, she continued up the steps.

When the worst of the storm had finally passed, Margaret fell asleep in Adam's arms. He returned to his own bed, but managed to sleep only fitfully through the night. The weight of his responsibilities lay heavily on him.

He finally gave up on sleep sometime before dawn and made his way to the parapet, where his wife had seen fit to end her life.

The air up on the high tower felt as if it had been washed clean by the rain. Adam blew out the candle of the lamp he'd carried with him, and went to the wall. He had not bothered to dress, other than putting on braes and chausses, but he was immune to the bite of the cool air on his bare chest and back.

Wearily, he gazed down into the darkness and wondered how life on Bitterlee could have been so terrible that Rosamund would throw herself from this very wall. Adam loved the isle. He knew every rock, every plant, every stream. 'Twas all beautiful to him, even the isolation.

He knew now that the solitude had been difficult for Rosamund, and he should have made a greater effort to bring visitors to her. He should have realized it and sent her to her father's home for visits, especially when he'd been called by King Edward to Scotland.

Why had he not understood how important companionship was to her? He'd thought that with a husband and child to care for, she would be satisfied. She would not need the company of her parents or of her London circle. He had believed her temperament would improve once she became a mother.

What a fool he'd been, an ignorant lad with no knowledge of how to keep a wife content. If ever he married again, all would be different. He would be certain to surround his wife with friends, if that was her wish.

Unbidden, an image of Cristiane Mac Dhiubh came to mind. He wondered if she would make friends in York more easily than she would manage here at Bitterlee. Just because her uncle was Earl of Learick did not mean that Cristiane would gain immediate acceptance. Adam suspected that she would seem just as appallingly Scottish to all her Yorkish relations as she did to him.

Yet, to be honest with himself, she was not exactly appalling. She was most definitely Scottish, but he could not hold that against her. He'd seen with his own eyes how the people of St. Oln had treated her—a half-English outsider. He'd glimpsed a deep well of inner strength that she carried and drew upon whenever circumstances warranted. It made her more attractive to him than any superficial attributes he would have chosen in a woman.

Not that she was shy of superficial attributes. He was

quick to arousal when he thought of her physical presence. From her expressive eyes to her graceful neck, her rose-tipped breasts to the feminine swell of her hips, the mere thought of her had the power to turn him to rock-hard awareness.

Adam raked one hand through his sleep-disheveled hair. The earliest birds had come awake, and he knew the sun would soon rise. He had Bitterlee matters to attend this day, and needed to concentrate on them—rather than on Cristiane Mac Dhiubh. She was a temporary distrac—

"Oh! My lord!" gasped a feminine voice.

Adam turned to see Lady Cristiane stepping onto the parapet with a lamp in hand. She must have been unaware of his presence until the lantern had thrown its light on him.

"Good morn, my lady," he said. With the light shining on him he could not see her, but he wondered if she wore the same look of appreciation and hunger that had been in her eyes when she'd seen him half-clothed before.

He heard what might have been a gasp, then she suddenly blew out the lamp, casting them in darkness again.

"'Tis early," he said, more gruffly than he intended.

"Aye," she replied. "The quiet of the morning woke me."

'Twas a strange way of thinking on it, but Adam supposed she was right. When the rain stopped, it had become eerily quiet. He turned and faced the sea again, wishing there was enough light to see her. Was she as meagerly clad as he?

'Twas a notion that had an immediate effect on him. *Damnation!* he thought. *Why had he not gone to Watersby when he'd had the chance?*

"The sun…" He cleared his throat. "The sun will rise soon."

She moved closer to the wall and set the lamp on the ground next to her. "Hear the kittiwakes? They're ready to feed."

Her voice was soft and intimate, like a lover's. He would never grow accustomed to her manner of speech. Most of the time 'twas not terribly Scottish, though she had enough of a burr to make it not quite English. 'Twas all too enticing, with its smooth musical lilt—rolling sounds that washed over him like the cool waters of the waterfall north of the castle.

Adam gripped the stone edge of the parapet and forced himself to think of something else. "We have seals, too," he finally said, "on the outer island."

"Ach, ye donna!" Cristiane said, forgetting to mask her burr. She turned to face him excitedly and put one hand on his arm to steady herself.

"We do," he said. Though he already had a death grip on the rock wall, the muscles in Adam's arm bunched at her touch, and heat flared in uncomfortable places. He wished he had a tunic to better cover his reaction to her touch. "'Tis not much of an isle," he added, turning away from her, "but a pile of rock off the north coast. For some reason, the seals like our insufferable weather."

"'Tis not insufferable!"

"Last night's storm—"

"Was truly amazing," she said with awe in her voice.

Had he heard her correctly? She was not about to run from the isle as soon as she could get away?

"You've been on Bitterlee less than a day," he said quietly, drinking in her scent. Her hand remained on his bare arm, and he harnessed the urge to find her fingers and take her hand in his, to touch his lips to the back of it. "How can you judge?"

"I cannot, not really," Cristiane said, restraining her burr once again, "but 'tis a beautiful place... Oh, Adam, look!"

The first rays of the sun splayed out over the water, giving an eerie cast to the scene. Within moments, though, the sky turned a brilliant pink, casting various shades of red and gold over the sea.

"'Tis breathtaking," she sighed.

True enough. Adam could not recall seeing anything quite as grand as Cristiane Mac Dhiubh enjoying her first sunrise on Bitterlee. Her eyes were wide, framed by gold-tipped lashes. Her lips were full and moist, and entirely too alluring.

She turned slightly toward him, her body close, too close for his own to ignore. He felt his hands grow moist and his heart begin to pound. The rushing surf was naught compared to the roaring in his own ears.

In the growing light, he saw that she was covered from neck to toe by a thin linen kirtle, yet her enticing form would never be hidden from him again, no matter how well covered it might be. Burned into his memory was the way she'd looked in the firelight the morning he'd seen her undressed.

'Twould take only the slightest movement of his hand to pull her close, a trifling tip of his head to bring his lips into contact with hers.

And every fiber of his being demanded that he do so.

He could divest them both of their clothes in seconds, yet Adam knew this was not an acceptable tack. Cristiane was under his protection.

"Is there a path down to the beach?" she asked, her voice subdued, her breath warm on his chest.

"There is no beach," he said roughly. He balled his hands into fists and stepped away. "Not up here near the castle. And no way down to the water, anyhow."

"But—"

"Just rocks and birds down there."

He lied. 'Twas possible to get across the rocks and down to the water. He had tried to convince Rosamund to go down with him when they were young and newly married, but his wife had had no interest in dallying near the water with him. She had shunned the lovely pool by the waterfall, too.

"I'm sure you will enjoy the gardens, though," he said in a conciliatory tone. 'Twas not an easy climb down to the beach, and he did not want her to risk it, especially not alone. "There is a great deal of new spring growth, and we have a large pond..."

The sunlight was more golden now, and Cristiane seemed to realize suddenly how inappropriately dressed she was. She'd been at ease in the dark, but now, when she knew he could see her, she felt the need to cross her arms over her breasts.

When she licked her lips unconsciously, Adam's entire body clenched, and he forced himself to look away. Though she was decently covered, the linen shift was thin, and it fit entirely too snugly for his peace of mind.

She seemed to know it.

"I—I'd best be going back to my chamber..." she said as she stepped away. "Before, er, I..."

He heard her bare feet softly retreating, and when the stairway door closed, he was able to breathe again.

Cristiane did not stop until she opened what she thought was the door to her room. Mortified to have stepped into some other bedchamber, she turned and fled, quickly finding the door to her own.

She knew her color was still high, and she pressed her hands to her cheeks to cool them. She resolved in future to avoid these early morning interludes with Adam Sutton, since they only served to embarrass her.

Yet she could not regret the few moments she'd spent enjoying his warmth as he stood nearly naked beside her.

His body was so different, so intriguing. Where she was soft and smooth, he was hard and muscular, and covered with hair. She'd ached to touch him, to run her fingers up the hard planes of his chest through that mat of hair, and see if he was as solid as he looked.

Heat flooded her cheeks anew and Cristiane stepped over to the basin of fresh water. She washed her face, cooling herself at the same time, then took a long draught of water before dressing.

She had to get away from here.

A clean kirtle that had once been a deep green color lay on the trunk at the foot of her bed. The fabric had faded and was worn thin in places, but was in much better condition than the gown she'd been wearing these last weeks. Hastily, she pulled it on over her head and then fastened the laces, finding it as snug a fit as the underkirtle.

Refusing to be disappointed by this gift, she vowed nonetheless to begin sewing as soon as Adam found some cloth for her to use.

She sat down and pulled on her shoes, taking half a moment to appreciate Adam's kindness in buying them for her. She quickly laced them, then left her chamber in search of a way out. She did not want to chance another embarrassing encounter with Adam.

There were so many passages and doors here in the

keep that it was unnecessary to go through the great hall
in order to leave. She knew she had only to find the
correct passageway, and it would lead her to an outside
door. Following an instinctual sense of direction, she
made her way to the main floor, without meeting anyone.

The sun was barely over the horizon when she finally
let herself out of the keep through a door near the chapel,
with the intention of making her way down to the water.

There'd been no path to her favorite places at St. Oln,
either. Yet she'd followed her father down to the sea all
those years before, finding footholds across the rocks
when she'd been just a child. There was no reason she
could not do the same here on Bitterlee.

"M'lady…"

Startled by the low voice and the sound of footsteps
on the gravel behind her, Cristiane whirled to see Sir
Elwin there. He looked well rested and content.

"Lord Bitterlee sent me to show ye the sights."

She swallowed. "I thank you, Sir Elwin," she said,
"but 'twill not be necessary. I can roam—"

"Ah, but the lord gave express orders that I'm to escort ye 'round the gardens and such."

"But—"

He took her arm and ushered her back onto the path.
"No buts," he said.

They headed for the garden and all its tame glory.

Adam was grateful that after the night's rain, the waterfall would be heavier than usual, and cold. 'Twas
what he needed to purge himself of the heat he could
not seem to control whenever Cristiane Mac Dhiubh was
near.

The dogs ran ahead of him as he limped up the narrow
trail that continued along the escarpment north of the

castle, and soon turned onto a narrow footpath through a thick wood. After following the path a short way, he heard it—the thundering of the water as it hit the stony floor a hundred feet below, filling a pool that overflowed into a river that rushed all the way down to the sea.

Taking a moment to rub the soreness from his thigh, Adam stopped, perched in a notch between two trees and gazed down at the sight of the falls. 'Twas so beautiful, he was sure Eden must have looked like this.

The dogs did not allow him to rest for long. Anxious for a good run, they circled him and whined until he left the path and continued on his way. He soon descended to the rock floor, taking care not to slip as he climbed down.

Ren and Gray were well ahead of him, loping through the shallows, then shaking their coats, spraying water everywhere.

The roar of the falls was deafening this morning, owing to the increased flow of water. The cold mist sprayed him before he actually stepped into the falls, and he appreciated the shock of it. He started removing his clothes as he walked behind the curtain of water, and when he was fully naked he braced himself, then stepped under the heavy spray.

The icy blast shocked him. He let out a roar, then shook his body like one of the dogs, relishing the release from tension. He stood under the downpour as long as he could stand it, then dived into the clear, deep pool that was fed by the waterfall. He vowed to stay there until he rid his mind and body of one wild-haired Scotswoman.

Even if his important body parts froze and fell off.

Chapter Nine

In spite of Sir Elwin's interference, Cristiane enjoyed her morning of exploration. The storm had caused some damage to the gardens, with fallen branches and small floods, but men had already begun setting it to rights. Even so, the grounds were lovely, with newly sprouted flowers and plants.

Far from the keep was a large pond, inhabited by a brood of ducklings that peeped incessantly as they swam frantically in circles, not far from the bank.

"Where is the hen?" Cristiane wondered aloud as she approached the reedy edge of the water.

Elwin shrugged absently.

Cristiane knew the babies would never leave their mother unless...

She pulled off her shoes, hiked up her skirts and stepped into the water.

"Lady Cristiane," Elwin called in as much surprise as alarm, "do ye think—"

"Pay me no mind, Sir Elwin," Cristiane said. "I'm accustomed to the water, and I'm a good swimmer, besides."

Elwin muttered something she could not quite hear,

but Cristiane ignored him. Wading in to her knees, she discovered a thick log floating in the water. 'Twas tangled up in a mass of weeds, and the body of the mother duck was caught there.

'Twas no wonder the little ones kept circling 'round. Cristiane looked back at them now, and realized just how young they were. Only a few weeks hatched, if she was not mistaken, and they would die without the hen's attention.

Cristiane could not let that happen. They were too precious to leave to such a fate.

She knew she could not be of much help, for she had only a few days at Bitterlee—just long enough to sew a new kirtle or two—before traveling on to York. One look at Sir Elwin told her that the knight would have no interest in nurturing the little ducklings, nor did the gardeners appear to have the leisure to attend to them.

Yet there had to be some way to save them.

"If yer done muckin' about, m'lady," Elwin said, pushing himself off the tree trunk where he'd been leaning and watching, "I'm fair starved and wouldn't mind breakin' my fast sometime soon."

Cristiane was hungry, too. She would consider the problem of the ducklings, and come up with some solution.

The sun was high when they returned to the keep. As she and Elwin walked toward the chapel, she saw Adam standing at the foot of the main stone staircase, surrounded by a group of people. His hair was wet and combed back from his freshly shaved face, and he wore a clean dark tunic and black hose. He looked as if he had just stepped out of his bath.

She had always thought him a beautiful man, but with

this aura of power about him, he was especially appealing. She wished she were not so distasteful to him.

She could not blame him for his dislike of all things
Scottish. He'd lost many Bitterlee men to the war, and
had been badly wounded himself. To add to all that, his
wife had died while he was away. Though he was too
fair a man to blame the Scots for Lady Rosamund's
death, he must resent having been away at war when she
died.

"Who are all those people?" Cristiane asked Elwin.

"They're from Bitterlee town," he replied. "Likely
come to tell his lordship what damage the storm did
down there."

Four men and one woman comprised the group. The
woman was young and pretty, with hair the color of
honey, pinned down and properly tamed. She was
dressed in a clean, well-fitting gown of bright blue, and
Adam seemed to pay particular attention to what she
said.

Cristiane wondered if the young lady were of the gen-
try. She certainly looked it, and judging from the way
Adam inclined his head to listen to her, the woman was
somehow special to him. Absently, Cristiane rubbed the
center of her chest, as if she could rub away the sudden
ache that began there.

Abruptly, she turned and darted up the stairs and into
the great hall, where servants were beginning to lay out
the noon meal. The dogs saw her and ran to her, sniffing
her shoes, offering their heads to be petted. Taking a
deep breath, she gave them their due, then turned away
from them and approached the table.

Little Margaret was there with her nurse and Sir Gerard. Also seated was a gentleman Cristiane had not yet

met. He had the look of clergy, with his tonsure and the cut of the coarse, dark brown robe he wore.

The priest's expression was a sour one, nearly matching that of the nurse, Mathilde. Gerard had the same sullen look about him that Cristiane had noticed the previous evening. Margaret Sutton seemed oblivious to the gloomy adults, and sat alongside them, gazing with unfocused eyes into the distance.

Cristiane knew her own appearance was anything but appropriate for table. She should have gone to her chamber to make repairs, but there was naught to be done about it now. She had no other clothes to wear, and her hair would not be subdued, not without combs, or string to tie it. Besides, she did not want anyone to think she would waste their time—and put off the meal—with useless primping.

Without ado, she took a seat, leaving Elwin to go where he would.

Adam could have done without hearing of all the disasters that occurred in town during the storm. Fallen trees, roofs blown off, floods. And, of course, minor damage had occurred as well. All would require precious manpower that was scant at best.

Yet he knew that Sara Cole would be no less than accurate in her assessment of the damage to the town. She was not a native of Bitterlee, but born a bastard into a family of traveling mummers. However, she was a gifted healer and midwife. In the five years since Sara's arrival here on the isle, she had gained the trust and admiration of the townspeople.

It had been Sara who had attended his wife at Margaret's birth, and had done all she could to rouse Rosamund from her indifference in the weeks afterward.

But 'twas not Sara who occupied Adam's mind as he entered the great hall. If he'd thought he'd be immune to Cristiane Mac Dhiubh after his dunking in the cold water, he was mistaken. He was every bit as susceptible to her even now, with her hair loose, the bodice of her kirtle nearly splitting at its seams and her hem riding a good hand's breadth above her ankles. All that was needed was for her to let out a bloodcurdling Scots battle cry, and the barbaric image would be perfect. He *could not* feel such a strong attraction to a Scotswoman.

He watched Cristiane hesitate a moment before sitting at table. She took a deep breath and seemed to bolster herself as she took a seat without guidance from those who should have assisted her.

The servants kept their distance, avoiding speaking directly to her. Mathilde said naught, and Father Beaupré kept his silence as well. Finally, Gerard muttered something in his usual sardonic manner, and Cristiane replied quietly, keeping her eyes down, her expression carefully neutral.

Adam tamped down his protective instincts and at the same time fought the desire to turn and head back out the door and down the keep's great stone steps.

Instead, he forced himself to approach the dining table. He greeted Cristiane and introduced her to the priest in their midst. "Father Beaupré did not join us last eve, Lady Cristiane," he said distantly, "so you did not have occasion to meet him." Her hands were trembling slightly, but Adam made a point to ignore it. He turned his attention to his daughter as the priest stood and gave Cristiane a slight bow.

"How do you do, my lady?" Beaupré said gravely.

"Very well, thank you," Cristiane replied.

Adam saw that Margaret's attention was once again engaged by their guest. He frowned with puzzlement.

He had not seen his daughter's eyes sparkle with such interest since the days when she'd sat playing in her mother's bedchamber, with Mathilde looking on.

Heartened by her reaction, he sat down and spoke to his daughter. "Margaret, do you remember Lady Cristiane?"

A slight nod of the head was the child's answer. Adam would not have believed the silence at the table could grow any deeper, but as he spoke to his daughter, it did. A frown of disapproval crossed Mathilde's face, and a mask of indifference covered Gerard's. The priest had already dug into his meal and was ignoring everything around him.

Margaret, as usual, said nary a word.

But that little nod of the head… 'Twas more than he'd gotten out of her in all the months since his return from Falkirk. He dared not hope for more.

Adam turned from Margaret, then watched as Cristiane gathered a cloak of serenity about her, the same kind of calm he'd noticed when she'd held her hand out and touched the doe near the river. "Did Sir Elwin give you a thorough tour of the gardens, Lady Cristiane?" he asked.

Adam had promised to take her himself, and when he looked up, he read that accusation in her eyes. But the attraction he felt for her was too powerful. He had to keep away from her as much as possible, else… He would not give form to any thoughts of what would happen. They were sinful and without honor.

Cristiane did not believe the company at table could have been more stiff or unfriendly. She would have declined the meal had she not already sat and been introduced. However, 'twould be the height of discourtesy to leave now, and her parents had taught her better.

Oh, how she missed her mother and father. She felt a

pang in the region of her heart when she thought of them, and blinked back a sudden rush of tears. If only they were here to guide her. She'd never felt so abandoned, so alone.

She looked up again at Adam and saw a familiar remoteness in his eyes. He did not want her here. She did not know what his reason was for taking her from St. Oln, but 'twas clear that he wanted her gone from Bitterlee.

And that hurt. She'd done naught to earn his scorn, other than being an inconvenience.

She should be accustomed to that. She'd been unwelcome at St. Oln, and Cristiane was beginning to fear that she'd be unwelcome in York, too. Her Scots blood would never be forgiven. Not by her uncle; not by this quiet lord with the stormy gray eyes who'd rescued her from a thoroughly dismal existence at St. Oln.

She bit her lip and turned her eyes to the meal, even though she had no appetite for food. Perhaps 'twould be best if Adam found an escort who could take her to her uncle right away. There was no need for her to stay here and sew new gowns. When she arrived at Learick, her mother's brother would certainly understand her circumstances at St. Oln, and make allowances for her shabby attire.

Cristiane sighed and resigned herself to her fate. Somehow, she would make the best of circumstances. Her mother had provided well for her future, and Cristiane would do her the honor of following her wishes. All that was necessary was to endure these next few days at Bitterlee, and then go to her uncle's estate.

"...from Mistress Cole," Sir Gerard was saying. Cristiane had been too preoccupied with her own thoughts to hear more, and she did not catch his meaning.

"Aye," Adam replied. "She said there's a good deal

of damage. Raynauld and some of the men are already in town, helping to drag away some of the downed trees.''

''What of the fields?'' Gerard asked. ''Ruined?''

''Nay,'' Adam replied, ''though some are flooded. They will be all right if it does not rain again for a few days.''

Their conversation continued, and Cristiane added naught to it. She picked at her meal, occasionally exchanging glances with Adam's wee daughter.

A fey one, she was, with gray eyes exactly like her father's, though her brows were the palest gold. Her head was bound tight in the same kind of white wimple she'd worn before, so Cristiane could not see her hair, and her clothing was dark and severe. Again, she was a miniature image of her nurse, who urged her—unsuccessfully—to eat.

The lass was too thin, Cristiane thought, with skin so transparent that her tiny blue veins were quite visible through it. Her eyes were dull, except for an occasional spark of interest when something caught her attention. Cristiane wondered if the plight of the orphaned ducklings would pique her curiosity.

''I saw something interesting by the pond this morn,'' she said when Margaret happened to look up at her. ''Something unusual.''

The child's eyes flicked toward Cristiane for a moment before she blinked and resumed her empty stare. Mathilde made a fuss of cutting up the food in Margaret's trencher, but the little girl clamped her lips closed and refused to be fed. Everyone else grew perfectly still, as if Cristiane had committed the worst possible blunder.

She did not care. From what she had seen, very few of the people here at Bitterlee had the remotest notion of hospitality. Or courtesy. For the duration of her stay on the isle, she would say and do as she pleased.

"If your papa doesna mind, I could take you out to the garden and show you after we eat," Cristiane said. "'Tis truly amazing."

Again, Margaret's interest flared and was quickly subdued again. Adam had not seen her act this way before, and he leaned back in his chair to observe his daughter's interchange with Cristiane unobtrusively.

Cristiane tore a piece of bread and dipped it into the juices of the trencher, then lifted it to Margaret's lips. "Eat, lass," Cristiane said. "If you want to come with me and see what I saw this morn, you must keep up your strength."

Adam held his breath as he watched Cristiane work some kind of magic on his daughter. Margaret allowed Cristiane to place the morsel in her mouth, even as Mathilde spoke. "We have our devotions this afternoon, Lady Cristiane," she said. "Therefore, Lady Margaret will not be able—"

"Devotions will wait," Adam said, cutting off the nurse's admonition. "Margaret and I will accompany Lady Cristiane to the pond this afternoon." The situation in town would wait, too.

He saw a flush color Cristiane's cheeks, but she continued offering juicy bites to Margaret, who accepted them. When 'twas clear the child would eat no more, Cristiane stood and took the little girl's hand, easing her down from her chair. "I'd rather not rush you, my lord," she said, "but Lady Margaret and I are ready to go."

Cristiane picked up a loaf of bread from the table, then walked purposely from the great hall, towing Margaret along with her.

Adam pushed away from the table and followed as she made her way through the baileys and out to the garden. She spoke to Margaret as she walked, but he could hear only a word now and again. It did not matter. She'd sparked Margaret's interest, and he hoped his daughter would not be disappointed.

Hell's bells, he hoped *he* would not be disappointed. He had lived without hope for far too long.

They reached the pond and Cristiane sat down on the ground in the weeds near the bank. The sun was bright and a warm spring breeze blew in from the mainland. 'Twas hard to believe that only last eve a storm had knocked down trees and wiped out two houses in town. He could only hope there would be no more rain for a few days.

Adam stood back, watching, as Cristiane took Margaret's hand again and got her to sit on the ground. She unlaced her own shoes and indicated that Margaret should do the same. When the child sat listlessly, not responding, Cristiane performed the task herself.

Barefoot now, Cristiane stood again. She took Margaret's hands and pulled her up, then tore a piece of bread from the loaf and handed it to her. The little girl took it and looked up at Cristiane, her eyes still somewhat vacant, though there was a hint of curiosity now.

If Adam had ever thought a heart could not burst, he was unsure of it now. For he felt as if his own would pound right out of his chest as he watched his little girl come back to life.

"You'll see," Cristiane said as she walked to the water's edge. She beckoned to Margaret. "Come...."

Margaret hesitated, but finally took her outstretched hand and stepped into the water, holding the piece of bread high. She shuddered and looked as if she would panic, and Adam fought the urge to rush to her side.

But Cristiane spoke to her in a low, reassuring tone. Adam wished he could hear what she said, but did not want to disturb the first real communication he'd seen his daughter carry on since her mother's death. He held back.

Cristiane showed Margaret how to pull her skirts up to her knees and hang on to them with one hand, and Adam watched as his child mimicked her. They stepped deeper into the water and Cristiane threw out a morsel of bread. Suddenly, a brood of tiny ducklings swam 'round a tangle of branches and weeds, and darted toward the bread.

Surprised, Margaret sucked in a breath, just as any other child her age might have done.

Adam moved closer. He could clearly hear the cheeping of the ducklings over the water, and every word Cristiane said.

"Tear off a bite and throw it, wee Meg," Cristiane said.

Wee Meg? His daughter was always called Margaret, but Adam wouldn't question it now. Cristiane could give her any Scottish name she chose, if only she could get Margaret to return to him.

After a moment's hesitation, Margaret did as she was told, and the ducklings made a dash for the newest tidbit. Margaret's body was held tightly. She did not speak, but a controlled excitement radiated from every pore.

"Go ahead, throw another," Cristiane said.

This time, the bit of bread landed closer, and the ducks swam even nearer. Margaret took another sharp breath and looked up at Cristiane with questions in her shining eyes.

"Their mama is gone," Cristiane said, "so they have no one to feed them."

Margaret looked back at the ducklings, which were now chirping madly and swarming like bees. Adam wondered if his daughter had any awareness of the similarity between the ducklings and herself.

"We'll help them, shall we?" Cristiane said. "And they'll be fine."

Margaret quickly got the knack of feeding the ducks, breaking more of the bread and throwing it in, aiming so that the ducklings swam a short distance away. She did not laugh, or even smile, as any other child would, but Adam could not help but think she had made a huge leap of progress during this short interlude.

He looked over at Cristiane, her back straight, her skirts up around her shapely knees. Curly red tendrils of hair had escaped their bindings to trail over her shoulders and down her back. Her rounded hips were clearly delineated when she bent to help Margaret. She suddenly gave a quiet laugh of delight, and Adam had to restrain himself from joining her where she stood.

But he could not interrupt, not when she'd managed to do what no one else on Bitterlee had been able to.

Margaret's entire chunk of bread was soon consumed by the hungry ducklings. She looked up at Cristiane, frowning. "More," she said.

Adam's heart pounded in his ears. He'd not heard a single word from Margaret's mouth since his return from Falkirk. Yet now she spoke. To Cristiane Mac Dhiubh.

Chapter Ten

The child was so thin and frail, Cristiane had had some doubts whether she would manage the long walk to the pond. But Meg—for that was how Cristiane thought of her—had managed to hold up.

Cristiane didn't notice Adam following until after she'd hiked up her skirts and stepped into the water, but 'twas too late now for decorum. He wouldn't expect it from her, anyway. She'd been undressed or partially dressed in his presence far too many times for him to think she had any sense of propriety about her.

Besides, hadn't she just convinced herself not to care what anyone here on Bitterlee thought about her?

"Will you not join us, my lord?" she called to him.

For one who was always so strong and confident, he seemed oddly hesitant to approach her and Margaret.

"You do not mind if your papa helps us feed the bairns, do you, Meg?" she asked.

Margaret stared toward the ducks and gave an almost imperceptible shake of her head.

"See, my lord?" Cristiane said, smiling. "Join us!"

Part of her wished he would remove his own shoes and hose, but he could not do that without being wholly improper. Still, Adam came to the edge of the water and stood watching, his presence both reassuring and dangerous to her peace of mind.

"Meggie lass," Cristiane said, "give your papa some of the bread."

Margaret looked up at Cristiane, then back at the ducklings, which were swarming again. She tore off a small piece of her bread and stepped back to the bank to hand it to her father.

Whatever danger Cristiane imagined Adam posed to her, it was gone when he touched his daughter's hand. Cristiane felt a tug in the center of her chest when she saw the expression in his eyes. They brimmed over with love and caring...and helplessness.

Cristiane could not imagine what ailed the child, and wondered if she'd always been like this. At first, she'd thought Margaret dull witted, but clearly, that was not the case. Perplexed, Cristiane wondered if Margaret's problem was spending too much time with that awful Mathilde.

Cristiane resolved to see that Margaret came out to the pond every day she remained at Bitterlee. Mayhap enough time out-of-doors would have a positive effect on the child. She might even say a few more words if she were motivated enough.

"Let's show your papa what to do, shall we, Meg?" she asked as she waded over to them. "Take his hand...." Cristiane took Margaret's hand and guided it to Adam's. "Help him throw it."

Adam waited for Margaret to move. Suddenly, she lifted his hand and "helped" him toss the bread to the wildly peeping ducklings. Then she covered her mouth with her hand as her eyes became dull again.

Adam's throat was choked by emotion. He did not

think he'd ever experienced such joy. He longed to pull Margaret up into his arms and hug her tightly, but did not want to frighten her deeper into her shell. Holding her during a storm was one thing. This was altogether different.

She had made progress today. After months of trying to get his child to respond to him, it had taken a stranger—Cristiane Mac Dhiubh—to make her come alive.

"Margaret," he said thickly. "'tis been my pleasure to help you feed the ducklings. Shall we come again tomorrow?"

Acknowledgment flashed in Margaret's eyes, then she quickly put her head down and did not answer. But it did not matter. He was heartened by her behavior, because only yesterday she'd have given no response at all.

Stepping aside to let Cristiane usher Margaret out of the pond, he stayed clear of them while the Scotswoman straightened their skirts and put both pair of shoes back on. He caught a puzzled look from her, but followed quietly behind as they returned to the hall.

Mathilde and Gerard awaited them. The nurse took charge of Margaret and propelled her toward the chapel, and the child kept her head down and went along without protest.

Cristiane would have spoken up, but Gerard cornered Adam before she had a chance.

"Mistress Cole awaits you in the solar," Gerard said.

Adam glanced toward the staircase, then turned back to Cristiane. "I cannot thank you enough, my lady, for…taking Margaret to the pond. And—"

"What ails the lass, my lord?" she asked. "Why is she—"

"Adam…" Gerard said harshly.

Adam ignored him. "My daughter has been low spirited since my wife…since my wife's death."

"Do you mean she has not spoken since then?" Cristiane asked, frowning. "She has not smiled or played or—"

"It pains me to see her thus. She was always such a vibrant child," he said. His frustration and helplessness were clear in his voice. "I have not known what to do…"

"'Tis her grief, my lord," Cristiane said. She was so close to her own grief that she could easily understand Margaret's. The child must miss her mother terribly. "It may take some time for her to recover from it."

"'Tis been two years!" Adam said bitterly.

"Aye," Cristiane said. "I know how it feels…when ye canna pull yerself out of it."

He looked at her as if he did not believe her.

"You don't understand. Her mother was never…" he speared his fingers through his hair. "Margaret was practically an infant when her mother died—"

"Adam," Gerard interrupted, "the child is a simpleton. There is naught you can do for her. Leave her to the nurse and—"

"Leave us, Gerard!" Adam said in anger. "I will see Sara when I am through here."

Cristiane would have preferred not to witness an altercation between Adam and his uncle, and was even more uncomfortable at the look of pure repugnance in Gerard's eyes when he gazed at her. She knew she was not popular with the people of Bitterlee, but Sir Gerard's blatant antipathy bruised her anew. Tears threatened, but she blinked them away, refusing to be cowed by his blatant hostility.

Gerard stalked away, though Cristiane would not have been surprised to find the man lurking somewhere nearby, poised to sling an unkind remark at her at the first opportunity.

"I'll not keep you any longer, my lord," she said, turning away. "I'll just return to the pond while the sun is still warm."

"Cristiane." Adam took hold of her arm before she was able to take a step. "What you did today…" His dark gray eyes shone with gratitude. "Taking Margaret to the pond…did you know 'twould make her come alive again?"

Cristiane smiled weakly and shrugged. "Nay, my lord. I only knew how I'd have felt at her age. Seeing that brood would have gladdened my heart. I only hoped 'twould do the same for Meg."

Adam could well imagine Cristiane as a bright, red-headed sprite, laughing, dancing out into the water to dally with the fowl that swam there. He raised his hand and gently touched her jaw with his fingers. Color rose in her cheeks and her breath quickened. He was tempted to touch his lips to hers.

Merely in gratitude.

But a kiss would be anything but proper. Adam forced himself to step back, freeing her arm from his light touch. The prudent thing would be to leave her here and head for the solar and see what Sara wanted. 'Twas likely she had come to visit Penyngton, and Adam wanted to know her thoughts on his condition.

Yet he was reluctant to leave Cristiane. His hands ached to touch her, his mouth to taste her.

Cristiane's lively blue eyes turned wary as he looked at her. Try as he might, he could not keep himself from taking hold of her arm again, and pulling her to him.

He tipped his head down as she lifted hers. She moistened her lips.

An eternity passed as they closed the space between them. He felt her breath on his lips, knew her sweetness before they touched.

Her mouth was soft. 'Twas hot and wet.

His free hand found the nape of her neck and pulled her close. He felt her body tremble as he opened his lips and urged her to do the same. Her tongue met his shyly, and he thought he might burst with the sudden intensity of his arousal.

Her hands moved tentatively, reaching up to his shoulders, pulling him closer. A soft whimper escaped her and Adam deepened the kiss. His hands caressed her nape, then slid down her back to her hips. He cradled himself in her softness, resisting the urge to pick her up and carry her to his chamber, where he could make love to her all afternoon.

But he would not. They were practically strangers, destined to be no more than acquaintances. She had been kind to Margaret, but would soon depart Bitterlee…with his blessings. And when she left for York, Lady Cristiane Mac Dhiubh would essentially exist no more.

''*Adam!*'' Gerard's voice caused them to leap apart.

Chapter Eleven

Cristiane's embarrassment was profound when Sir Gerard interrupted her tryst with Adam in the great hall. She should have known better than to allow her attraction to go so far. 'Twas unseemly to behave in such a manner with a man who was not—who would never be—her husband.

Shakily, she fled the hall. Somehow, she managed to make it all the way to the pond after Adam's sensuous onslaught, taking refuge on the ground at the base of an ancient oak. Curling her legs under her, Cristiane relived the moment when his lips had touched hers, when he'd pulled her close and let a feverish groan escape.

Where would their sensuous interlude have led if Gerard had not intruded? To a private alcove in the castle? To a bedchamber? Cristiane knew Adam's wife had been dead two years. Had loneliness, coupled with her own convenient presence and naiveté, driven him to take advantage of the moment?

'Twas difficult for Cristiane to care what the reason was. She'd been strongly attracted to Lord Bitterlee since the moment he'd rescued her at St. Oln, and feared she would have given herself to him, regardless of his reasons for wanting her.

His body was hard and unyielding. He was as strong and powerful as any man she'd ever known, and Cristiane still felt an intense desire to pursue the course of their attraction.

'Twas wrong. Whatever she felt for Adam was not reciprocated. She was not so naive as to believe aught else. His kiss had started as an expression of his gratitude, and naught more. 'Twas only the physical attraction between them that had turned it into more.

"Sir Charles is naught but skin and bone," Sara Cole told Adam. "He tells me he's been suffering through night sweats for quite some time, and now he's coughing blood," she added. "I would say 'tis a kind of lung fever, my lord."

"Why did he not tell me he was ailing?" Adam asked, pacing the chamber restlessly. He was frustrated both with his friend's reticence and with Cristiane's inflamed response to his touch, his kiss.

He was an idiot to have touched her so intimately. Now that he'd tasted her, he doubted he could ever forget how she'd felt in his arms.

Sara shook her head. "I do not know," she replied, frowning. "He never told... I can tell you that without proper rest and attention, he will d-die."

"Is there naught that you can do for him?" Adam asked, horrified by the prognosis given his closest friend. 'Twas clear that Charles's fate lay heavily upon Sara, too.

"Aye," she replied. "Some. There is a decoction that I will mix especially for him. I'll bring it here every day and give it to him myself."

"Thank you, Sara," Adam said. "But is there anything the rest of us can do, here at the castle?"

Sara smiled, causing the dimple high on her cheek to deepen. It reminded Adam of the same mark on their father, as did the color of her hair. For she was his half sister, and had come to Bitterlee five years before in order to meet the noble father who had abandoned her mother.

When Sara had first arrived, their father had been too ill to accept or deny her claim, but in his delirium, he had spoken the name Nichola—Sara's mother's name.

Adam had not been able to deny that Sara was his sister. She had his father's green eyes, the same dimple and his coloring. There could be no doubt that Sara was a Sutton.

Yet she had not come to Bitterlee with the intention of being welcomed into the family. Nay, she had merely wanted to meet the man who was her sire. But when she found him ill, and near death, kindhearted Sara had stayed to nurse him until the end.

Subsequently, she'd made a life for herself in town. And if anyone suspected she was Thomas Sutton's daughter, no one had mentioned it in all these years.

"You can help keep his spirits up," she said. "See that he is offered his favorite foods. Do whatever is necessary to keep him happy, content."

Adam gave a quick nod. It would be done. Adam could not imagine Bitterlee without him. Beyond being seneschal of Bitterlee, Charles Penyngton had been a loyal and true friend.

Adam walked with Sara to Penyngton's room and opened the door a crack, only to find that Charles was asleep. Closing the door quietly, he took her by the arm and led her down the stone staircase. With luck, he would send Sara on her way, and resume his interlude with Cristiane.

It only remained to be seen whether that kind of luck would be good or bad.

Cristiane was not normally prone to prowling indoors. She preferred the elements, whether fair or harsh, wet or dry. Yet Bitterlee Castle fascinated her.

And she was restless.

Her father's keep at St. Oln was a primitive shelter compared to this. Domhnall Mac Dhiubh had possessed one tower, with a few mean chambers abovestairs, and one wooden staircase, the place where he'd met his death.

As she wandered through the keep, Cristiane discovered several rooms off the great hall, many with long, narrow windows covered with panes of glass that could be opened like those in her own chamber, when the weather permitted. A row of secret alcoves lay beneath the main staircase, and beyond that was a large chapel.

'Twas as grand as the church at St. Oln. Nay, more so.

The Bitterlee chapel was made of stone, with a huge, ornately carved altar at one end. Tiny flames from a hundred beeswax candles flickered in the semidarkness of the chamber, and the aroma of incense was strong. Long, ornamented plaques painted with the images of Christ and the Madonna hung on the walls beyond the altar.

Cristiane felt compelled to kneel in this exalted setting. Bowing her head, she prayed for the strength to resist her fleshly urges and endure her stay at Bitterlee without falling into temptation. Her attraction to Adam was naught short of sinful, and there was no future in it.

Determined to put that moment of lunacy out of her mind, she offered prayers for the souls of her parents, and for wee Meg, that she would soon overcome her grief.

Crossing herself devoutly, Cristiane rose and left the chapel, following the long corridor with the alcoves. When she reached the great hall, she saw Adam and the young woman from town. This must be Sara.

They were speaking quietly together, and Adam had a proprietary hand at her elbow. It should not have been such a surprise, nor should Cristiane been so dismayed by the sight of Adam with that woman.

Yet she was. For all her resolve to avoid physical entanglements in future, it hurt to know that he had only trifled with her.

"'Tis doubtful any border Scots enjoy such bountiful fare," Gerard said as he speared a succulent bite of fish with his knife. *"Nor should they."*

Cristiane tried to ignore his harsh words, but they stung, as they were meant to. Yet she kept her head down and continued with the evening meal, alongside Meg and Adam.

"Lady Cristiane had naught to do with any English deaths," Adam said. "Her village had no part in the conflict with King Edward."

"Ah…so the lady is an innocent," Gerard said, his sarcasm ripe, "who knows naught of that devil, William Wallace."

Cristiane slapped her knife on the table, and was about to retort, when Adam intervened. "You will be unwelcome at my table, Uncle, if you persist in baiting our guest.''

''*Your* guest, Nephew,'' Gerard said with a sneer. ''Your very convenient guest.''

Cristiane was not certain of his meaning, but made a guess, based on Gerard's interruption of the kiss she'd shared with Adam. Her heart sank, knowing that Gerard's assessment of her was a fair one.

A lady of good breeding would never have been caught kissing a man.

She suddenly had to get away, get out of the stifling confines of the hall. Adam's conversation had been stilted, and now Gerard was plainly insulting. She could not take much more.

Cristiane stood and excused herself from the table. Knowing how poorly dressed she was, how badly she fit in and how much she was reviled here, she had to summon every ounce of brazen nerve she possessed to walk away.

She kept her trembling to a minimum as she fled to the chapel and out the door nearby.

''That was uncalled for, Gerard,'' Adam said angrily. He shoved back his chair. ''If it should happen again, I'll put you off the isle.''

He walked away, following in Cristiane's footsteps, unsure what he would do once he found her. She'd been visibly upset, though he believed she'd managed to conceal her hurt from all in the hall but him. However, he was too aware of her for her reaction to escape his notice.

His limp slowed him down, so that by the time he reached the castle gates, she was out of sight. Undeterred, he continued on the path—the only way for her to go, unless she'd walked around the keep and slipped back inside.

Somehow, he doubted she'd do that.

As the path grew steeper, he slowed slightly, due to the soreness in his thigh. The wound had come a long way, but still needed more time before 'twas completely healed. He could only hope that the limp, and the pain he felt when he overtaxed himself, would eventually subside.

When he came to the turnoff toward the waterfall, he stopped and considered which way she would have gone.

Then he opted for the path to the waterfall.

The sun had not yet set, and so 'twas slightly cooler in the shady forest, though the day had stayed warm and sunny. It should have cheered her.

A multitude of wild creatures fled from Cristiane as she walked, and birds chirped overhead. The scent of pine was strong, but there were many deciduous trees as well, just coming into bloom. Cristiane should have enjoyed it more, but she could not shake the wretched feelings wrought by Gerard's words.

She heard the rushing water of a river nearby, and assumed she would come to it soon. Instead, the path changed direction, and Cristiane found herself walking along a high, craggy escarpment, across from a magnificent waterfall.

She held her breath in awe and watched as the water dropped majestically from a high ledge to a rocky chasm below. 'Twas an amazing sight. She'd never seen anything like it near St. Oln.

Cristiane began to search for a path that led down to the base of the falls, where a pool of clear, blue water fairly beckoned her. She loved to swim, but had only been able to do so in the ocean, where the waters were often very rough, and in the icy river south of St. Oln.

She found no clear path to the bottom of the waterfall, but 'twas not difficult to find her way down the rocky incline. A child could have done it. With the falls roaring in her ears, Cristiane walked across the smooth rock floor and stepped behind the wall of falling water. Crouching down to take off her shoes, she wished she were not so alone. 'Twould be a joy to share this wonderful place with someone.

Fiercely tamping down her sudden spate of loneliness, Cristiane walked barefoot all 'round the base of the falls, letting the mist spray her. 'Twas cool and refreshing, and she let it cleanse her of the ridiculous longings she would never allow to take form in her mind.

Anyone could see that Sara suited Adam. She was beautiful, and well-dressed, and Cristiane could not doubt that she was a gently bred lady.

Cristiane was merely a breach in the rhythm of Adam's life. He'd had some reason for going all the way to St. Oln to take her away, and now his duty was completed. He would send her to York and his life would return to normal. She had been a fool to think there could be anything more…not that she ever had, not really.

She stepped over to the pool, which was carved out of the rock. It seemed to take only the overflow from the base of the falls, so 'twas an ideal place for swimming—deep and calm, and warmed by the sun.

Crouching, she cupped her hands in the water and drank deeply, then settled on a long, flat rock just outside the spray of the falls. If anything could bring her peace, this place ought to do it.

She calmed her thoughts and forced herself to relax, letting her body go limp as she listened to the roar of the falls. As she watched, a small red fox picked its way down the rocks to the pool. It, too, took a long drink, stopping frequently to look up at her. Feeling no threat, it continued to drink, then scrambled around the site, its natural curiosity driving it to examine every little nook in the rocks.

Without warning, the fox suddenly dashed up the rocky wall opposite Cristiane, leaving no sign it had ever been there.

With a somewhat lightened heart, Cristiane walked back to put on her shoes, then climbed up to the path, promising herself she'd return for a swim on the morrow.

Mayhap she would bring wee Meg, if she could pry her away from Mathilde for a while.

Adam stepped off the path. He'd reached the place where he could see the waterfall from above, and thought he'd try to catch sight of Cristiane before going all the way down. He wedged himself between two trees that served as a convenient perch, and trained his eyes on the base of the waterfall.

All his breath rushed out of his lungs when he saw her there. Her fresh, young beauty struck him once again, and his body reacted predictably. Pushing himself away from the trees, he could hardly wait to go to her and take her in his arms. He could think of naught but her impassioned response to his kiss.

He'd never encountered anything like it, and he'd been married more than three years. He did not doubt that Cristiane's untamed appearance would be matched by her responses if he took her to his bed.

One taste of her was not enough. One touch of her silken hair and soft skin had only inflamed him to desire more. He longed to spend hours learning the secrets of her body, sharing the delights he knew were possible, but had never experienced.

Halfway down to the path, he stopped himself. He had no business thinking of Cristiane Mac Dhiubh in this way. She was not the woman he would wed, and she was a nobly bred lady who deserved better than having a ruttish male pawing her.

She would not have to put up with him *or* Gerard much longer. As soon as Adam's knights had done their duty helping to clean up the isle after the storm, he would send a few of them with Cristiane to York. 'Twould be only a few days more.

Then he would be finally rid of this constant state of agitation.

Chapter Twelve

"'Tis a mess, is it not, my lord?" Sara Cole said to Adam as he stood in front of her house on the hillside just above the harbor. 'Twas already dusk, and he'd known better than to ride to town at this time of night. He would be lucky to get back before dark.

Yet his restlessness had forced him to act. Every pore of his body demanded that he go to Cristiane and satisfy the lust she aroused in him. Luckily, good sense ruled. He would not violate her innocence while she resided here at Bitterlee, no matter how strong the urge.

"And the fields…" Sara continued. "The women and children have been working to clear the brush and debris."

"Aye," Adam said distractedly. "'Twill take everyone's help to clear the mess."

He turned away and led his horse down the hill toward the cottage that had sustained the most damage.

Sara was not mistaken about the conditions here. Fortunately, no one had been hurt in the storm, and all the ships had survived. Losing a fishing vessel would have been even more devastating than the damage to the cottages, especially at this time of year. Until the harvest, grain would be short. Bitterlee would depend primarily upon fish for its sustenance.

Still, the repairs that were needed would seriously tax the manpower on the island. 'Twould be several days before he could spare anyone to take Cristiane to York.

Adam helped the men finish stacking the logs they had cut from one of the downed trees, then walked to the tavern to share a few mugs, glad for a respite from his thoughts.

Adam had not returned to the castle the night before, and Cristiane learned that he'd stayed the night in town. In spite of herself, she wondered how much Sara had had to do with his decision not to return home.

'Twas not her concern, Cristiane told herself as she climbed out of bed. Adam Sutton could be naught to her, even though he made chaos of her senses. His life here on the isle would go on without her once she left for York, and she would hardly be remembered, if at all.

Except, perhaps, by Gerard, who would think of her with disdain.

She swallowed and wrapped her arms around herself, tamping down a wave of emotion so unexpected it took her off balance. If only she still had her mother... Cristiane had never needed her more than now, when everything about her life had changed, and was about to change again. She needed Elizabeth's wise advice. She missed her desperately.

Blinking away the foolish moisture that welled in her eyes, Cristiane opened the window of her chamber. Once again, a beautiful day had dawned. Determined to avoid Adam's nasty uncle, she dressed quickly and slipped down the stairs, only to be confronted by the very man she'd hoped to elude.

"At least we were not all murdered in our beds as we slept," he said, sneering.

"Wh-what?" Cristiane asked, alarmed by Gerard's remark. "Are there—"

"If *I* were lord of the isle, I would certainly not allow a bloody Scot under my roof…unguarded."

His meaning suddenly became clear, and Cristiane bit her lower lip to keep it from trembling. She spun away from the hateful man and ran outside, closing her ears to the jeering remarks that followed her.

She had done naught to him, or any other Englishman, yet he hated her as if she herself had wielded a sword in William Wallace's army.

Rushing blindly, Cristiane once again found herself on the path that led to the waterfall. Instead of heading inland, she kept walking along the escarpment that overlooked the sea, searching for a likely place to climb down.

Before long, she came upon a break in the edge, where there appeared to be good footholds and a few sturdy bushes that she could hold onto if necessary. Still shaking from her confrontation with Gerard, she picked her way down.

Cristiane was surprised to discover that the descent to the beach posed no more difficulty than the rocky slopes at St. Oln. She had expected much worse, after Adam's warning that there was no way down to the water.

Had he wanted to keep her away from here for some reason?

She made it all the way down to the beach, where a narrow strip of sand, broken by huge, black boulders, met the sea. Carefully choosing the right pillar of rock, she stepped onto it and sat down, leaning back to take refuge in the beauty of the clear blue sky.

For a few short moments, she was able to keep her mind carefully blank. As the breeze ruffled her hair and tossed her skirts, she did not think of her mother or father, or of Sir Gerard's meanness. She did not allow thoughts of Adam to cross her mind. She just lay quietly on the rough surface of the rock and watched absently as herring gulls circled in the air, their screeches echoing over the water.

But her troubles soon returned.

Cristiane took off her shoes and stepped down to walk aimlessly along the edge of the water, occasionally glancing up at the rocky slope she'd scaled. This spot was so isolated, she could easily believe herself to be the only person in the world.

She did not doubt she was the loneliest person in the world. At least at St. Oln, she'd had her mother and father. Here, she had no one.

Suddenly there was a lump the size of a duck's egg in her throat, and the pain of grief welled in her chest. She missed her father's great belly laugh and her mother's quiet counsel. They may have been an odd little family, but her parents had enjoyed a deep affection for one another, and they'd loved their daughter.

How would she ever go on without them?

Tears had never been Cristiane's solution to a problem. Yet she felt them welling in her eyes as she thought of her parents, cold in their graves. Her vision blurred as she gazed out over the sea and considered her future, and the bleakness that was sure to follow her to York.

She would not belong there any more than she be-

longed in St. Oln...*or* on the Isle of Bitterlee. She was
a misfit, a lost soul. She would be lucky if she were met
with indifference in York, rather than outright abhorrence.

Many a time had Adam spent the night in town, accepting the reeve's hospitality, and his best bed. Adam
had been anxious to return home last night, but he'd had
one—mayhap three or four—too many cups of good Bitterlee ale to make the ride up to the castle in the dark.

He'd done naught but think of Cristiane Mac Dhiubh
all night—while he was awake, and in the restless
dreams that had plagued him hour after hour. He'd
awakened in an agitated state, anxious to act, but unsure
what to do.

'Twas barely daybreak when Adam returned to the
keep. He checked on his daughter and found her fast
asleep, then discovered that Cristiane was nowhere in
the castle.

He had not intended to seek her out, but was powerless to resist the pull. Only a few servants were about
when he walked out to the duck pond, but Cristiane was
not there. Suspecting that she'd gone wandering beyond
the castle walls again, Adam started up the path, looking
for her.

He doubted she would come to any harm on the isle,
but he was responsible for her. He did not want any
mishap to befall her while she was under his protection.

Besides, those dreams of the previous night haunted
him. He'd seen her soft curves again, and had tasted her
mouth, but in the dreams, they had not stopped with one
kiss. He had touched her, had run his tongue across the

pebbled tips of her breasts, his hands down the soft curves of her buttocks.

And that was naught compared to the way *she* had touched *him*. He'd been ready to explode upon awakening.

Adam quickly reached the waterfall, finding it deserted. He stripped off his clothes and slipped into the pool, once again cooling the heat that had simmered within him since he'd met Cristiane Mac Dhiubh.

He decided she must have walked farther along the path, mayhap down to the beach. She had seemed quite determined about that, and of course there was a safe route down the rocky escarpment. He had not told her about it because he hadn't wanted her going down there alone.

'Twas his mistake.

He climbed out of the pool, refreshed and without the headache that had annoyed him since awakening an hour earlier in the strange bed. He dressed and went up to the path, following it to the only place where Cristiane could have climbed down to the beach.

He did not see her, but scrambled down the rocky face of the escarpment anyway, withstanding the ache it caused in his injured thigh, certain that she must be here somewhere. He made it to the sand and stopped to lean against one of the huge rocks that stood upright out of the water. Glancing first one way and the other, he finally saw a patch of color in the distance.

Cristiane.

He let his throbbing leg rest a moment before setting off down the rock-strewn beach, toward her perch.

She had chosen one of his favorite spots, near a small inlet where the Cuddy ducks liked to come in and feed.

She was sitting on a flat-topped boulder, her knees drawn up and her head resting upon them. Her red curls trailed wildly down her back.

She did not hear him as he approached, and he called out so he wouldn't startle her.

Her head jerked up as if she'd been slapped. Her mouth moved, but he couldn't hear what she said. Even from a distance, Adam could see that her eyes were red and swollen, and her face covered with tears.

The most enticing face he'd seen since he'd watched her at the waterfall the day before…

Frowning with concern, he increased his pace, even as she turned away. She rubbed away her tears with the skirt of her gown, then slid off the rock and onto her feet to meet him, smiling shakily.

"Y-your leg, m-m'lord," she said, determined to speak first. "Should you have climbed—"

He took hold of her upper arms. The sight of her distress infuriated him, and it bothered him even more that she attempted to keep her anguish from him.

He'd made a solemn vow to keep her safe, to prevent any further cruelties. Yet he'd failed. He'd spent the night carousing and lusting after her, while something must have occurred to make her miserable. "What is it?" he demanded. "What's happened?"

Her chin quivered, but she swallowed hard, searching for control. "Naught, m'lord. 'Tis naught."

"Has my uncle—"

"Nay," she replied. "I only…" She tugged herself out of his grasp and moved a few paces away. Turning to face the sea, Cristiane crossed her arms over her breasts. "'T-tis beautiful here."

Adam did not know how to respond. Clearly, something had upset her, yet she would not speak of it. He would take her in his arms if he thought she would permit it, but her stance all but screamed for him to keep his distance.

"When d'ye suppose ye'll be able to t-take me to York?"

He was dumbfounded by her question. "I thought you would stay a few days," he said carefully. Just as he was about to speak of the gowns he thought she'd make, he stopped himself, realizing 'twould only serve to remind her of her shabby appearance. She was upset enough without adding aught more.

"I'd hoped you'd...spend some time with my daughter," he said instead. "You've had more effect on her than anyone since my wife's death."

Margaret ate barely enough to survive, and she shunned normal childish activities.

Yet Cristiane Mac Dhiubh had been on Bitterlee less than a full day before she'd managed to get Margaret to eat. She'd drawn Margaret out of her silence, if only to speak one word. 'Twas naught less than amazing. Adam could not let her leave before seeing how Margaret would react to her today.

He would deal with any wrong done her, if only she would consent to stay a few days and see what further effect she might have on his daughter.

Luckily, Cristiane was not unaffected by Margaret's plight. Adam could see that the notion of staying to help Margaret was compelling.

"You managed to get her to eat yesterday," he said, approaching her cautiously. "Would you try again today?"

The muscles in her throat moved convulsively, then

she brushed away another tear from her face. "Aye, m'lord," she replied shakily. She raised her chin and sniffed once. "I'll sit with her at mealtimes and take her to feed the ducklings."

"Thank you, my lady," Adam said. "And as to whatever upset you—"

"'Twas naught," Cristiane said. "Just a wee bit of foolishness."

Adam doubted that, but kept his counsel. Mayhap she would speak of it another time.

Chapter Thirteen

The sky was overcast when Cristiane led Meg to the duck pond. The old nurse had resisted allowing the child out for the afternoon, but Adam prevailed. Cristiane could feel him walking behind, carrying extra bread and a couple of linen towels, trying his best to be unobtrusive.

As if such a thing were possible. She felt his presence with every fiber of her being.

She'd have thrown herself into his arms earlier that morn, if only it would not have been wholly inappropriate to do so. She knew the warmth and security of his embrace would have comforted her, but she also knew it would have led to more.

"Do you think the ducklings will still be here?" Cristiane asked Meg. She already knew the answer, because she'd brought food for them earlier.

But Meg didn't reply.

"Have you still got your loaf?" Cristiane asked.

The lass held up her hand for Cristiane to see the bread she carried. She did not acknowledge her father walking behind them, nor did she speak. But Cristiane detected a hum of excitement in the child's bearing, the light of interest in her eyes.

When they reached the edge of the pond, Margaret sat down on the ground and removed her shoes without being prompted. The two adults exchanged an astonished glance over her head, and Cristiane felt an odd sensation unfurl in the region of her heart.

For now, she felt as if she belonged here.

Basking in the joy of the moment, she sat next to Margaret and removed her own shoes. She had to hurry in order to catch up to Meg, who had already hiked up her skirt and stepped into the water.

"Meggie! Wait for me!" she called, concerned about the frail bairn in the water alone.

But the ducklings swam right over to her, capturing her full attention. She waded farther in, throwing scraps of bread to them. Adam stepped forward to intervene, but Cristiane was quickly ready, and stepped into the pond before him.

"'Tis glad they are to see you, Meg," Cristiane said.

Margaret made no reply, but waded deeper as she continued tearing bread from her loaf and throwing it to the ducklings. Cristiane stayed next to her, ready to grab her if she should lose her footing.

"Step carefully, lass," Cristiane said. The farther they went into the pond, the muckier the bottom. "You don't know if—"

All at once, Margaret slipped. Cristiane lunged, keeping the child above water, but losing her own footing. She went down with an awkward splash, up to her neck. Adam stormed into the water to help, drenching his shoes and hose and most of his tunic.

Meg clapped one hand over her mouth and her eyes

grew huge and terrified. The little ducks scattered, quacking frantically at the disturbance.

Adam swore under his breath.

And Cristiane smiled at the absurdity of the incident. She'd been trying to keep up with reticent Meg, yet the child had gone on ahead of her. Meg had stepped out a little too far, but might have kept her footing well enough without Cristiane's clumsy assistance.

Naught had gone right for her today. To her intense mortification, Adam had caught her on the beach indulging in a spate of self-pity, weeping her heart out. He'd managed to sway her from leaving Bitterlee right away, using his daughter's plight to induce her to stay.

And now she was sitting on the murky bottom of his duck pond, with a frightened five-year-old and a comely English nobleman looking on. It could not be more ridiculous.

Catching Meg's eye, she laughed aloud.

The child still seemed stunned. Then Adam laughed behind her.

"Your bread is still intact, Meg!" Cristiane said amid her laughter.

"Though Lady Cristiane's dignity is not," Adam jested, and Cristiane sent a well-aimed splash toward him.

Adam did not mind, not after he saw the hint of a smile on his daughter's face. Margaret was actually amused by Cristiane's antics! If it would not have been wholly unfitting, Adam would have gathered Cristiane in his arms in gratitude for showing him the key to unlocking Margaret's heart.

Just as he had the day before.

"Dinna laugh at me, my wee bairn," Cristiane teased, her burr as thick as that of Wallace himself. She stood up out of the water. "Or I might be compelled to splash ye, too!"

"Oh!" Margaret cried, unsure what to do. Adam did not interrupt, aware that Cristiane had some kind of unique rapport with Margaret. "I..."

"'Tis all right, lassie," she said, affectionately touching Margaret's head. "Dinna worry. I wilna dunk ye."

But Cristiane's dunking had molded her clothes to her body. She might as well be naked for all that her thin gown covered her, for she'd worn her old brown kirtle from St. Oln, not wanting to ruin the better gown she'd been given at Bitterlee.

Her hair was wet and pushed away from her face, leaving her throat and collarbones bare. Adam could think of naught but touching his lips to that delicate notch where they met, then trailing his mouth down to her breasts. He would not stop there. His hands would trace the sweet curve of her back and her bottom, and he would close the gap between them, pressing tightly, inflaming her. Torturing himself.

Adam looked away, across the pond. This temporary loss of his senses could only be due to his pleasure in witnessing Margaret's changed behavior. While he recognized and appreciated Cristiane's uncommon beauty, he was resolved to keep her at Bitterlee only as long as her influence over Margaret continued to be so vital.

When he looked back at his daughter, Cristiane was unfastening Margaret's wimple. 'Twas not long before she was pulling it off and tossing it onto the bank. "That's much better, Meggie," she said as she ushered her out of the pond. "You have beautiful hair."

Margaret touched her head tentatively, as if unfamiliar with it. Adam frowned.

"I always wished I had pretty hair like yours," Cristiane continued. "All silky and gold like the brightest rays of the sun."

Margaret remained silent while Cristiane spoke, though she kept her eyes trained on Cristiane, her attention fully captured by the vibrant Scotswoman. "I had a lovely green veil once, a long time ago..." she said, as Adam picked up a towel. "And combs to hold my hair in place."

"Combs?" Margaret said.

Adam stopped moving when Margaret spoke.

"Aye, combs," Cristiane said, as if it weren't the most amazing thing in the world to hear her speak. "You know—they're made of bone and if you place them just right, your hair will be beautiful."

"Beauti...ful." The little girl's speech was awkward, unpracticed. But clear.

Cristiane took the towel from Adam and continued drying herself, while Margaret watched her every move. "Your papa brought you some hair ribbons from his trip."

Adam had forgotten them, but when Margaret looked up at him with yearning in her eyes, 'twas all he could do to keep from running to the keep and digging them out of his saddle pack.

"Aye," he said. "I'll give them to you when we go back. Would you like that, Margaret?"

His daughter nodded solemnly.

"Lady Cristiane," he said, "'tis not warm enough here in the shade for you to stand about in wet clothes. We had better get you back to the keep and out of that gown."

Cristiane blushed at his words, and he belatedly realized his double entendre. "Come," he said, wrapping a dry towel around her. He took Margaret's hand and was gratified when she did not resist.

Cristiane walked near them, though she held back, as if she knew she did not belong.

"Charles!" Adam said as they entered the great hall to find Charles Penyngton on the settle before the fire. "You should be abed."

"Aye, my lord," Penyngton replied, "but I wanted to see you this morn. And," he added, with a twinkle in his green eyes, "I knew there was no other way to meet Lady Cristiane."

Adam glanced over to where Cristiane stood, wrapped in the toweling cloth and holding Margaret's hand. Margaret looked more like a natural five-year-old now, damp and bedraggled, with her hair loose and disheveled. Her eyes were no longer expressionless. She was coming back to him.

He was sure of it.

"Forgive me, my lady," Penyngton said, "if I do not stand."

"Lady Cristiane, this is Charles Penyngton," Adam said, "seneschal of Bitterlee."

"And cousin to your mother," Penyngton added, gaining a sharp, puzzled glance from Adam. "'Tis sorry I was to hear of her passing."

"I...I thank you, sir," Cristiane replied haltingly. A faint crease appeared between her brows, and Adam could see that she was baffled by his claim of kinship.

Adam had not known of Penyngton's connection to Cristiane's mother, either, though it made perfect sense. How else would he have known of Cristiane's plight? He must have kept up correspondence with Lady Elizabeth all these years.

"I remember Elizabeth when she was just a girl at Learick," Penyngton said. He covered his mouth with a cloth as he suffered a fit of coughing. "Mayhap you will have an opportunity to pay me a visit in my chamber and I will tell you about your mother…and her journey to Scotland all those years ago."

"I—I would like that, Sir Charles," Cristiane said, her voice betraying her surprise, as well as her curiosity.

"My lord," Penyngton said, facing Adam, "Bill Williamson brought this parcel up from town a short while ago."

As soon as Adam saw it, he knew it contained the two gowns he'd had made for Cristiane. Actually, the gowns were not complete, merely cut out and started for her, since he'd been unable to provide Williamson's wife with Cristiane's exact proportions. Merely close approximations.

He set the parcel on one of the chairs and opened it. Inside, he found that the seamstress had used both bolts well. The gowns seemed nearly complete; all that was left was to stitch up the sides.

"I had these made for you in town," he said, looking up at Cristiane. He lifted first one and then the other, to show her.

She wore the same expression as she had the time he'd given her shoes—close to tears, barely in control of her emotions. He thanked heaven for that. He did not think he could stand to see her overcome by tears as she'd been this morn on the beach.

"They're not, er, finished," he added awkwardly. "I could give only approximations of your si—" He stopped himself when he realized what he was about to say. Like a sudden storm, the image of her body, partially clothed, came upon him. Every muscle clenched as he thought of her intimate dimensions.

By the expression in her eyes, he knew she was remembering the moment, too. He felt singed by the heat he saw there, and touched by the intensity of her emotion.

Another coughing spell, more virulent than Penyngton's first, broke the contact between Adam and Cristiane. Adam frowned as he watched his old friend wracked with misery, and he finally insisted upon helping him back to his bed.

Cristiane hugged the bundle to her breast, then glanced at Meg, whose eyes were downcast. Not another soul was in sight, so she said, "Come with me."

The child did not hesitate, but followed her up the two staircases and into her chamber, where Cristiane set down her bundle. She let out a laugh that was half a sob, and looked at the gowns again. "Your papa is a thoughtful man," she said to Margaret.

The gowns were made of fabrics that were entirely unfamiliar to Cristiane. All she knew was that one was an incredible blue, with green sleeves and gold edging at the neck. The other was the most vibrant yellow she had ever seen, so soft 'twas like the down of a Cuddy duck.

The loveliness of the two gowns brought tears to her eyes. She'd never had anything so precious—besides her two books.

"Weep-ing?"

Meg's voice startled Cristiane. She had nearly forgotten the child was with her, yet there she stood, beside the table at the bedside, her golden hair in a wild tangle, her eyes as large as goose eggs.

"Nay, lass," Cristiane said, turning to her and taking

her hand. "'Tis just that I've had nothing so fine as these two gowns—oh! A beautiful chemise, too!" she said, noticing the undergarment for the first time. She hugged it to her breast and blushed. "Your papa..." Had seen with his own eyes that she needed it.

She set the unfinished gowns back on the bed and unlaced the old kirtle she'd been wearing when she'd been drenched in the pond. Glad she'd had the foresight to put it on, rather than the more acceptable one that had been provided for her, she peeled it away, along with the old undergarment.

"I donna suppose ye've had occasion to see anyone naked before," she said, when she saw that Meg's mouth had dropped open. "Well, 'tis naught to be ashamed of." She pulled on the dry chemise and then the kirtle over it. "I did a good bit o' swimming without clothes back home."

Margaret still said naught, but her amazement showed in her eyes. Cristiane finished lacing her gown, then touched the child's shoulder. "Come," she said. "'Tis time we got you into something dry. Show me your chamber, lass."

Meg took her hand and led her down the dim hall to the room where Adam had comforted her during the storm. The child pushed the door open and the two went inside. 'Twas dark. Cristiane walked to the window and pulled open the heavy drapes that shrouded the room.

"This is where you sleep, then?" she asked, looking at the stark furnishings of the nursery. A large wooden crucifix dominated one wall, a prie-dieu standing beneath it. At least that was what Cristiane thought it must be. She'd never seen one, but had heard her mother's description of the little kneeling stands where a lady might say her devotions.

This one was made of wood, just like the cross above it, and was unsoftened by any padding whatsoever. She caught wee Meg eyeing it, and Cristiane frowned, wondering how much time the child spent kneeling there.

The room also contained a narrow bed with a rough woolen cover, a small trunk that stood under the window and a plain washstand near the bed. No rushes covered the cold floor.

Meg went to the trunk and pulled out fresh clothes. She stood still then, seeming not to know what to do.

"Here, lass," Cristiane said. "Pull out the laces.... That's it," she added, when Meg began to unlace herself. "Your papa will be proud when he learns what a bonny lass you are."

When the child was in her clean kirtle, Cristiane picked up a comb from the night table and began to comb through Meg's beautiful blond locks as she hummed a tune her mother used to sing to her. She felt content, as if she belonged, as if this could be her own child, her own home.

'Twas a foolish fancy, she knew. But for a few minutes, she would enjoy the peace she felt here with this wee lass whose grief was as keen as her own.

"There you are!" Nurse Mathilde swept into the chamber, her presence dominating the whole room. "I became worried when I could not find you, Lady Margaret. You should have—"

"Wee Margaret was with me...and Lord Bitterlee," Cristiane said, cutting off the nurse's tirade. Cristiane did not care for the woman's tone, though her words were not inappropriate. But she made it seem as if Meg were at fault for causing worry, when the nurse had to have known Adam had taken charge of his daughter.

Mathilde sniffed, then joined her hands under her

breasts and slipped them into her sleeves. Meg kept her eyes on the floor. Waiting.

"I'll just finish combing Meg's hair," Cristiane said, deciding to brazen it out, "and take her down to her father for the noon meal. It *is* nearly time, is it not?"

Mathilde said naught for a moment, and Cristiane held her breath. She'd never asserted any sort of dominance over another person before, and was not certain the nurse would accept her authority now. But Mathilde bowed and acquiesced.

Cristiane let out the breath she had not realized she'd been holding, and watched as Mathilde quit the room.

"Well," she said brightly. "That wasna so verra difficult, was it?"

"Keep her here," Penyngton said breathlessly as he climbed into his bed. "My lord, you could do worse."

"Aye," Adam agreed, aware that the seneschal was referring to Cristiane. "But not much."

"What are you saying? Lady Cristiane is perfect."

Adam shook his head. He *knew* she was perfect, but not as his countess. She'd be well suited to his bed, but naught more.

"Did you see how Margaret kept her eyes on her?" Penyngton asked. "How she watched Lady Cristiane's every move?"

Adam had not, only because he'd been so occupied with watching Lady Cristiane himself. He'd dwelt upon the way her sodden gown had clung to every curve, and had thought of tasting the tiny drops of water at the base of her throat. He had hardly thought of Margaret's reaction to her.

The untamed aspect of Cristiane that repelled him

from taking her as his wife demanded that he take her to his bed. Yet he could not. She was no harlot for hire.

"You never mentioned she was your cousin." Another reason Adam would never touch her.

"Twice or thrice removed," Penyngton replied with a shrug. "I maintained an occasional correspondence with her mother."

Adam clasped his hands behind his back and stepped away from the bed. "When did you plan to inform me of your illness, Charles?" he said, changing the subject. "Clearly, this...this cough...did not come upon you suddenly."

Penyngton pressed his lips together tightly. "There was so much that needed doing here, my lord," he said. "And with your own injuries...and the situation with Lady Margaret...I just thought—"

"That 'twould not matter to me that you were ill?"

"Nay," he replied quietly. "Only that it seemed more important for you to go to St. Oln and remove Lady Cristiane from her situation there than to stay here worrying over my health."

Adam rubbed the back of his neck. Charles suddenly looked much older than his forty-five years. His light brown hair was dull now, and there were strands of silver that Adam had never noticed before. The seneschal's cheeks were hollow and sunken, yet his eyes sparkled with the same feisty intelligence that had characterized all his years of service to Bitterlee.

"What has Sara Cole said about...all this?" Adam asked, still trying to absorb the enormity of Charles's illness.

"She calls it a consumption of the lung," Penyngton said. "I must rest, try to eat, and I will have to drink some awful concoction that she'll bring to the castle daily.''

Adam braced his hands behind his back and nodded, as Penyngton began to cough again. "You *will* rest, Charles," he said. "There is naught for you to do now, anyway. I'll take care of whatever comes up—"

"And my cousin?" Penyngton asked. "What of Lady Cristiane?"

Adam resumed his pacing, his brow deeply furrowed, his mouth drawn into a serious line. "Leave her to me."

"Well, well...it seems we dine informally this noon," Sir Gerard said as he joined Cristiane and Meg at table. His words were slurred, as if he'd already consumed too much ale. He belched loudly, the sound echoing through the hall.

Cristiane braced herself for his next remark, and vowed to remain silent, regardless of how cruel it might be. She had already challenged Mathilde's authority over Meg, and was not about to cause a disturbance with Gerard. She hoped that if she said little, the odious man would leave her be.

Adam had not arrived to take part in the meal, and servants began to serve without him. Trays of steaming food were set on the table, and a footman placed a pitcher of ale at Gerard's elbow. He poured himself a full cup, though Cristiane was of the opinion that he needed no more.

"Try this, Meg," she said, deliberately turning away from Gerard. She offered a bite of fish to the child. Margaret opened her mouth and took the morsel, while Cristiane remained uncomfortably aware of Gerard's scrutiny.

"Where's old Tildy?" Gerard asked. "In the chapel, on her knees again?"

Cristiane realized he was asking about Mathilde, but before she could reply, Gerard spoke again.

"Can't imagine what she's done that requires so much penance."

"I—"

"*You,* on the other hand—along with all the rest of your Scots butchers—have plenty for which to atone."

His speech had become even more slurred, and Cristiane recognized the mean tone that often accompanied drunkenness. Some men became maudlin, some jovial. Too many became cruel.

Gerard was one of those, and Cristiane had no intention of remaining here at table, suffering his ire.

Without giving it another thought, she gathered the trencher she'd been sharing with Margaret, grabbed the lass's hand and took her away from the table. Ignoring Gerard's command to return, she drew Meg to the door and stepped outside.

It looked as if it might rain, but Cristiane and Meg walked through the castle gate and up the path. They had not gone far when Cristiane stopped, allowing Meg a moment to rest. The child held back, unaccustomed to this kind of exertion, yet there was a light of excitement in her eyes. And the hint of a smile about her lips.

Meg's expression lightened Cristiane's heart, and she knew she had done the right thing in bringing her out here. She could hardly wait to see how Meg would react to seeing the waterfall.

Adam could not find Cristiane. And according to Gerard, she had Margaret with her.

He did not know exactly what had transpired between

Cristiane and Gerard, but his uncle was livid. Before Adam had been able to extricate himself from the great hall, he'd heard more than enough about the Scots she-devil who was poisoning the very air of Bitterlee.

Gerard had been involved in many a campaign in Scotland, so Adam knew he felt justified in his hatred of the Scots. Yet 'twas not reasonable to vent his ire upon Cristiane. She'd had no part in any of Wallace's campaigns against the crown. She was as much English as she was Scot, and everyone here needed to recognize that fact.

Adam walked through the garden and toward the pond, where he hoped he would find Cristiane and Margaret. Certain that Cristiane would be upset by her confrontation with Gerard, he wanted to get to her as soon as possible. After all, something had upset her earlier that morning, and he was likely to find her in tears again, distraught over the incident with Gerard.

He stopped short when he thought of it. What would he do to comfort her? She'd refused his touch this morn, and had asked about leaving for York. 'Twas likely she'd be even more anxious to go now, and Adam had no idea how he would dissuade her.

He needed her. Margaret was responding to Cristiane in a way he'd not seen in two years.

Cristiane had to stay.

The old wound in his leg pained him fiercely after all his activities that day, but he continued on until he reached the duck pond, only to find it deserted. The little ducklings swam toward him when they saw him, clearly expecting a treat, but he hadn't brought any food.

He walked to the far side of the pond and sat down on a stone bench to rest his leg, rubbing the pain from it, wondering where Cristiane and Meg could have gone.

Chapter Fourteen

Cristiane had very little personal experience with children, though she'd seen plenty of them at play in St. Oln. Meg Sutton did not know the first thing about playing.

She'd come down the trail to the waterfall, followed Cristiane behind the sheet of falling water and stood staring at it. Cristiane was certain that any other child would have stepped closer and put out her hand to reach into the curtain of water.

"Come, Meggie," Cristiane said. She pushed up her sleeve and tested the water, indicating that Meg should do the same.

The child followed suit finally, giving a squeal and jumping back when the cold water hit her. Cristiane was afraid at first that the experience had been too shocking, but one look at Meg's face told her the lass was delighted. True, her stance and expression remained tightly controlled, but there could be no doubt that she had enjoyed it.

Cristiane breathed a sigh of relief.

"Come back," she cried happily. "'Tis only cold.

'Twill not hurt you, though you might get a wee bit wet.''

Meg stepped closer to Cristiane, grabbing hold of her skirt. Then she put her hand into the stream of water again, and laughed aloud.

'''Tis wonderful, is it not?'' Cristiane asked.

Meg nodded, her face a mirror of joy. The significance of this response was not lost on Cristiane. She hardly knew Margaret, but she was aware of Adam's worries regarding his daughter. She'd been locked up with grief, and it seemed that she was starting to let it go.

"I know you can speak, lass," Cristiane said, laughing. She threw her head back. "Say, 'This is wonderful!'"

Meg ducked her head shyly, but Cristiane swooped down and picked her up, swirling her around behind the waterfall, making them both laugh heartily, their voices echoing off the rocky walls.

"Wonder-ful!" Meg cried.

"I knew you would love it," Cristiane said, letting her down. "Shall we take off our shoes and get our feet wet?"

Without speaking, Meg reached down and unlaced her shoes. She pulled each one off and tossed it away from the falls, then stepped up to Cristiane to take her hand.

There was no point in remaining at the pond, so Adam walked painfully back to the keep. He had to believe Cristiane would keep his daughter safe—and he hoped that whatever effect Cristiane was having on Margaret would continue.

Aware that naught but a hot soak would improve the condition of his leg, he climbed slowly to his own chamber in the north tower, after giving orders for a hot bath to be made ready for him. He would heat the tortured scar sufficiently to relax, then rub in some of the ointment Sara had made for him.

Sometimes it actually worked.

Adam entered his chamber and walked to the open window. The sky was overcast, but there was no rain yet. He unfastened his tunic and pulled it off, then removed the light linen undertunic while he waited for the footmen to bring in the tub and hot water.

His saddle pack lay in a corner near the bed, and Adam suddenly remembered the ribbons for Margaret. He did not know what had possessed him to purchase them, for Meg always wore a wimple—just like her mother and her nurse—unless it was from some odd notion that if her hair flowed free, so would her words and deeds.

He knew it made no sense, but he'd bought the colorful strips of cloth anyway. He took them from his satchel and left his room. He walked down the corridor, past the chamber that had once belonged to his wife, then on to the nursery.

Stepping inside, he was struck by the austerity of the room. 'Twas entirely different from the kind of surroundings he'd had as a lad, but Rosamund had insisted on leaving the furnishings to Mathilde. Adam had acquiesced on this point, aware that whenever he denied Rosamund her wishes, she'd become more forlorn, more withdrawn.

He placed the ribbons on Margaret's washstand, hoping that when she discovered them, Cristiane would help her put them in her hair.

"My lord!" Mathilde stopped abruptly near Margaret's chamber, clearly surprised and chagrined by

Adam's state of undress. She blushed furiously and stared at the floor.

"I am just leaving, Mathilde," Adam said. He frowned. It struck him then that Rosamund's reaction to his naked flesh had always been the same as the nurse's.

'Twas very different from Cristiane's.

He cleared his throat. "I brought some ribbons for Margaret's hair. I would like you to leave her wimple off in future. 'Tis unhealthy to have her head covered so tightly all the time."

"But my lord—" Mathilde ventured, glancing quickly up at him, keeping her eyes carefully trained on his face.

"I'll hear no more of it," Adam said as he stepped away. "My daughter will be spending more time with me, too, Mathilde. Every afternoon, in fact. Allow for it in your daily plans."

Mathilde may have replied, but Adam did not hear her as he took the few steps to Rosamund's chamber. Turning the latch, he went inside the room where he'd never felt welcome.

Many of Rosamund's possessions remained here, including some clothing that had not been given away. He would like to give it all to Cristiane, but Rosamund had been a much smaller woman. None would fit the Scots-woman.

He glanced around, remembering insignificant details about Rosamund—her delicate features, her tiny hands and feet. Pale, white skin, soft and smooth as down. Her hair had been the same as Margaret's—white-blond, like an angel's. Always covered. Untouchable.

A small wooden casket lay on the windowsill, and Adam opened it. Inside were the two combs he'd hoped to find, along with some jewelry Rosamund's family had not taken.

The wooden combs were of little value. They were simply carved and highly polished to a dark sheen. Yet he knew Cristiane would appreciate them. There had to be thread and needles here, too, and after a quick search, he found them.

Closing the door against unwelcome memories, he walked down the dark corridor and stopped in Cristiane's room, leaving the combs and the sewing supplies on the table. The package of unfinished gowns lay on the bed. Besides the parcel, there was little sign that anyone occupied the chamber, just Cristiane's discarded kirtle and the ragged underclothes she wore with it.

Adam lifted the thin linen bodice, feeling the frailty of the cloth, remembering the way it had so perfectly— so arousingly—framed her naked body. His physical reaction to that memory was so quick and so profound that he dropped the chemise.

He suppressed the erotic thoughts he had no right to entertain, and jabbed his fingers through his hair. Then he turned and stalked back to his own chamber, where his bath awaited.

Though Cristiane would have stayed at the waterfall with Meg until dark, she could imagine Adam calling out all his men to search for them if they did not return soon. Besides, it looked as if rain was coming, and Cristiane did not want Margaret caught out in it. Who knew if it would storm as violently as it had the night she'd arrived on Bitterlee?

With a promise to return the next day, or as soon as the weather permitted, Cristiane helped Meg put on her shoes, and returned with her to the keep.

Hoping to avoid encountering anyone—Gerard in particular—they went in through the door near the chapel, then walked quietly to the great hall.

"I'd rather avoid your uncle, lass," Cristiane whispered, which resulted in a tiny giggle from Margaret.

Cristiane looked down at her, marveling at the changes that had occurred in such a short time. Why had no one taken the time to treat the lassie like the child she was? Of course she was silent and withdrawn. She knew naught else.

Cristiane resolved to speak to Adam about this as soon as she saw him next.

Finding no one in the hall, they climbed the steps, then followed the route to the north tower, where the family chambers were located. "If I can find a needle and some thread," she said quietly to Meg, "I'm going to sew one of those gowns. Then I'll be presentable tonight at table."

Meg nodded.

"Would you like to help me with it?"

Cristiane's heart was warmed by the child's smile. She lifted the latch of her chamber door and pushed on it, then was shocked to discover that she'd chosen the wrong room.

She pushed Meg behind her and tried to get her jaws to work. Adam had just stepped out of his bath and stood fully nude next to the tub. She could not take her eyes from him.

"I—I..."

Adam did not speak, either, nor did he attempt to cover himself. Never having seen a naked man before, Cristiane was struck by the masculine beauty of his body—the finely sculpted muscles, the rough hair that furred his legs and chest and nested that most virile part of him.

She wondered how he managed to keep it contained when he was fully clothed. It did not seem possible.

More embarrassed than she'd ever been before, she finally found her voice and spoke as she pulled herself out of the chamber. "Y-yer pardon, m'lord."

"Pa-pa?" Meg asked, and Cristiane was too rattled to feel any astonishment at the child's unexpected speech.

"Aye," she said, feeling the heat in her face. "'Twas your papa."

She did not know how she would ever face him again.

"Come," she said, pulling Meg to the next door. She opened it cautiously, then stepped inside, closing it behind them.

Adam did not know whether to feel chagrin or to relish the obvious hunger he'd seen on Cristiane's face when she'd looked at his fully aroused, naked body. By the time she'd stammered her way out of his chamber, her face had been covered by a furious blush, but at least she had not been frightened.

He was certain, however, that she would never come out of her own chamber again without coercion. He would deal with that later.

For now, he had much to think about.

Penyngton had a valid point about keeping her at Bitterlee. Unquestionably, she was taken by the isle, and all its rough beauty. He doubted that even their winter weather would intimidate her. She had made more progress with Meg—Margaret, he corrected himself—than anyone else in the two years since his return from Falkirk. She had no family anywhere, other than the Earl of Learick, whom she did not know, and would not miss if she did not see him.

Adam recognized the obvious problems with making her his countess. She was still a rough Scotswoman, uneducated, underbred, and as much a villein as any of the people of the isle. At least she seemed that way, for all her noble blood.

The islanders would not only have difficulty accepting her as their mistress, they would have difficulty concealing their hostility. To them, she was a bloodthirsty Scot. Even the servants at the castle had not yet come 'round, and Gerard seemed to delight in baiting her.

But once Penyngton had brought it up, it seemed that Adam could think of naught else than making Cristiane Mac Dhiubh his wife. He craved her in a way that was wholly unseemly—and likely unwelcome, knowing what he did about wives—but he was unable to dismiss this notion from his mind.

Chapter Fifteen

Meg saw the combs first.

Cristiane could not imagine where they'd come from. She picked them up and admired their smooth texture, and knew that she would be able to confine her hair appropriately with them.

It had to have been Adam again. Bit by bit, he was seeing to it that she was equipped with all she would need when she arrived in York.

Embarrassment choked her once again. Not only did she look every bit as barbaric as a Norse raider, she had gawked at his naked body like a dizzy-eyed maiden. He must think her the most laughable creature he'd ever met.

Cristiane was relieved to receive an invitation to dine with Sir Charles Penyngton in his chambers. She would not have to face Adam before they'd both had sufficient time for the incident in his chamber to recede into distant memory.

She used the afternoon wisely, sitting next to the open window, sewing on her new gowns as she and Meg listened to the sounds of a gentle rain. Meg was a great help, holding the pieces together while Cristiane slipped pins into the delicate fabric. They worked well together, with Meg's expression becoming more open with every hour.

She still spoke rarely, and only one word at a time, but it seemed to Cristiane that it was progress.

The blue gown was nearly finished when Mathilde came to take Meg away. "'Tis time for your instruction with Father Beaupré," she said, taking Meg's hand. Cristiane could not interpret Meg's reaction from her facial expression, since she had cast her eyes down. Cristiane would have kept the child with her, but was unsure how much change she could bring about in only two days.

Before letting Meg go with the nurse, she placed her hands on the child's bony shoulders. "I'll come into your chamber and say good-night after prayers, shall I?"

Meg raised her head and gave a small smile. "Yes," she whispered. "Please."

"At least tell me you are considering it, my lord," Penyngton said as he watched Adam pace the floor next to his bed. A small table had been brought into the chamber that adjoined the seneschal's office next to the great hall, and two chairs to accommodate the two who would dine with Penyngton.

"All right, Charles," Adam replied, "I am considering it. But I promise naught."

"Understood."

Adam knelt and built up the fire against the cool, damp air. He found the gentle rain pleasant, but 'twould not do for Charles to take a chill. He was anxious for Cristiane to arrive, but did not want Charles to know it. The decision whether or not to take her to wife was a grave one, not to be taken lightly, and he would not raise Charles's hopes, only to decide against it.

A light tap at the door brought Adam to his feet. He crossed the room and opened it, to discover a very different Cristiane Mac Dhiubh standing there, blushing as red as one of the beets in Cook's garden.

Her hair was arranged in an intricate coif of golden-red locks, gently restrained by the combs he'd left in her chamber. Soft, curly tendrils framed her face beautifully.

The blue silk had been transformed into a lovely but simple gown with long, fitted sleeves and full, flowing skirts. The bodice fit Cristiane's form tightly to the waist, leaving her neck and shoulders delightfully bare.

There was naught barbaric about her now.

Even her eyes were demurely shuttered, betraying not the slightest hint of her thoughts. If not for her blush, Adam might have believed the incident in his chamber had never occurred.

"Come in, my lady," he said.

"Lady Cristiane," Penyngton said from his bed, "'tis good of you to come."

"Thank you for inviting me," she replied as she walked toward him. Adam was taken with her grace and poise. He'd seen hints of these qualities before now, of course. But she'd always seemed more Scottish than English.

That had changed.

"Be seated, my dear," Penyngton said. "I would visit a bit before the meal is served."

"Thank you, Sir Charles." She sat near the bed, dismissing Adam completely from her awareness. "I'm anxious to hear what you knew of my mother. When she spoke of her home in York, 'twas always with sadness.

All I know is that she was banished to St. Oln, disowned by her father.''

Penyngton shook his head. '''Twas a harsh punishment,'' he said. ''Though no one, not even your grandmother, challenged it.''

''What happened?''

Penyngton coughed into a clean cloth. ''Let us save that story until after we've dined,'' he said when he'd recovered. Adam recognized Charles's delaying tactics and knew that, for some reason, he did not wish to speak of Elizabeth of York now.

''How do you fare, Sir Charles?'' Cristiane asked. Her sense of protocol and courtesy was flawless. Adam could almost believe she'd been tutored in the most cultured house in England.

He sat back in his chair and observed her graceful movements as she conversed with Penyngton, pouring him a mug of water, standing to assist him in adjusting a pillow. He heard her musical voice, with barely a hint of the Scots burr that was so offensive to his people. The sound of her soft laugh drifted over him like talented fingers, eliciting a physical response. 'Twas all he could do to keep from groaning aloud.

''—at the waterfall?''

Cristiane and Penyngton both looked at him as if expecting a reply.

''Sorry...I was not paying attention.''

'''Tis naught, my lord,'' Penyngton said. ''Just that Lady Cristiane is taken by our waterfall, and it seems that Lady Margaret gained some enjoyment from it today, as well.''

''That's where you were this afternoon?''

''Aye, m'lord,'' Cristiane replied, looking at him directly for the first time since entering the chamber. ''We carried our meal out there, and sat behind the falls to eat.''

Adam frowned with puzzlement. "My daughter ate? Out-of-doors?''

Cristiane shrugged as she nodded. "Every bit of what we brought with us.''

Penyngton was smiling triumphantly behind her. Adam had to admit 'twas just short of a miracle that Cristiane had managed to reach something within Margaret, to somehow draw her out of her shell. Mayhap Charles was right in his assertion that Cristiane should remain here. Adam did not know if this change in Margaret would continue, especially if Cristiane left Bitter-lee.

"And…and how did my daughter find the falls?''

"She found them delightful, m'lord,'' Cristiane said. Her smile touched her eyes and every other part of her face, making it glow. If he'd thought her beautiful before, he could not think of a word to describe her now. Radiant, mayhap. Magnificent.

The meal was served and they ate, conversing politely about the weather and the damage done to the town by the storm. Cristiane finally got over her discomfiture at having to see Adam so soon after…*seeing* him. He was modestly covered now, dressed in a fine black tunic trimmed in blue and gray, and black hose. His hair was combed neatly back from his handsome face, and she could tell that he'd recently shaved his afternoon whiskers from his jaw.

She was unused to seeing a man's naked face. Her father and all of his men were bearded, and 'twas near impossible to discern their features.

Adam's were well defined and striking. And if she

looked at them overlong, her heart pounded and her throat went dry.

"Your uncle Roderick, the Earl of Learick," Penyngton said when the meal was done, "is your mother's brother."

Cristiane nodded. She knew this much.

"He was older by several years," Charles continued.

"Why did my mother's father banish her?" she asked.

"She fell in love with the wrong man," Penyngton replied.

Cristiane leaned forward and listened with rapt attention as Penyngton told of Elizabeth Huett's doomed affair with Learick's huntsman.

"Alan was older and should have known better," Charles said, "but your mother was quite a beauty in those days. She was a spirited and daring girl, who enjoyed running her horses and joining the hunt. I am certain he tried to resist her, but 'twas impossible. They were thrown together more oft than not, and...the inevitable occurred."

Cristiane swallowed. Penyngton's words shocked her. She had never known her mother had loved another besides her father. It caused a wealth of confusion in her mind and a stab of pain in her heart, yet she had to hear what Penyngton had to say. She felt compelled to know all.

"When the earl—her father—discovered them, he demanded that Elizabeth renounce Alan," Charles continued. "In all honesty, I believe Alan tried to get your mother to see reason, but she would not. She ran away from her father's house to Alan, hoping, I suppose, that he would take her away...that they would wed."

"Charles..." Adam's voice broke in softly, but Cristiane hardly heard his voice.

"The earl found out before—"

"Penyngton..." Adam warned. "You're upsetting the lady."

Cristiane realized then that there were tears on her face. She sniffed and brushed them away. "What happened, Sir Charles? Why did they not wed?"

Penyngton gave a quick glance in Adam's direction, but continued. "Alan was killed by an arrow that night. 'Twas put about that he was taken for an intruder at Learick Castle, and your grandfather refused to give any more details. Your mother was locked in her chamber until a suitable bridegroom could be found.

"Within weeks, she was on her way to wed the laird of St. Oln, in Scotland," he said, "a man who was willing to take the dishonored daughter of an English earl."

Cristiane stood abruptly and walked to the fire. She said naught, for there were no words in her heart, only a tortured coil of anguish and confusion. Adam was suddenly behind her, his hand at her waist.

"Was there some very good reason for...?" he began angrily, turning to speak to Penyngton. Then he let out a long breath of frustration and turned abruptly back to Cristiane. "Come," he said, "you need some air, and I...I'll walk with you."

He picked up a lamp, and she went with him mutely. He kept one hand at her lower back, guiding her up the stairs, pondering what possible reason Penyngton could have had for telling Cristiane her mother's sad history. The lady already grieved her parents' recent deaths. Why dredge up this sorrowful tale now?

'Twas still raining, so they did not go outside. They walked down the corridor to Cristiane's chamber, and Adam opened the door, guiding her into it. She stood unmoving, just inside the room, her eyes gazing blankly at nothing.

He cleared his throat. "My lady…"

Absently, she looked up at him. "Aye?" she said quietly. A slight frown marred her perfect forehead.

"Will you be all right?"

"Oh, aye," she replied. There was surprise in her voice, as if she had just noticed she was not alone. "Just fine, m'lord. You needn't… I mean, 'tis a bit of a shock, learning of my mother's…of her, umm…"

"Lover."

Cristiane nodded. "I never knew there was anyone but my father."

Adam did not know what to say. Clearly, Cristiane was distressed after learning about her mother and Learick's huntsman. Both her parents were dead now, and it had happened so many years before that—

"My mother never quite fit in at St. Oln," Cristiane said. Her voice was quiet and sad. She ran one hand along the opposite arm, as if to ward off a chill. "My father adored her. He'd have done aught for her, if only…"

Her nose reddened and her mouth twitched, as if she would weep, and Adam expected to see tears. But they did not fall. He closed the distance between them and drew her into his arms, though he knew he could do naught to protect her against the sad memories. She shuddered once and he held her more tightly.

Adam did not know how long they stood thus, but his intentions of giving solace soon changed to something different, something more. Her body felt soft and yielding against his own, and he could not keep from running his hand across her shoulders and down her back.

She made a small sound and slipped her hands 'round

his waist, holding him close as she lifted her face from his chest. Her eyes were clear and dry as she looked up into his.

He wanted her as he'd never wanted another woman. But it was not to be.

Cristiane slept badly. She'd sat up through the deepest hours of the night, listening to the rain, thinking about her life and all that she'd known in St. Oln. She'd finally found sleep near dawn.

Her eyes were swollen and her head felt stuffed with goose down when she awoke late the next morning. But the day was warm and the sun shining, and Cristiane was not one to dawdle inside when the weather was fine.

She washed quickly, but before she was fully dressed, a tap at the door interrupted her.

'Twas Meg.

Cristiane glanced up and down the corridor outside her chamber, but saw no one else. She could not imagine where Mathilde was, but did not question the nurse's absence. "Come in while I put on my shoes," she said, wondering if Adam was nearby.

Meg entered and climbed up on the bed.

"Would you care to walk with me this fine morn?" Cristiane asked, smiling at the child.

Meg smiled back and nodded.

"Well, then, you'll have to say so." Cristiane had gotten a word or two out of the child the day before, and saw no reason to let her continue getting away with her silence.

"Go...walk-ing?"

"Aye," Cristiane said, grinning broadly. "We shall go walking." 'Twas another small success, but she was pleased nonetheless. She took Meg's hand and they went down the two flights of stairs to the great hall, where one servant was sweeping out old rushes and another dusting the massive mantelpiece. No one else was in sight.

They went out the main door of the great hall and walked down the massive stone staircase, just as a group of knights rode into the bailey on horseback. One of them stopped and removed his helm when he saw them.

Gerard Sutton.

Cristiane refused to retreat, even though the malevolent look in Gerard's eye was intimidating. She took a firmer hold on Meg's hand, tightened every muscle in her back and continued down the stair, determined to go 'round him.

He turned his horse and stepped ahead, then dismounted directly in front of her. Cristiane had no choice but to step back.

"Sir Gerard," she said. 'Twas neither greeting nor pleasantry. She merely stated his name to somehow fortify herself.

Gerard did naught but stand in her path, folding his arms across his chest, presenting a daunting obstacle. "'Tis a fairer place than your precious Scotland, is it not?"

"Aye, Bitterlee is more than fair, Sir Gerard," she said, raising her chin defiantly. She would not be cowed by his belligerent attitude.

"My nephew is in town," he said, "working to clear away the debris from the storm."

"'Tis good of him," Cristiane replied, stepping away.

"And he enjoys the company—nay, the homage—of the townswomen," Gerard continued. "Especially that of Sara Cole. A lovely *English*woman."

Cristiane's step faltered for an instant, but she proceeded on her path, drawing Meg along with her. What did it matter to her whether Adam was in town with a thousand adoring women? He was lord of Bitterlee. 'Twas his domain, and there was no doubt in Cristiane's mind that the people loved him.

But she could not help but wonder whether Sara Cole's feelings for Adam were more meaningful, as Gerard had implied.

She and Meg walked up the path toward the waterfall, and Cristiane put her troubling thoughts from her mind. She'd dwelt enough on the circumstances of her parents' marriage, and did not care to spoil the morn with thoughts of Adam with Sara Cole.

The sun was high when they reached the waterfall, and they climbed down the rocky slope to get to the base. Meg gave a happy cry and ran to the falling sheet of water, anxious to thrust her hands into it.

Cristiane was struck by the sharp contrast in the child's behavior from yesterday.

"Come on," she said with a laugh, following Meg to the back of the falls. "Let's take our shoes off before they get soaked."

They did so, then spent the better part of an hour walking over the flat rocks at the base, thrusting their feet into the falls, then into the pool.

"I don't suppose you can swim?"

Meg looked up at her with wonder. "Nay," she said.

"Then 'tis high time you tried it."

Chapter Sixteen

Adam learned that his daughter and Lady Cristiane had left the keep more than an hour before. He gave his horse over to a groom, then headed out on the footpath toward the place where he knew they'd go.

It did not take long to reach the notch between the two trees, where he could see down to the waterfall.

The heavy fall of the water blocked the sound of any voices, but Adam was certain they would be here. He settled himself into the perch where he could look down and see them, and was startled to realize they were both in the pool. He had barely reacted to the sight of Margaret, *swimming*, when Cristiane lifted her out, then climbed out of the water herself.

They were both naked. Laughing.

Adam watched, transfixed, as Cristiane squeezed the water from Margaret's hair, then raised her arms to do the same to her own. Her body gleamed white in the bright sunlight, her breasts full and high, her waist narrow, flaring to smooth, feminine hips.

Her legs were shaped as he remembered them, longer than they seemed under her long skirts, strong and well formed.

The sight of his daughter, with her too-thin child's body, laughing and dancing circles around Cristiane, was nearly overpowering. Cristiane's smile was bright and engaging. She truly delighted in Margaret's antics.

Adam felt as if his ribs expanded beyond their bounds, then snapped back too tightly. He forced himself to turn away, even though the sight of Cristiane's lush body lured him, tortured him. He would not allow himself to intrude upon this moment of privacy, even though every drop of his overheated blood urged him to do so.

Steadying himself, he decided to remain in place until they left the waterfall, or at the very least, until they clothed themselves. At that point, perhaps he would join them at the base of the falls.

Cristiane finished lacing Meg's gown and bade her to sit in the warm sunshine, on an outcropping of rock, away from the mist of the falls. It felt good to be sitting here with Meg, to be not quite so alone anymore. If only Adam... Nay, she would not even begin to think it.

"You've a natural talent for swimming, Meggie my sweet," she said as she sat next to the child. She picked up some of Meg's pale blond hair and began to fashion it into tiny plaits. "You float upon your back as well as those wee ducklings in your garden pond."

"Ducklings!" Meg cried, then clapped a hand over her mouth.

"Ach, aye," Cristiane replied. "We'll feed them later. They won't starve yet."

"Now!"

"Nay, my wee one," Cristiane said with a laugh. "We'll sit here in the sun for a bit, then return to the castle so that no one will worry over our absence."

Adam would not miss them, since he was occupied in

town, but Cristiane did not want to make an enemy of Mathilde. She knew she was treading on thin ice with the woman.

But 'twas so peaceful here at the falls that Cristiane could not face returning just yet. She made herself comfortable next to Meg and took in her surroundings. Birds chirped high in the trees above them. Squirrels chattered, and the small red fox that Cristiane had seen before skittered down the rocks to drink from the pool.

''Do you see it?'' she asked Meg. ''The little fox?''

Meg nodded.

''Stay very still and mayhap it will come closer.''

The fox finished its drink and looked up. It caught sight of Cristiane and Margaret, and stood perfectly still. After a few moments, it stepped closer, and then closer still.

Margaret and Cristiane did not move or speak, but there was a look of pure rapture on the child's face.

Curious, the fox moved closer.

Suddenly, it turned and ran, scrambling up the opposite side of the rocky fissure.

Cristiane laughed aloud, and Meg joined her. ''Tomorrow, we will have to bring some tasty little tidbit for Sir Fox,'' she said.

''Tomorrow?''

''Aye, if you like.''

''And the ducklings?'' Meg asked, astonishing Cristiane by stringing her words together.

Cristiane laughed and gathered the girl into her arms for a hug. ''Aye, the ducklings, too,'' she said, stroking her hair.

A sound from above startled them, and Cristiane looked up to see what caused it.

Adam was working his way down the rocky face toward them. Cristiane tried to calm her racing heart as she watched his approach, reminding herself that 'twas his daughter he was after.

He certainly had not come to see the Scottish outcast he'd brought to Bitterlee, in her shabby brown kirtle. She reached self-consciously to her hair, all tangled up across her shoulders and down her back, and wished there was some way to hide the awful mess.

"Papa!" Meg said quietly. Adam would not be able to hear her, but he would be able to see the expression of delight in her eyes.

The warmth of Adam's smile made Cristiane think her heart would melt.

He reached their rock and sat down, keeping Meg between them. Cristiane reminded herself that she was merely a visitor here. 'Twas true that she'd had some creditable effect on Margaret, but 'twas no hardship to do as Adam had asked, and spend time with the lass. In truth, over the past few days, she'd come to love wee Meg, every bit as much as she loved the child's father.

Lady Cristiane stood abruptly and walked away from the place where they'd all been sitting only a moment before. Adam did not know what was wrong, only that tension coiled throughout her body.

Her hair cascaded down her back in spectacular redgold waves, the wispy ends brushing the base of her spine. Adam could not keep himself from envisioning the naked woman cavorting on these rocks, taking joy in the moments spent with his daughter.

She turned suddenly, but kept some distance between them. "Have you decided when I shall leave for York, my lord?" she asked. There was a breathlessness and an urgency to her question, and Adam wondered what had prompted it.

Surely naught untoward had occurred today to make her want to leave Bitterlee. She seemed to truly enjoy Margaret's company, and Adam would put no limit upon their time together.

Gerard had been in town all through the morn, making a nuisance of himself while everyone else worked, so he could not be blamed. Adam doubted the servants would have been bold enough to insult her openly, either.

He wondered if Cristiane was anxious to go to York in order to question her uncle about the events leading to her mother's banishment from home. He supposed that was as good a reason as any, especially after the sketchy story that Penyngton had told her.

"Cris-ty?" Margaret asked, tugging on his tunic. A serious frown creased her forehead.

Adam looked down at his daughter and smiled at her shortened name for Cristiane. "Aye," he said. "Cristy."

"Papa," she said with agitation. "Cris-ty is...going?"

Margaret's speech startled him, and he gazed at her without responding. Then he looked back at Cristiane. "Mayhap we can find a reason to keep her here a while longer," he finally said.

Cristiane, her hands clasped before her, approached. "Another day, m'lord," she snapped. "But then I must prevail upon you to provide m-me an escort. There is no further reason for me to remain on Bitterlee. I've d-done what you've asked..." she tipped her head toward Margaret without speaking of the favor he'd asked of her. "But now—" she breathed deeply "—I must take my leave."

Adam took Margaret's hand and stood. Together they approached Cristiane's tense, but unwavering form.

He was not ready to let her go.

"There is much more to Bitterlee than the paltry bit you've seen, my lady," he said quietly. "The isle is particularly fine in spring, and anyone can see that you enjoy our little island. Please...consider remaining with us a few more days."

"Stay," Margaret added, and Adam silently thanked the little girl for her additional plea. He was certain Cristiane would not refuse her.

Yet he could see that she was torn between staying and wanting to go. He had not realized how important it was for her to meet her Yorkish relations.

"All right," she said, as if she believed she was making the worst mistake of her life, "I'll stay. But only for a few more—"

"Swim to-morrow," said Margaret, her odd, choppy speech still surprising him.

"Aye, if the weather's good...." Cristiane conceded.

"Mayhap I'll join you," Adam said, wondering what her reaction would be.

"Nay!" Cristiane's face suffused with color.

Adam carefully schooled his own into a perplexed expression. "'Twould be my very great pleasure to join you," he said, meaning every word. He could only imagine the pleasure he would have in that pool, naked with Cristiane Mac Dhiubh. "I would enjoy seeing my daughter swim."

"'T-tis...a time for ladies only," she stammered, though she attempted an assertive tone.

Adam decided not to toy with her now. But he *would* return on the morrow, and stand guard while his ladies cavorted unclothed, here on the rocks.

* * *

Adam and Margaret fed the ducklings that afternoon without Cristiane. Wee Meg's eyes had pleaded with her to accompany them, but Adam had said naught. Cristiane knew she would not be at Bitterlee for much longer. 'Twould not do for Meg to become too dependent upon her.

The best thing was for Adam to take up what Cristiane had inadvertently begun, and he obviously knew it. So instead of going along and enjoying the fine day, and the company of Adam and Meg, Cristiane spent the afternoon alone in her chamber.

Besides, she could not bear to spend another hour with them, not now…not when her feelings were so fresh, so raw.

She realized that she'd been falling in love with Adam Sutton from the moment he'd taken her arm in St. Oln amidst the hostile people of her village. He had not judged her harshly, despite her Scots blood, regardless of the losses he'd suffered because of her people. He had kept her safe on the journey to Bitterlee, had been kind to her, treating her with deference, entrusting her with his daughter.

He'd been naught but chivalrous and noble since the moment they'd met. How could she help but love him?

While Adam and Meg went to the kitchen for a loaf of bread, Cristiane entered the keep alone. She had promised to stay longer on Bitterlee, but she knew it could not be for too many more days. 'Twould only hurt the worse when she finally left.

Cristiane hurried across the length of the hall, hoping not to meet anyone, but Gerard stood near the steps, blocking her way. She stopped short when she saw him.

"In a hurry, *my lady?*" he sneered.

Cristiane started to move past him, but he grabbed her arm.

"Come, come," he said, pulling her toward the table, "and join me in a cup."

"Nay," Cristiane replied, trying to tug her arm away. "I must respectfully decline, Sir Gerard. I have sewing to—"

"Your stitchery will wait," he said, his thick brows coming together in a daunting frown. "Is it not possible for a Scotswoman to show any courtesy or *respect* at all?"

Cristiane shook her head and freed her arm. "Your pardon, Sir Gerard," she said, containing her anger, "but I..." She swallowed hard. All she wanted was to get away without any harsh words exchanged. "I must go."

He gave a low laugh. "Ah, now I see what my nephew sees in you," he said. "Fire enough in those eyes to entice him to your bed, yet—"

Shocked by his words, Cristiane nearly slapped him. Instead, she spun away and darted up the stairs, loath to hear any more of his degrading talk.

"He may bed you," Gerard called after her, "but he'll never wed a savage like you!"

She stopped stock-still on the stair for an instant, cut to the core by Gerard's caustic laugh. Then she clambered up the stairs as quickly as she could, but did not escape before his parting words slammed into her heart.

"'Tis fortunate he did not promise your mother he would take you to wife," Gerard bellowed. "He only said he'd bring you here and *then* decide if you were suitable."

'Twas nearly suppertime when Adam arrived in Charles Penyngton's bedchamber, to find Sara Cole attending him. She was simply dressed, as usual, in a well-made kirtle of good cloth. Her neatly combed hair was only partially visible beneath a modest veil.

The room felt overly warm due to the fire in the grate, but Charles needed the extra heat. His visitors made do.

"Margaret speaks now," Adam said as he paced the length of the chamber. He felt entirely at ease with Charles and Sara. And though he did not officially recognize her as his sibling, they had become close over the last few years.

"That's wonderful news, my lord," Sara said, handing a cup of steaming brew to Charles. "What happened? Did Mathilde… Oh! Your Scottish lady!"

"'Tis amazing, the effect Cristiane has had on her," Adam said. "My daughter actually *talked* to me about ducklings, and a red fox that she saw near the waterfall. And swimming… Cristiane is teaching her to *swim!*"

"And you question whether or not to make her your wife," Penyngton said, choking on the healing decoction. The seneschal shook his head. "You must know, my lord, that any relation of mine would be a worthy—"

"Charles, 'tis not a question of her worthiness." Adam stabbed his fingers through his windblown hair. "She is as worthy as any woman I've known—honest and caring, and she loves the isle."

"But…?"

"*But*…she is so confounded Scottish!" he said. "And…" *Untutored, unrefined, untidy* were the words that came to mind, but he did not voice them. They were unkind, and 'twas not Cristiane's fault she'd been born to a humble Scottish nobleman.

Adam resumed pacing, and no one spoke. Charles continued sipping from his mug, and Sara remained in her chair next to the bed. The occasional crackle of fire was the only sound as Adam traversed the chamber twice.

"One minute her burr is as thick as mud, but the next, she sounds exactly like the granddaughter of an earl," he said. "She looks the part of a barbarian from the north...." Although now that she had a decent gown to wear, and combs for her hair, he had to admit she did not look nearly as wild as she had merely a week ago.

Except when she stood at the waterfall, bared to nature and all the elements. He pinched his eyes tight and suppressed a groan as his body responded to the vivid memory of Cristiane's naked beauty and the taste of her kiss. "I cannot imagine the people ever accepting her as mistress of Bitterlee," he said, his voice oddly harsh.

"Mayhap in time they will," Sara said.

"Lady Rosamund was never truly part of Bitterlee in all the years of your marriage," Charles said. "There was naught about the isle that pleased her."

Adam nodded absently, his stomach churning at the thought of watching Cristiane ride away with an escort of his men. She would sail to the mainland, her hair blowing freely, her skirts hugging her legs as she stood in the wind during the crossing. From there, she would leave for York, and he would never see her again.

"She is anxious to go to her uncle," he said, thinking of all the times in the past week that she'd spoken of leaving.

"Why would she?" Charles asked. "She has never met the Earl of Learick, and after what happened to her mother..."

"She speaks of leaving for York...."

"Idle talk," he said. "Ask her to stay. Or send her to me, and I'll make your proposal for you. As her nearest relation—nearest *available* relation—'twould be entirely fitting for me to do so.''

As Adam paced across the room again, he did not notice Charles and Sara exchanging a curious glance. He could only think of Cristiane sailing away from the isle, and how dull and vacuous Bitterlee would seem once she was gone.

''What will she have in York?'' he asked. ''An uncle and some cousins—''

''Aye,'' Charles said. ''Two of them. Both young men.''

Young men. If not the cousins, then some other young man. Someone who had the sense to see beyond her unrefined exterior. Someone who would learn to care for her, who would take her to wife....

Adam's jaw clenched involuntarily. He stopped his pacing directly in front of Charles. ''Do it then,'' he said. ''I'll send Lady Cristiane to you before we sup. You will act as her guardian in this instance and make her an offer—''

''If I may, my lord...'' Sara interjected. ''If it were me, I would rather receive a proposal from my bridegroom, not from a distant cousin who deigns to act as my guardian.''

Adam ran a hand over his whiskered jaw. ''I...when Rosamund and I wed...our fathers negotiated the match.''

''Well, since neither of you has a father...''

The silence in the room was palpable for a moment.

''Aye,'' Adam finally said as he straightened his tunic. ''I will do it. I will speak to her tonight.''

Cristiane sat next to the open window of her chamber, bent over her sewing, her heart in shreds. She knew 'twas impossible to stay here any longer, feeling as she did about Adam and his daughter. It had been a mistake to insinuate that she would remain any longer than necessary, especially now that she was aware of the arrangement Adam had made with her mother.

He'd had ample time to decide whether to take her to wife. Clearly, he'd decided she was not suitable. 'Twas true she had few womanly skills. Though capable of putting these gowns together, she could never have sewn them from a bolt of cloth. She had no knowledge of embroidery or of brewing, nor did she have experience in ordering a household.

She could read Latin, but what use was that to a man who had a learned seneschal?

The people of the castle avoided her, the servants went out of their way to snub her, and his uncle despised her. Though she worked to curb her Scottish tongue and speak as her mother had taught her, her burr slipped out at inopportune times. And there was naught to be done about her hair, unless she kept it covered at all times.

She rubbed the back of one hand over eyes that were suddenly moist, then sniffed. She resumed her sewing, anxious to finish the last gown, a lovely creation of fine golden cloth. As soon as it was done, she would be ready to leave for Learick.

'Twould be difficult to leave Adam and Meg. Cristiane did not think she'd ever seen a child so needy. The poor lass grieved for her mother, her father barely knew how to deal with her, and her nurse...well, poor Mathilde was not well suited to bringing up a child. She treated Meg as a tiny adult.

At least Meg had started to come out of herself. The grief would always be with her, but she was moving past the pain that had been locked inside. She would not need Cristiane much longer.

As for Adam…they'd shared one amazing kiss. That was all.

Clearly, it had not meant the same to him as it had to her. Nor had any of the other moments they'd shared over the last few days.

Cristiane wiped her eyes once again, then decided she needed a change of setting. Remaining indoors at a task she found tedious only served to worsen her mood.

She picked up a comb and worked to restore her hair to order, anchoring it with the combs Adam had given her. Brushing a few stray threads from her gown, Cristiane decided that all her paltry attempts at grooming were for naught. She was still a plain Scottish lass—unwelcome on English soil.

She would walk down to the pond, or mayhap to the beach. She had no intention of dining in the great hall, where Sir Gerard and his caustic tongue would be at the ready. Nor did she feel she could face Adam just yet.

Considering that there was a bit more daylight left, she took one of her books from the trunk at the foot of the bed, blew out the candles in the lamps, then turned and opened the door.

"Adam!"

Adam rubbed his palms against his thighs. He could not understand why he had ever thought Cristiane uncivilized. Or untidy. Cleanliness had never been a shortcoming, but now she was beautifully dressed in a gown she had helped to make, and her hair was cunningly arranged and contained. Clearly, she was more gently bred than he had credited her.

"I apologize for, uh, startling you," he said. "'Twas not my intention, er..."

God's teeth, he was stammering! He cleared his throat. "Might I escort you to the hall?"

She did not respond immediately, her movements strangely awkward for a woman who always moved so well, so gracefully. Something was amiss, though Adam had no inkling what it might be. Unless Gerard...

"I—I am not hungry, my lord," she finally said. "I'd planned to go down to the pond..." she lifted the object she held in her hands "...to read."

Masking his astonishment, he took the book from her. "Roger Bacon," he said, looking at the cover. "You read *Opus Maius?*"

She gave a small nod. "I thought I'd spend the last hour of daylight with this..."

He handed the beautiful, leather-bound volume back to her and jabbed his fingers through his hair. She could read, he told himself. *Latin.*

"I..." She stopped and licked her lips nervously, hugging the book to her breasts. "I must admit I've not done as Friar Roger teaches...."

"What?" Adam asked incredulously. She'd thrown him entirely off balance. "Learned Arabic? Studied mathematics?" That she'd read *Opus Maius* at all was beyond comprehension. *He* had only heard of this Franciscan scholar, and he knew of no woman who bothered with such lofty ideas. He leaned one hand against the lintel of the door, his brows drawn together in bewilderment.

"Nay, m'lord, I've not studied Greek or Arabic."

"But you *have* studied mathematics."

"Some."

Abruptly, he took her arm and drew her out of her

chamber. How could he have misjudged her so? He'd taken her measure by her appearance only, never bothering to look any deeper.

Adam kept hold of her as they walked to the stairs and descended, until they reached the great hall. "Where is wee Meg, m'lord?" Cristiane asked. "Will she not eat?"

Wee Meg... It sounded so very Scottish, yet 'twas merely an endearment. Had he mistaken *everything* about Cristiane?

"Nay," Adam replied distractedly. "She is asleep in her bed. Her eventful day wore her out."

"Oh. Well...is there some other, er, problem?" Cristiane inquired. Her forehead furrowed in a thoughtful frown, and his eyes were drawn to a tiny mole just above one golden brow. He did not know how he'd missed the delightful spot before now. He envisioned himself touching his mouth to it, smoothing the worry from her brow.

"I only want to talk to you," he said, tearing his eyes away.

Several of his men were assembled in the hall for the meal, but food was not in the forefront of Adam's thoughts. He wanted to get Cristiane away from the crowd, where he could collect his thoughts and ask her to become the lady of Bitterlee.

Nay. 'Twas too formal a proposal. Instead, he would ask her simply to wed him. But hearing the words in his head made him realize that approach was too indifferent. He was the intended bridegroom, therefore he needed to make it much more personal, as Sara had advised. Trying the words again, he decided he would ask her to do him the very great honor of becoming his wife.

And then he would give her his reasons.

Chapter Seventeen

He refrained from touching her as they walked along the cobbled path through the garden, uncertain of his ability to make his proposal without scaring her off. He knew how Rosamund would have reacted if he'd touched her in an overly familiar manner at their betrothal. He did not want to elicit the same reaction from Cristiane Mac Dhiubh.

Nay, he would take some time with Cristiane. Wooing her, softening her, until she would welcome his advances.

"Were all seven ducklings still here this afternoon, m'lord?" Cristiane asked when they reached the pond.

"Aye," he replied. "We fed every one of them."

"Good," she said. "If they can survive another week, I think they'll be all right."

He nodded in agreement. She seemed to know a great deal about wild creatures, and held a special affinity for them.

Rosy light from the setting sun glinted on Cristiane's hair, and several tendrils had come loose from the combs. They framed her face softly, accentuating the delicate shape of her ears, the line of her jaw.

His fingers ached to touch her.

He knew how it felt to kiss her, to hold her. But he also knew how a wife responded to such advances. Rosamund had despised any physical intercourse with him. He was determined to exercise whatever restraint was necessary to keep Cristiane from becoming frightened of him.

"There is a bench on the far side of the pond," he said when they reached the place where Cristiane and Meg had waded in to feed the ducklings.

"Oh," she replied. "I haven't been to the other side yet."

Still, Adam refrained from touching Cristiane as they continued on the path, circling the water as he absorbed everything about her. She was surefooted, matching his pace as they walked. Not dainty, he noticed, though her skin was very fine and her bones sturdy.

She would have no difficulty bearing his children.

"Do you not have swans here?"

Adam flushed with color, and was glad Cristiane was looking across the pond and not at him. "Nay," he said. "To my knowledge, Bitterlee has never had any."

"There were none in St. Oln, either," she said, "or I'd have known them."

"I have no doubt you would," he replied. "How did you learn so much about the birds and beasts?"

"From my father," she replied. "He was a learned man, for all the warring he was forced to do."

"Oh?"

She nodded. "A scholar, he was," she said, slowly making her way along the path. "He even studied for a time in Paris...before he wed my mother."

"So that explains the book?"

"Aye," she said. "*And* the reason my mother was

sent to him, though I didna understand it entirely until Sir Charles explained the circumstances to me.''

''How so?''

''My uncle—my mother's brother,'' she said, ''knew my father in Paris years ago. That was never secret.''

They reached the bench and sat down facing east, where the sky was a deep wash of blue upon gray.

''My mother never hid the fact that she'd had a falling-out with her father, which was why she left Learick,'' Cristiane continued. ''I never knew the particulars of their…disagreement…though I'd always known 'twas her brother who'd arranged for her to go to St. Oln.''

Adam said naught, but watched the play of the sky's changing colors in her eyes. 'Twas clear that the loss of her parents was still fresh in her heart, yet it seemed to do her good to speak of them.

''She wasna happy there,'' Cristiane said. ''She never felt that she belonged.''

If Cristiane refused his proposal, would this be the reason? Because she knew how it was to be an outsider? He had every reason to believe he could make his people come to accept her. With Sara's help, they would forget she was half-Scot, and would think of her only as the mistress of Bitterlee. His wife.

''And now I know the other cause of my mother's sadness,'' Cristiane said. ''The way her father dealt with her lover…'' She shuddered.

Adam was certain she would be just as much an outsider in Learick. The fact that she was the lord's niece would not make her seem any more English to the people of Learick, especially now, with so many English lives lost in King Edward's campaign against Scotland. And there would be many at Learick who would remember her mother's indiscretion with the huntsman. Who knew how that would affect the way they treated Cristiane?

"I suppose I'd worry about my parentage," Cristiane said, glancing away, "but I know my mother went to Scotland and married my father several years before I was born."

There was naught he could say about that, so he took the book from her hands once again, opened it and carefully turned the pages, reading a short passage in Latin aloud.

"Theologians sometimes discuss the substance of our earth," Cristiane translated with ease, "trying to locate heaven. They want to know if it lies on the equator. They ask, where is hell? Do the heavens have power over things that can be born and die? Or over the rational soul…"

"Your Latin is far superior to mine, my lady," Adam said.

"I doubt you have much use for it," she said, blushing at his compliment.

"You are right about that," he said. "'Tis fortunate I have Sir Charles to do all my writing for me."

"Was it he who corresponded with my mother…who made the arrangements for me to be brought here?"

"It was," he said, and it seemed a good time to make his proposal. "Lady Cristiane…"

The book lay open on his lap, unnoticed now, though the wind fluttered its pages. She looked up at him and unconsciously moistened her lips.

He cleared his throat. "You and Meg—Margaret— get on well."

"Aye," Cristiane said. "She's a bonny child."

"And the isle…it pleases you."

"'Tis true," she sighed. "If only there was time to explore every corner of it! But I'll soon leave for York and—"

"Cristiane," he said. He nearly took her hand in his, but thought better of it. "You need not leave Bitterlee."

Her brows came together for an instant over puzzled eyes. "But I—"

"Stay," he said. "Remain on the isle and become my wife."

Cristiane would have clapped her hands with joy if only Adam had shown some enthusiasm, some personal need for her, beyond that of taking care of his daughter.

His manner was cool, distant, as if her answer was of little consequence. She looked up into his eyes and saw something in the stormy gray depths, a flash of something she'd not seen before and could not identify.

If only he would touch her, mayhap even kiss her again. She longed to feel his arms around her, feel the length of his body pressed against hers. She needed to know that he wanted her as badly as she yearned for him. Then she would know how to answer.

Her reaction was foolish.

Many a marriage—even that of her parents—had been based on less. Titles, estates, political power…these were good reasons to wed. Truly, when she arrived at her uncle's estate, there would be far less reason for any man to wed her, for she had no land, no dowry, no political connections. If anything, she would merely be an unwelcome Scot.

'Twould be much the same here, though the days spent with Meg, and the beauty of the isle, might be compensation enough.

Whatever spark had been in Adam's eyes was gone

now, every expression carefully concealed. But Cristiane had seen it, and she believed there was more behind Adam's proposal than the convenience of gaining a new nursemaid for Meg.

His assessment was partially correct—the isle pleased her, and she got on exceptionally well with Meg. What he did not know was that she loved him, and would have stayed even if he had not asked her to wed him.

"I have no dowry, my lord," she said quietly. His jaw was rough with dark growth, and she could almost feel its texture without even touching him. Without noticing, she leaned closer, wondering how his whiskers would feel against her skin.

"A dowry is not necessary," he replied, his breath mingling with hers. 'Twas warm and inviting, and Cristiane could not keep herself from inching even closer.

"'Tis unlikely that the people of Bitterlee will ever accept me as mistress here." Her voice was a mere whisper. Blood pounded in her ears as she watched his eyelids lower, and he gazed at her lips. Surely he wanted to touch her. In another moment he would ki—

"That will change in time," he said, suddenly standing. He stepped a few paces away, then turned and looked at her, his hands gripped into fists at his sides.

She could not help but notice that the pulse in his neck was racing and his expression was earnest. Cristiane could almost believe her answer to his proposal was of the greatest importance to him.

She did not understand why this should be so, but did not care to question it now. 'Twas enough that she would be allowed to stay. "Well then, my lord," she said, looking into his stormy gray eyes, "I'll stay. I'll be your wife...."

* * *

"Papa coming too?" Meg asked as she took Cristiane's hand. They went through the great hall and out the main door, walking through the bailey toward the path that led to the waterfall. The sun was high and warm, and 'twas a perfect time for swimming.

"Nay, Papa said he would see us later," Cristiane replied. "He had some matters to attend in town."

Her heart was full as it had not been in months, and there was naught that could spoil her day, not even the distance Adam kept between them. 'Twas no matter, Cristiane thought. She could only believe that would change after they were wed.

In the meantime, she and Meg would have their swim, would play near the waterfall for a while, and at supper Adam would announce their betrothal.

She smiled at the thought.

"Taking the half-wit for a stroll?"

Meg let go of Cristiane's hand and buried her face in Cristiane's skirts when Gerard spoke.

Cristiane did not know how the man managed to sneak up on her so often, but he'd done it again—caught her unawares, startling her with his cruel words.

"Try to keep a civil tongue, Sir Gerard," she said, somehow managing to stop her voice from quavering. "Or 'twill be said the isle was named after you." She peeled Meg's hand from her skirts and led her forward again.

Some of the men in the bailey must have heard the interchange, because there was laughter behind them now, and Gerard's angry voice in reaction to it. Cristiane did not know how she had summoned the nerve to speak in such a way to Gerard, but she was not sorry for it. And if he ever said another disparaging word about wee

Meg and her lack of speech…well, Cristiane would not be responsible for her actions.

She took Meg's hand in her own and continued down the path. Meg held on as if her very life depended upon it.

"I wonder if our bonny wee fox will come today," Cristiane said once the castle wall was out of sight.

"Have you any…bread?" Meg asked, still cowed by the confrontation with Gerard.

Cristiane laughed, then stopped and hugged the child. "You are a quick one, my lass!" she said, treasuring the thought of becoming this child's mother. She felt a fierce protectiveness toward her, and woe to anyone who would dare to hurt her. "Aye, I brought bread."

They came to the place where the path turned and continued toward the waterfall. They climbed down to the rocks and wandered near the falls for a few minutes, while Cristiane glanced 'round, looking to see if the area was entirely isolated before shedding their clothes to swim.

Cristiane suspected the English would consider swimming naked barbaric, but naked was how she'd done it at home. Besides, she had no spare clothes—and no extra chemise—to wear in the water. Meg probably had one. Cristiane would find out about that before they came here again.

For now, though, they were alone, the sun was shining and the day could not have been more fine. "Come on, Meggie," she said to the child as she pulled off her shoes. "There's a lovely blue pool waiting for us!"

There was no reason to wait three full weeks to wed her.

Early that morn, Adam had dispatched a man to the

bishop in Alnwick, with letters from the priest of St. Oln, and Lady Elizabeth, and another from Father Beaupré, attesting to the lawfulness of the match. It should only take a few days for the journey, then to see the bishop and gain his permission. 'Twas possible to be wed by week's end.

Adam would wait no longer. He did not think he *could* wait any longer.

He gazed down at the pool where Cristiane and Margaret swam. He'd promised himself only to keep watch over them, but found he could not keep his eyes from straying down to them.

And why should he not?

The one was his own little daughter, the other his betrothed, soon to be his wife…

Even though she stayed mostly in the water and out of sight, Adam's body reacted in a manner that was becoming familiar. It had been years since he'd felt this way. He wanted Cristiane fiercely, but there was no doubt that she would be terrified by the intensity of his need.

He vowed to keep control.

They would have many long years together, and Adam would not spend them the same way he'd passed his years with Rosamund, with her ignoring and avoiding him.

He wanted Cristiane.

And he believed that, with care, he could foster and encourage the glimmer of interest he'd seen in her eyes. He knew 'twas not impossible for a wife to desire her husband. He'd seen evidence of it with some of his men. Elwin, for instance. The men often made veiled remarks regarding his lusty wife.

But Adam's mother, as well as his own wife, had abhorred their husband's touch.

Adam wanted this marriage to be different. He wanted Cristiane to feel every bit as eager to touch him as he was to touch her. He wanted to hold her through the night as they slept in his bed. He did not know why this ideal held such appeal—his parents had certainly never done it, nor had any other nobleman of his acquaintance. He'd never spent an entire night with Rosamund. *She* had never once visited his bed, and on the occasions when Adam had gone to hers, she'd made it clear he was unwelcome to stay the night.

Adam had no doubt that keeping Cristiane Mac Dhiubh close to him as they slept would be too great a pleasure to deny.

He would see that she became accustomed to him, to his presence. It would need to be done gradually, so as not to alarm or frighten her. He would spend time with her, walk the beach with her, make certain their first night in their marriage bed was as pleasurable for Cristiane as it was for him.

He rubbed one hand across his mouth and over his chin. He was getting ahead of himself.

Stepping away from the notch in the trees where he had kept watch over the path as well as the waterfall, Adam decided to put his plan into action now.

He grinned as he started down the rocky incline to the floor of the falls, certain that, with his daughter there to make her feel secure, he could begin to make Cristiane feel safe with him. Alone.

Meg took to swimming like a wee duckling. Cristiane was delighted with her progress, and knew 'twould not take many more lessons before the lass could be trusted in the water alone. Meg floated belly-down on the water, dunking her face, propelling herself with her arms and kicking with her legs.

The water in the pool was cool, but not unpleasantly so. Meg tolerated it without going blue, so Cristiane let her stay in a while longer, playing splashing games with her. She doubted Meg had ever had this much fun in her few years of life.

Old Mathilde was much too dour for a child like Meg, and Cristiane decided to speak to Adam about her. Today, when she'd gone to find Meg for their swim, she'd found her on her knees on the stone floor of the chapel, praying for the soul of her dead mother.

Common sense told her that that was not a likely way to get wee Meg to move past her grief.

The child splashed and laughed, and suddenly her eyes went even brighter.

"Papa!" she squealed.

Chapter Eighteen

Cristiane whirled in dismay. She was fully naked in this clear water, and Adam Sutton stood directly above her.

Her clothes were draped over a rock a good fifteen paces away, along with the two drying cloths she'd brought for herself and Meg.

"Watch me!" Meg cried, putting her face in the water and showing her father what she could do, while Cristiane could do naught but offer the same support she'd given before. 'Twas awkward, holding on to Meg while keeping herself shielded from his view, but she managed somehow.

"Very good!" he said. "And is Lady Cristiane a good swimmer, too?"

She cast him a look that challenged his question.

"Yes!" Meg cried. "She dives deep!"

"Ah…" Adam said. "Shall I join you? I li—"

"Nay, m'lord!" Cristiane exclaimed in alarm. The last thing she wanted was for Adam to disrobe and step into the pool.

Meg suddenly shivered, and Cristiane knew she

needed to get out of the water and into the warm sunshine.

"'Tis time to stop, my lassie," Cristiane said, propelling the child toward the edge of the pool. "Your papa can pull you out."

"Nay, Cris-ty," she said with a pout. "You!"

"Not this time, my wee one," Cristiane said, ducking down so that the water reached her chin. "Put up your arms and let your father take you."

Adam was too close to the pool for Cristiane's peace of mind. She crossed her arms over her breasts, but had never been so conscious of her nakedness. She felt the coldness of the water, too, and knew she would soon have to get out, as well.

She watched as Adam lifted Meggie out and took her to the rock where the towel was set out. He wrapped his daughter up and rubbed her body from shoulders to ankles, and Cristiane could only think how 'twould feel if he did the same for her.

At that moment, he looked up, locking her gaze with his, and seemed to know exactly what she'd been thinking. Blushing wildly, she submerged herself to cool off.

Adam stood in the sun, drying Margaret. He knew Cristiane could not remain underwater forever. Nor could she remain in the pool much longer. 'Twas too cold.

She would have to come out and face him sooner or later.

"Are you warm enough now, Margaret?" he asked, aware that his own body was more than just warm.

"Yes," she replied. "Cris-ty?"

"She'll come out soon," he replied. If not, he would just have to go in and get her.

She emerged at that moment, and Adam did not know whether or not to consider himself fortunate.

"Cris-ty!" Meg called.

Cristiane smoothed her hair back. "Aye, lass," she replied, her eyes glancing nervously up at him.

His intent was not to frighten her off, but to put her at ease…to make her realize she could trust him. "My lady," he said, "Margaret and I will give you a moment's privacy if you wish to leave the pool."

He gathered Margaret into his arms and stepped behind the waterfall, turning to face the stone wall. He called out, "Let us know when you are decent."

The rush of the water was so loud it prevented him from hearing Cristiane's movements. He bit the inside of his cheek and waited. He would just have to trust Margaret to tell him when it was safe to turn around.

"The fox, Papa!" Margaret cried, pointing.

Without thinking, he turned quickly, and through the curtain of falling water, he saw that Cristiane was wrapped in a meager linen towel that covered her body only from her chest to her knees. She stood perfectly still, her eyes on the pool she'd just left.

Adam glanced that way and saw a fox scurrying to the pool, apparently oblivious to the people around it.

"Stay still, Meg," he whispered.

Carefully and quietly, Cristiane picked something up from the pile of clothes on the rocks. She took one step, holding out her hand. The fox stopped drinking, eyeing her warily.

Cristiane took another step closer, and the fox sat up, sniffing the air. Suddenly it turned and dashed back up the rocks. Holding her towel around her, Cristiane took the last step to reach the place where the fox had stood, and dropped a crust of bread there.

Adam thought his chest might burst when she bent to do so.

Quickly, he turned back before Cristiane was aware of his gaze on her body—her plump breasts, her trim legs, the curve of her buttocks. "Are you warm enough, Margaret?" he asked.

"Aye, papa," she replied. "Want to…see the fox."

Surprised by the number of words she'd strung together, he did not reply right away, but let her down to the rocky floor. She immediately headed for Cristiane.

"You may come out now, m'lord!" Cristiane called, tying her last lace. She looked utterly charming with her hair in glistening waves, curling around her face. Adam wondered how she would react if he were to take her in his arms now.

"Cris-ty!" Meg cried, running to Cristiane. "Fox!"

"Aye, you saw it, did you?" she asked.

Margaret nodded. "Gone."

"It's gone now, but do not doubt it will be back," Cristiane said. "Do you not agree, m'lord?"

"I would not be surprised," he replied absently. He could not possibly want Cristiane more than he did at this moment. 'Twas fortunate that little Meg was present, else he'd have been hard-pressed to keep to his plan of accustoming her gradually to his presence.

"Today?" Margaret asked, and Adam forgot exactly what they were discussing.

"Mayhap," Cristiane said. She sat down on the rock where her clothes had been, and put on her shoes. Margaret dropped down next to her. "And if he finds that crust, he will be back for more."

"Oh!" she replied. "Like…like ducklings!"

"Exactly."

"Cristiane," Adam said as he sat down, keeping his

daughter between them, "shall we tell Margaret our news?"

"Umm...'tis up to you, m'lord," she replied shyly.

'Twas as if she did not believe she would truly become his wife. Adam experienced a moment of alarm. "You have not changed your mind, have you?"

"Nay, m'lord," Cristiane quickly replied.

She believed he looked relieved. For an instant, he had not seemed quite so distant, so...official. She knew Adam cared for his daughter, and she supposed it would distress him to learn that the one person who seemed to have a positive effect on Margaret had changed her mind and would be going away.

Cristiane could not change her mind, even if she wanted to do so. She could not bear to leave Adam, or to leave Meg and the isle.

"Meggie lass," she said, glancing up at Adam, "your father has something to tell you."

Margaret turned to look at him, and he brushed one hand across her forehead, pushing back the wet strands.

"Lady Cristiane has decided to stay with us on the isle," he said. "She will become my wife...your new mama."

"Ma-ma?" Meg said vacantly. Then she frowned. "Ma-ma...in heaven with Our Lord."

"Aye, Meggie," Cristiane said. The child's words sounded as though they'd come straight from Mathilde's lips. "Your true mama is in heaven. But I will be here with your father, to look after you."

The child said naught, but gazed at the spot where the fox had taken its drink. Then she turned to look at the waterfall, staring blankly.

Adam's expression was one of puzzlement.

"Meggie," Cristiane said, taking the child's hand in

her own. "Do ye not want me to stay?" She swallowed
hard. What if the child did not want her? Would Adam
withdraw his proposal?

The child finally turned. Her gaze was focused,
steady. "Stay," she said. "And feed the ducklings!"

"I've petitioned the bishop at Alnwick to waive the
banns," Adam said as they followed the path back to
the castle. Meg wandered ahead of them, stopping every
now and then to pick a flower that interested her.

Cristiane's heart did a little jump when she thought
of Adam speeding up their marriage. Normally, 'twould
take three weeks for the reading of the banns.

"'Tis possible that we can be wed by week's end,"
he said.

Was he anxious to have her as his wife, or just eager
for Meggie to have a mother? Would he have sent her
to York if Meg had decided she did not want Cristiane
to stay?

He gave her a sidelong glance. "I will not be a demanding husband, Cristiane," he said.

"Oh, but I—"

"I would rather we did not start our marriage with
any uneasiness or…fear…between us."

"I am not frightened of you, m'lord." She could not
imagine why he thought she'd be afraid of him. He'd
never given her any cause to fear him.

She thought she heard him take a sharp breath, but
could have been mistaken, though there was no doubt
he felt awkward with her. He limped along, quietly for
a while, and Cristiane thought about the one kiss they'd
shared. It seemed so long ago.

She did not think he had disliked it, even though he

had not attempted to repeat it. She wondered how he would react if she were to step in front of him and, somehow, get hold of him and…kiss him again.

"You have had an astonishing effect on my daughter in a short time," he said, jarring Cristiane from thoughts of a more sensual nature.

Cristiane shrugged. "The lass spends too much time on her knees, praying for her mother."

"I knew that Mathilde emphasized prayer and devotions.…"

"Aye," Cristiane replied. "But too much. She spends hours at her prayers."

Adam frowned. "I had not seen it. I assumed…" He shook his head. "'Tis inexcusable. I should have been more aware of what was happening."

Mayhap that was true, but from what Cristiane had learned from her mother, English fathers had little to do with their own offspring. Nursemaids raised them, and young lads were sent off to neighboring estates to be trained in the knightly arts. 'Twas unusual for Adam to spend any time at all with Meg.

Cristiane wondered about these last two years since the Battle of Falkirk. She knew Adam had returned to Bitterlee newly widowed, and wounded besides. 'Twould have been overwhelming to deal with his own grief as well as his daughter's. Mayhap he still grieved for his wife.

"You were badly injured at Falkirk, m'lord?" she asked. When he did not reply, she went on. "I would imagine your recovery took a good deal of strength."

"Aye," he said. "But it does not excuse my negligence with Margaret."

"It goes a long way toward explaining it," she said.

She knew by his limp that whatever had happened to his leg still bothered him. She wondered about the scar on his jaw and what other wounds he'd received while warring for the English king in Scotland.

"I once broke my arm," she said, "when I was just a bairn. The bone came clear through the skin. I remember 'twas sore after it healed. My mother put liniment on it and rubbed it every day, and my father made me use it, exercise it."

"Your arm seems well enough now," he said, glancing at the faded scar on her forearm.

"Aye.... You might think of doing the same for your leg," she said tentatively. "If you have liniment, I could..." She stopped when she realized that she was about to tell him she would be happy to apply ointment and do the rubbing for him. She felt heat spread from her chin to her forehead.

Adam slowed his gait and turned to her without speaking. 'Twas clear that he knew what she'd been about to say, and Cristiane could not tell how the idea set with him, for he kept his face carefully expressionless.

"That is, if y-you had some liniment, you could try r-rubbing it...."

"I have liniment," he said, though his voice seemed different than before. Quieter, deeper. A muscle in his jaw flexed as she watched.

Cristiane placed one hand over her stomach, vaguely aware of an odd sensation there. "Mayhap s-someone should, er, someone could—"

"Cris-ty!" Meggie shouted, ending the awkward moment. The child ran toward them and gave the handful of flowers she'd gathered to Cristiane. Then she scampered off, with more energy than she'd shown before.

* * *

Cristiane gave Meg over to Mathilde's care and entered her chamber. A young handmaid was already there, pouring hot water into a tub. She smiled shyly.

"Your bath, my lady," the lass said, dipping into a slight curtsy.

"Thank you," Cristiane replied warily. None of the castle servants had been the least bit friendly to her, and she did not trust this sudden show of deference.

"May I...would you care for help with your laces?"

Cristiane could do naught but stare at the maid, wondering if she was imagining this interchange. Slowly, she turned, allowing the girl to unlace her.

"I took the liberty of finishing your gown," she said.

Cristiane glanced at the neatly folded cloth that rested on the trunk at the foot of the bed. "Why, thank you," she answered. "I..."

"If I might be so bold, my lady," the girl said, "'tis a wonderful thing you're doing for Lord Bitterlee's daughter."

Cristiane was too astonished by her words to reply.

"The change in her..." the girl continued. "I cannot see how it can matter that you're a Scot."

"Well, I..."

"The child's not been right since her mum died," she said, "but what you've started...I think she'll be all right now."

"I hope so," Cristiane exclaimed. "She's a bonny one."

Cristiane's borrowed gown came off and she walked toward the tub while she unlaced her chemise. She did not feel the need for a bath now, having just been swimming, but she was not about to turn down the one offer of friendship she'd received since coming to Bitterlee.

"What is your name?" Cristiane asked.

"I'm Beatrice, my lady," she replied. "But call me Bea, like everyone else does."

The great hall was full, and a special meal had been prepared for the occasion of Adam's announcement. He knew it would take time for the people of Bitterlee to accept Cristiane, but he intended to demonstrate his commitment to her. And if necessary, he would challenge anyone to deny his right to make her his wife.

Gerard gulped his ale as he stood near the main dais, sneering at Adam. "You can do better," he said.

"If you're referring to my impending marriage, Uncle," he replied tightly, "then I must disagree. Lady Cristiane is my choice."

Gerard spat into the fresh rushes.

"A bloody Scot for a bride," he snarled derisively.

"Half-Scot," Adam muttered, turning away from his uncle. "And you'd do well to remember it when she is my wife."

"She'll wed you only to stay on Bitterlee, to become mistress here," he said. "Don't think I haven't noticed her wandering. The isle reminds her of her home…of all she has lost."

That thought gave Adam pause, and he wondered if Gerard had been spying on her from one of his various hideaways on the isle.

"She'll be no wife to you, Adam," Gerard continued. "'Twould be better to take yourself off to Watersby when you have need of a woman, rather than take this— this bloody savage to wife."

"Stay away from her, Gerard," Adam stated, then turned away. He spotted Raynauld seated at a table nearby, along with Sir Elwin and his wife, Leticia. He could count upon these men to support Cristiane. They knew she was no bloodthirsty Scot. Nor was she a cold-hearted opportunist.

'Twas true that she liked the isle…but what did that matter? The mistress of Bitterlee ought at least to feel comfortable on her island home. He would not tie himself to another wife like Rosamund, a faint-hearted woman who felt trapped and secluded here.

Voices suddenly grew quiet, and Adam looked up to see that Cristiane was standing in the gallery at the top of the stairs.

She was so beautiful that his throat went dry. She fairly shimmered in a gown of gold cloth that hugged her body from her breasts to her waist, then flared just below her hips. He nearly groaned aloud, wondering how she could be as alluring fully clothed as she was naked.

Her hair was tame, perfectly demure, and partially covered in the same golden cloth as her gown. She glowed with an aura of health…and nervousness, Adam realized.

He climbed the steps to escort her down, and saw that her hands were clenched at her sides. "My lady," he said as he turned and took her hand, placing it atop his own. "Do you see Sir Elwin there?" he asked as they descended. "Next to him is his wife, Leticia. And Raynauld beside them."

"Where is Meg?" she asked, and he saw her glance toward the main dais, where his uncle was sitting, hunched over a large mug.

"She will take her meal in the nursery this eve, with Mathilde," he replied, glad to have something to speak of, to take her mind off what awaited them below. "And no prayers for her tonight, beyond one quick one before bed."

Cristiane's brows raised, widening her eyes delightfully. "What will Mathilde do with her then?"

"I told her to teach Margaret a game or two," he said, wishing he could pull Cristiane into his arms and kiss away the lines of worry.

She smiled at his jest, a tense smile, but it pleased him when she no longer resembled a prisoner being led to the stake. He knew this was difficult for her. She was entirely among strangers, people who had yet to make her feel welcome.

And she was to become their mistress.

Raynauld came to the foot of the stairs when they reached the bottom.

Cristiane was as glad of his appearance now as she'd been when he'd shown up on the staircase of the English inn and helped Adam get her to safety.

This room was not as hostile as the inn...or was it? Gerard stared malevolently at her, and it seemed that everyone else waited in silence for her to commit some grave error.

"Lady Cristiane," Sir Elwin said as he approached, "may I present my wife, Leticia."

A pretty round woman with rosy cheeks and glossy black hair smiled shyly at her. "'Tis my pleasure to make your acquaintance, my lady,"

"No greater than mine, Leticia," Cristiane said, and with her words, the silence in the hall broke.

Everyone began to speak again. Servants moved about the tables, setting out platters of food and pitchers of ale. Musicians began playing, and a pair of jugglers thrilled the crowd with their antics.

"Shall we be seated?" Adam asked. He put his hand at Cristiane's back and felt her trembling. "The worst seems to be over."

They were approached by several of Adam's knights, and Cristiane was introduced to the reeve of Bitterlee town. She was as gracious and polite as Adam could possibly have wished.

He had hoped that Penyngton would be well enough to join them, to bolster Cristiane's morale, but the seneschal was too ill. His cough was worse, and he was feverish. For the first time since his friend's illness, Adam was truly worried for his life. He was pale and drawn, and coughing seemed to wrack the very life from him.

Adam had summoned Sara from town to come up and do what she could for him, and she'd promised she would remain with him as long as he needed her.

That was some relief, although Adam had hoped to introduce Sara to Cristiane tonight. He doubted that he would ever acknowledge her publicly as his sister, but he would certainly tell Cristiane of their relationship. Besides, Sara was a respected resident of the town, and Cristiane should know her.

The Bitterlee cooks provided a pleasing, impressive meal, yet Adam noticed that Cristiane merely picked at her food. She also sat stiffly in her chair, although her most avid detractor was nowhere near. Gerard had disappeared.

Adam glanced around the hall, and though there was plenty of entertainment, ale and good food, the guests were strangely somber. The people of Bitterlee were not ready to accept her as their lady, though the knights of his garrison were slowly coming 'round.

Adam turned to her. ''By what miracle do you manage to induce my daughter to eat?''

''My lord?'' she asked. The tiny mole at her brow moved as she frowned with puzzlement.

"You have hardly touched your meal," he said, "so I wondered what I might do to convince you to eat."

"Ach, I'm na..." She blushed and bit her lip. "I'm not hungry," she said, enunciating each word carefully.

"Cristiane," Adam said, placing one hand over hers. "I do not judge you by your speech. You needn't guard against the occasional slip with me."

Her chin quivered for an instant before she was able to get her emotions under control, and she glanced at the people in the hall. "I'm afraid it *will* matter to the rest of Bitterlee."

"Not for long," he vowed.

He removed his hand from hers and stood. Taking up his knife, he tapped on the side of his goblet to get the attention of the assemblage. The music stopped, the jugglers dropped their balls and conversation ebbed. Soon all was quiet in the hall.

"Thank you all for joining us this eve," he said. He spoke of the recent storm and the repairs being made. He joked about his soldiers doing the work of farmers. Finally, he said, "Our celebration tonight is to mark the occasion of my betrothal to Lady Cristiane of St. Oln."

When silence ensued, Adam continued. "The marriage will take place in ten days, at Holy Cross Church. My bride and I invite all to attend the wedding and the Mass in town," he said. "*And* the feasting afterward!"

Adam's knights began to applaud, but the clapping sounded hollow in the hall. The townspeople sat quietly, apparently stunned by their lord's news. Adam had not believed Cristiane's body could become any stiffer than it had been during the meal, but now she seemed brittle enough to break.

"A toast!" Sir Elwin called before Adam could act.

The knights and all their ladies stood as Elwin toasted

the lord and his lady's health, wishing them a long and prosperous life together. By the time he was finished speaking, all the other guests had stood and lifted their cups to Adam and Cristiane.

Though they drank reluctantly, Adam felt 'twas a beginning. He could not ask for more.

Chapter Nineteen

Rain threatened. Cristiane could feel the change in the air, and the heaviness matched her mood.

Standing on the parapet where she'd met Adam her first morning on Bitterlee, she breathed deeply.

"I thought I might find you here," he said quietly.

Cristiane whirled around at the sound of his voice, and saw Adam step away from the door and walk toward her, lit by the hazy moonlight.

"They will accept you in time," he said.

Cristiane said naught, but turned and placed both hands on the low crenelation. She was not so optimistic. Their disdain was clear. Yet she would not renege on her promise to wed him.

She knew she could not bear to leave him, even if every last person on the isle hated her.

"How many men did you lose at Falkirk?" she asked without turning.

"Seventy."

Cristiane's heart dropped. So many men. So many families affected. How would a Scotswoman ever win them over? Would they ever see her as aught but the enemy?

"Nearly all of the knights in the hall tonight went to Scotland with us as well," Adam said. "They do not hold you responsible for our losses."

"'Tis not a rational thing," she said. "I merely represent that which caused their sorrows."

"You are too insightful for your own good, Cristiane," he remarked, turning her to face him. His strong hands were gentle on her shoulders, and Cristiane wished that he would pull her close, mayhap even kiss her as he had done once before. "Their feelings will change. They will see what you've done for Margaret and…"

'Twas clear he did not want to kiss her, or he'd have done so by now. She did not understand why he'd kissed her that one time, unless he'd been carried away with the emotion of seeing changes in Meg. He'd certainly not thought of doing it since then.

Resigned to becoming a mere replacement for Meg's mother, Cristiane could not allow herself to dwell on her secondary position. She would become Adam's wife, and a mother to the lass. Mayhap in time Adam would come to care for her as she cared for him.

But she would not count on it.

Thunder rumbled low in the distance, presaging the storm to come. Adam let go of Cristiane's shoulders reluctantly. If he had not, he'd have done something he would certainly live to regret.

He reminded himself that patience was the key. He would court her as if she had a chaperon with her at all times, and never once give her reason to feel alarmed in his presence. Soon after the marriage, he would approach her as a husband, but not until then.

"Rain is coming," he said, exerting monumental control over his baser urges.

"Will it be as severe as the last?"

"I hope not," he replied. "There was enough damage done in town. We don't need any more."

"Has…has Meg always had a fear of storms?" she asked.

"You heard her, then, the night you arrived?"

"Aye…" she replied, turning away.

"Before I went away," he said, "before her mother died, she was never afraid. Now the sound of thunder sends her into a panic…. 'Tis not practical for one who lives on Bitterlee to fear a storm."

In the moonlight, he saw the crease between Cristiane's brows that indicated she was puzzling over some problem. It warmed his heart to know that she was concerned about his daughter, that she thought about the things that troubled her.

He would have taken her in his arms right then if he hadn't been afraid that his premature advances would drive her to the edge of this parapet.

Shuddering, he stepped away.

This time, when Cristiane heard the scream in the night, she knew what it was. Though she knew Adam would take care of Meg, she scrambled out of bed and lit a lamp anyway, before hurrying to Meggie's chamber.

Adam was there ahead of her, only partially dressed, already holding the child in his arms. His back was to her, but Meg saw her as soon as she walked through the doorway.

"Chris-ty!" the girl wailed.

"Aye, lass," Cristiane said. "I'm here."

Another crack of thunder rattled the window and Meg screamed again. "Papa!"

"I'm here, Margaret," he said. "There's naught to fear."

"Mama!" she cried, burying her face against Adam's bare chest. "Come back!"

"Cristiane is here, sweet," Adam said, glancing up, "and she is not leaving."

Cristiane sat down on the bed with Adam and his daughter, putting her arm around Meg's wee shoulders. "Try not to let the wind and thunder frighten you, Meggie," she said quietly. "'Twill not hurt you."

"It hurt Mama," she said against Adam's chest, so that it was difficult to understand her.

"Nay," Adam said. "Mama was hurt when she fell."

Cristiane looked sharply at Adam. She'd not heard Rosamund's cause of death before, and it surprised her to learn the woman had fallen to her death. Had it happened during a storm? Had she slipped on the rocks near the beach? Was that why Adam had told her there was no way down there?

"Was it storming when Lady Rosamund fell?" Cristiane asked him.

Adam shook his head. "I do not know. She died the week before my return from Falkirk."

"Mayhap we should find out."

The storm passed without doing any damage, and life went on as it had before. Cristiane and Meg fed the ducklings and swam at the waterfall, while Adam kept watch over them.

He learned that Rosamund had, indeed, jumped from the parapet during a violent storm. But why such a strong connection between storms and Rosamund's death should exist in Margaret's mind was unexplained.

Adam could only hope she would outgrow it, just as she seemed to be developing normally in other ways again.

As the days passed, Charles Penyngton's condition worsened, and Cristiane made only a few short visits, as they seemed to tire him. Sara Cole, however, spent a good deal more time at the castle, nursing him.

"Is there anyone in town who is not opposed to my marriage to Cristiane?" Adam asked Sara late one afternoon as he walked her to the main door of the great hall. Penyngton's fever had broken and he was resting comfortably, so Sara would return home until she was summoned to the castle again.

"Of course," she replied. "But there are those who will despise her forever, just because of her Scottish blood."

"You know these people, Sara," he said. "You live with them. Do you think their opinion of her will change in time?"

"They regard you most highly, my lord," she said. "I cannot imagine they would scorn your wife forever."

"I've noticed some of the servants warming to her," Adam mused. In fact, several of the younger maids had begun to show deference to her, and the footmen and grooms did not seem quite so hostile.

"As will the rest of the people of Bitterlee," she said.

"I hope—"

"Papa!" Margaret's voice broke into their conversation, and Adam looked up to see his daughter running toward him. Cristiane remained behind. She seemed wary, unsure.

Adam took Sara's arm and walked down the stone staircase to meet Margaret, who threw her arms 'round her father's legs. "Cristiane," he said, lifting Margaret into his arms. "Come and meet Sara."

Cristiane wished she had worn one of her better gowns today. Instead, she found herself meeting this paragon of Bitterlee wearing some woman's discarded, faded green kirtle. And her hair was its usual mess, having been subjected to the wind down near the pond.

"How do you do, Mistress Cole."

"Sara, please," she said. "'Tis a pleasure to meet you, my lady. Lord Bitterlee has spoken of you often."

Cristiane felt a pang of jealousy that she knew was unwarranted. He may have told Sara about *her,* but had hardly mentioned Sara in their own conversations. It gave her the impression that her betrothed shared long, intimate talks with this woman.

And Sara was beautiful, with perfect skin and lovely features. Cristiane knew her own appearance could not begin to compete with Sara Cole's.

"I'm sure there's not much for him to tell," Cristiane said, taking care to tame her burr.

"Oh, but there is," Sara replied. "Look how much you've helped little Margaret. I cannot believe the change in her."

She reached over and smoothed a lock of Margaret's blond hair away from her face, and Cristiane had the irrational urge to tell the woman to leave her daughter alone. 'Twas ridiculous. After all, Sara Cole had known Meg all her life. Cristiane was a newcomer.

Still…

"—told me of the ducklings you and Margaret saved," Sara was saying. "And about a fox that actually takes bread from your hand."

Cristiane's eyes opened wide and flew to meet Adam's. How did he know she'd been feeding the fox? The last time he'd gone with them to the waterfall, the fox had still been too shy to come near. He must have seen her—

She blushed from the roots of her hair to her neck. The only way he could possibly have known about her feeding the fox was if he'd seen her bathing with Meg. They still went every day that the weather permitted, and they swam naked in the water.

"I—I..."

"'Tis quite a talent," Sara said, "this way that you have with wild creatures."

"I suppose...." she replied. "That is, I..." She did not dare look at Adam or her color would deepen even more.

"Drink, Cris-ty!" Meggie cried, slipping out of Adam's arms and rescuing Cristiane from her shock. She had every reason to take her leave now, without seeming ungracious.

"If you'll excuse us, my lord," she said, "Sara. 'Twas a pleasure meeting you."

Cristiane climbed the steps holding Meg's hand. When they entered the dark hall, the dogs stood up and trotted over, anxious for Cristiane's attention. "A *way with animals,* indeed," she muttered. "No healing skills, no control over the servants, no—"

"Breeding," Gerard said. He sat in one of the chairs near the hearth, and Cristiane had not seen him. "Nothing at all to recommend you."

Meg tugged at Cristiane's skirts to draw her away from the unpleasant uncle, and Cristiane was more than willing to follow.

"Not like Sara," he said, slurring his words. "Much better suited to Bitterlee."

Even though they were walking away from him, Cristiane heard what he said. And this time, she couldn't have agreed with him more.

Adam found them sitting on the steps at one of the back entrances of the keep, sipping water from mugs. The two big dogs pranced around them, waiting for some attention.

He could not forget Cristiane's expression when she'd realized he'd seen them at the waterfall. Fortunately, she had not seemed angry. She had blushed, and there'd been heat in her eyes for the instant she'd allowed herself to look at him.

This was wholly satisfactory progress, he thought.

"We travel to Bitterlee town tomorrow," he said, sitting down next to Cristiane. Sara had proposed a fête in town to introduce Cristiane. She had found Cristiane charming, and believed that the townsfolk would quickly come to accept her if they had an opportunity to meet her.

"No, Papa!"

He should not have been surprised by his daughter's reaction, but she'd become so much more inquisitive and outgoing these last few days that he'd expected her to be interested in a trip to town. "Why not, Margaret?"

"We feed the ducklings!" she said. Her words were becoming less disjointed, much more appropriate for a child her age.

"I see," he replied. "And if we found someone who would feed them in your place?"

Margaret pondered the question.

"Because there is to be a festival in town," he added, raising his eyes to meet Cristiane's. "To celebrate my betrothal to Lady Cristiane."

"Oh, but Adam—"

"Don't tell me you cannot leave the ducklings for one day, either, Cristiane," he teased. He would do anything to remove the line of worry that creased her forehead, yet he knew how important it was for her to go into town and mingle with the people.

No one could hate her once they knew her.

"N-nay…"

"Do not worry," he said. "I'll be with you. Naught untoward will happen tomorrow."

It seemed to Cristiane that the town was overtaken with children. And quiet, cautious adults.

Cristiane could only be grateful that Gerard Sutton was not here to add to her unease.

The day was overcast and cool, but musicians played, and the jugglers and acrobats who entertained at the castle were there to help to enliven the gathering. Adam had been true to his word, and kept by Cristiane's side. No one had the gall to act in an overtly hostile manner. In fact, there were a few who'd actually been friendly.

"Many blessings on you," said a young girl as she handed her a clump of flowers.

"I thank you," Cristiane said, overcoming the vast lump that had suddenly appeared in her throat. "What is your name?"

"'Tis Gemette, my lady," the girl replied before running off.

Meggie clung to Cristiane's skirts, eyeing the children as they ran through the lanes, frolicking and playing as they would do on any feast day. Though she was not quite ready to join them, their activities fascinated her.

Trestle tables were set up in the center of town in front of the stone church, and women were bringing baskets of food—breads and dishes of fish, mostly—under Sara

Cole's supervision. Also helping were several of Adam's servants, who laid out food brought from the castle earlier in the day.

It would all have been very inviting if Cristiane had not been quite so nervous.

"My lord." 'Twas the reeve. Cristiane remembered being introduced to him at their betrothal feast. "Lady Cristiane, may I present my wife, Lucy Morton."

"I am glad to meet you," Cristiane said to the woman, who carried an infant in her arms and walked with a toddler wrapped around one leg.

"Likewise, my lady," Lucy replied, obviously feeling awkward.

"Your children are beautiful," Cristiane said. "But they must cause a good bit of work."

"Ah, that they do," she said, "and we have two more, besides."

"What are their ages, Madam Morton?" Cristiane asked.

As Lucy relaxed and spoke of her family, Adam gave Cristiane's arm a reassuring squeeze. Or mayhap 'twas more in the way of letting her know that she was doing well with his people.

Another young mother approached with her husband, and then another, and soon Cristiane was surrounded by women, all discussing the trials of motherhood on the isle. She hardly realized when she'd gotten separated from Adam.

"Heard you've done some good with little Margaret," one of the women said.

"Aye, well…" Cristiane began, "she's a sweet child, and 'tis no hardship to spend time with her."

"No wonder Lord Bitterlee decided to wed you," another woman said, clearly aware of how her words would strike Cristiane. "He's likely pleased to have someone—anyone—who can help the child."

"That nursemaid Lady Rosamund brought when she came to the isle—"

"Why, she's no good for a child at all—"

"Much too harsh."

Cristiane could make no response. 'Twas exactly what she thought, too, though she did not need some tactless townswomen to tell her that Adam had chosen her in order to provide a good mother for Meg.

"Shall we eat, Meggie?" Cristiane asked, taking Meg's hand. She needed to escape these harpies with their cruel words.

Trestle tables had been set up near the church. Cristiane looked over the crowd and saw that Adam was surrounded by townsmen, fishermen and farmers. "'Tis just us, then, Meg," she said, leading the child to a table. "Your papa will join us later, I'm sure."

As they were filling plates, Sara Cole came up and greeted them. "I'm so happy you and Lord Bitterlee were able to come today, my lady."

"Thank you, Sara," she replied. "'Tis a fine day for such a fête."

"I hope your ducklings do not miss you over much," Sara said to Meg. Then she looked up at Cristiane. "Lord Bitterlee told me that was a concern."

"Aye," Cristiane said weakly. Again she realized how much closer Sara was to Adam.

And all the while he seemed to want to keep his distance from *her*.

"Some of the children are playing by the river, Margaret," Sara said. "Mayhap Cristiane will take you down there and you can join them."

"Swimming?" Meg asked.

"Likely not," Sara said with a friendly smile. "Unless it warms up a bit."

After a while, since Adam was still occupied with the townsmen, Cristiane and Meg walked with a couple of the other women to the riverbank at the edge of town.

"The older boys like to swim here, my lady," said one of them, "because the sea is too rough."

"And too cold!"

"But the river is running swift these days with all the rain we've had," said another. "They'd best watch the current, or they'll be dragged out to sea."

"Aye, they'll be careful."

"They always are."

Cristiane urged Meg to join some of the smaller children, who were tossing small stones into the water at the river's edge. But Meg would not go without Cristiane.

The change suited Cristiane, who had grown tired of the veiled, and not-so-veiled, insults to her Scottish blood. She walked on to where a group of children were playing together. Meg was shy with them, but Gemette approached her right away.

"Hello!" she said. She handed Meg one of the smooth rocks she held in her hand. "I've been saving this one, but you can throw it."

Meg looked at her with eyes wide with pleasure, and took the stone. "What do I do?"

"Don't you know how to throw?" Gemette asked.

"I do," Meg said, though Cristiane had her doubts.

"Watch me first," Gemette said, apparently with her own doubts about Meg's abilities.

Cristiane smiled as she watched them, satisfied that Meg was content.

Lots of children were playing all along the riverbank.

Some older boys were fairly far upriver, playing a daring game on a high branch that hung over the water. Their mothers did not seem concerned. None of them were watching too closely, even though the boys' play seemed rather unruly and dangerous to Cristiane.

"Chris-ty!" Meg called. "Watch me!"

Cristiane turned her attention to Meg and Gemette and the other little lasses who'd joined them. Each one was trying to outdo the other, throwing farther, or higher, or into the exact same place in the water. Cristiane had to laugh at their giggles and antics, as well as at the fun Meg was having. She wished Adam were nearby so he could witness his daughter's delight.

She stepped away from the river for a few minutes, glancing back toward the center of town to see if she could get his attention, but he was nowhere to be seen. Disappointed, she returned to the water, just as screams broke the tranquillity of the afternoon.

"'Tis Gil!" the boys screamed.

"He's fallen!"

"He'll be carried away!"

Everyone who heard the panicked screams rushed to the riverbank to see what was amiss. Cristiane was closest to the water, and saw what appeared to be a limp mass of rags being tossed about in the rough current.

Without thinking, she ran into the water.

Chapter Twenty

The sound of shrieking voices carried into town. Adam, along with everyone else who stood milling about, hurried to the riverside. He searched the crowd for Cristiane and Margaret, but did not see either of them.

"My lord!" the reeve cried.

Distracted, Adam gave him his attention.

"'Tis your lady," he said urgently.

Adam grabbed the man by his shoulders. "What about her?" he demanded as a wave of alarm ran through him. "Explain!"

"One of the boys—Gilbert Raven—fell into the river," Morton said breathlessly. "Lady Cristiane went in after him."

"No!" Adam said, pushing his way through the crowd.

Filled with dread, he rushed to the riverbank, then ran alongside, following the surging flow down toward the sea. Cristiane would have to be an incredible swimmer to fight the current *and* save the lad. With his heart in his throat, he knew 'twould be a miracle if they were not washed out to sea.

He saw her then, a mass of bright blue rags, being

tossed about in the frothing white water. No one could survive the beating she was taking, not with the current so strong after the heavy rains.

He would not lose her now. Cristiane meant so much more to him than he'd ever thought possible. And Margaret—she was so attached, he could not bear to think what it would do to his daughter if something happened to Cristiane.

Adam pulled off his shoes and unlaced his tunic, fully intending to go in after her. But then the river tossed her again and she was thrown toward the far bank.

"Get me a boat!" he shouted. "A small gig… quickly!"

Men scrambled to do Adam's bidding, while he resisted the urge to jump in after her. He suddenly realized how futile that would be. *Damnation!* She had to be all right!

The crowd behind Adam was frantic. Gilbert's mother wailed in anguish over her son, whom she presumed was drowned. Her neighbors commiserated loudly.

No tears were shed, however, for Cristiane Mac Dhiubh.

Men arrived carrying two boats between them. As awkward as it was, they managed to lower them to the bank without damaging them, and push them into the water. Suddenly, someone shouted, "There they are!"

Adam looked downriver and saw something blue nearing the river's edge. He started running, ignoring the spears of pain jabbing through his leg. The whole town, it seemed, followed.

"Someone get blankets!" he shouted as he neared the place where he thought he'd seen her.

'Twas an area with no beach, only a rocky shoreline. There was no place for Cristiane to climb up out of the water, even if she were able to do so. He kept one eye on the water as he ran, watching for any sign of her or the boy. When he suddenly saw a flash of blue among the rocks, he made straight for it.

She'd managed to pull the boy to the rocky bank, but no farther. Her body was draped across one of the rocks near the river's edge, one arm still holding on to the youth, whose face was barely above water. The entire episode had lasted merely a few moments, but Adam felt he'd aged years.

"Cristiane!" he called, scrambling down the rocks to get to her. Two or three men followed him into the water, helping to drag her and the boy out.

They took her from him so that he could climb out of the river, and when they had her on the ground, she began to cough and sputter. The boy she had rescued was lying in his mother's embrace, vomiting violently.

Adam knelt next to Cristiane, wrapped her poor, shivering body in a blanket and took her in his arms. He put his lips to her forehead, thanking God she was alive.

"Chris-ty!" he heard Margaret cry out. Suddenly, his little daughter was next to him, weeping and cradling Cristiane's face between her small hands. "Papa?"

"She will be all right, Margaret," he said, as if he could control her fate.

She continued to shiver, and Adam knew he needed to get her inside, to a fire. He stood up, then lifted her unconscious body in his arms. Margaret followed as he walked toward Sara's cottage, unmindful of the quiet chatter and whispers behind him.

"Drink, Lady Cristiane," said a soothing feminine voice.

Someone lifted her head and brought a strong, warm drink to her lips. She sipped.

"Adam?" she said weakly.

"Aye, Cristiane," he said. "I'm here."

She opened her eyes. She was in a cozy room where light came from one small window and a hearty fire blazing on the hearth. "Where is Meggie?" she asked.

"She fell asleep awhile ago," he said. "She's here in Sara's cottage."

"And the boy?" she asked. She had to know if the boy she'd dragged from the river had survived.

"He'll live," Adam said, "no thanks to his lack of common sense."

"His father carried him home," Sara added more gently. "He's battered and bruised, but he'll recover."

Cristiane did not seem to have the energy to say or do more, though she wondered how she had managed to get out of the water. The last thing she remembered was hanging on to the lad, and being tossed so hard she lost her breath and all sense of direction.

"Rest now, Cristiane," Adam said. "When you're up to it, I'll take you home."

She closed her eyes and drifted off again, thinking of the welcoming walls of Castle Bitterlee. Home.

Cristiane awoke to the sound of low voices speaking in the distance. She opened her eyes and saw that there was no longer any light coming through the window. Night had fallen.

Adam stood next to the fire with Sara, their heads close together, talking quietly. Cristiane pushed herself up onto her elbows. She must have made some sound, for the two broke apart and came to her side immediately.

"How do you feel?" Adam asked.

"So tired," she said. "And…muddled. I canna seem to remember what happened."

She began to sit up, and realized she was naked under the blankets. Adam grabbed at the coverings and held them in place. Cristiane did not have the energy to blush appropriately. "Your wet things are still drying near the fire," he said. "One of the maids brought some fresh clothes from the castle."

'Twas likely Bea, the only one who seemed to have any regard for her.

"When can we go home?" Cristiane asked.

"Not until morning," Adam replied. "'Tis too dark to attempt a ride on the path. Besides, you need to rest."

"Aye," she replied. "The lad who fell into the river?" she asked, not remembering that she'd asked about him before.

"He's fine," Sara replied. "I saw him myself not an hour ago."

"I'm verra glad to know it."

"The boy's mother has been here several times to see how you fare," Adam said.

"That was good of her," she replied. "Is wee Meg still asleep?"

"Aye," he said. "I made up a pallet for her near the hearth. She'll sleep there all night."

"And what about you?"

"Don't worry," he replied, glancing up at Sara. "We'll make do."

Cristiane was alone when she awoke in the cottage the next morning. As she levered herself out of the bed, she discovered exactly how bruised and scraped she was.

She had been foolhardy to jump into the river after the boy.

Yet he'd have drowned had she not. A bit of soreness was little price to pay for his life and well-being.

Her yellow gown was lying across the foot of the bed, and next to it her newly made chemise, clean and dry. The blue gown she'd worn the day before was nowhere to be seen. Most likely ruined, Cristiane thought sadly.

She wondered where Adam and Meg were. She assumed they had spent the night here in the cottage, hadn't they? And Sara, too, she thought dismally. Sara was so much more a part of their lives than Cristiane could ever be. Sara was a part of Bitterlee, accepted by the people here.

And she probably would have had more sense than to jump into the river, risking her own life as well as the lad's. Adam likely thought Cristiane half-witted for her actions.

Ah, well, 'twas too late for regrets.

She only hoped Meg hadn't been too terrified. She hadn't thought of the child's reaction to seeing her jump into the river and disappear. She hoped she hadn't frightened her back into silence.

Cristiane climbed out of bed and began to dress, carefully pulling her chemise over one bruised shoulder and taking care with her skinned knee. She'd barely gotten the yellow gown up over her shoulders when someone rapped lightly on the door.

"Who's there?" she asked.

"Adam," he replied as the door opened. "And Margaret."

"Cristy!" Meg ran to her and wrapped her arms around her as Cristiane tried awkwardly to hold her gown in place.

"Margaret was worried about you last night. We had a devil of a time getting her to sleep," he said, coming closer. "And she's been after me to let her wake you all morning." He stood directly in front of Cristiane, reaching for the laces that tied her bodice, while Meg hung on quietly.

He did not seem angry at all, but his eyes were stormy this morn. Cristiane saw their expression only fleetingly, before he'd had a chance to hide it.

He cupped her face in his hands. "I don't think I've ever been so afraid as when they told me you'd jumped into the river," he said, his thumbs tracing circles on her cheeks. She could feel his breath on her lips, and she was certain he was going to kiss her. Her heart sped in anticipation of his intimate touch. She had yearned for this. "Promise me you'll be more caref—"

The door opened abruptly, and Adam and Cristiane broke apart. Sara stepped in, only to stop in her tracks when she saw them. "I…I beg your pardon, Lady Cristiane, I thought—" She turned to leave as abruptly as she came in. "Gilbert Raven's mother awaits you outside."

"I meant to tell you that," Adam said, when Sara had gone.

Rattled by the interruption, Cristiane had trouble clearing her thoughts. "Who is Gilbert Raven's mo— Oh, the boy in the river."

Adam nodded as his hands returned to the laces of Cristiane's gown. "She has something for you. A gift." He began tightening the cords from her waist up, working to a point directly between her breasts.

She sighed deeply, raising her chest, inadvertently increasing the contact between them. His eyes held hers for a moment, and Cristiane thought they were tinged with regret. He quickly finished tying her gown, and drew Meggie back from her fierce grip on Cristiane's legs.

"Shall we go?" he asked.

Cristiane nodded, raised her chin, straightened her backbone and started for the door.

Adam stopped her with one hand on her arm.

"You took an enormous risk yesterday," he said. "And even though you frightened the wits out of me—and Meg—I could not have been prouder. You prevented the day from turning into a tragedy."

"I…I did not think, Adam," she said quietly, pleased by his declaration. "I just acted."

"I was afraid, Cristy," Meggie said. "I couldn't see you in the water."

Cristiane crouched down to the child's level and looked into her eyes. "I know, Meg," she said, "and I'm sorry I frightened you. But the lad's life was in danger, and I had to do something."

Meg nodded as if she understood.

"You know I'm a good swimmer, lass," she continued. "I hope someone would have done the same for you if *you* had fallen in."

"Cristiane," Adam said, "promise me you'll think twice before doing something so dangerous again."

"Aye, Adam," she replied. "But I cannot promise that I won't do the same thing again. If there is no other way—"

"Just be careful," he said.

"I will."

Adam opened the door, holding it for Cristiane and Meg. Cristiane stepped outside, keeping Meg's hand in her own. The arrangement suited Meg, who was not about to let Cristiane go.

Gilbert's mother was not the only person awaiting her. Adam estimated a good three dozen men and women quietly milled about outside Sara's cottage, though Sara was nowhere to be seen.

"My lady," the boy's mother said, taking Cristiane's free hand and kissing it. "I cannot thank you enough for saving my boy. Without you, he'd have drowned for sure. He's not a good swimmer...."

"I'm glad I was there to do it," she answered, plainly embarrassed by the woman's frank adulation. Cristiane's speech was as *English* as Adam had ever heard it. "Please, say no more about it—"

The crowd surrounded her, and Adam detected a look of alarm in her eyes. She hugged Meg to her side and looked frantically about. Adam hoped she was looking for him.

He made his way through the crowd to her side. After picking Meg up, he slipped his other arm around Cristiane's waist, possessively, yet protectively, sensing she needed the reassurance of his presence.

He'd come so close to losing her. 'Twas not until the moment he realized she was in the river that he'd known how desperately he loved her, how devastating 'twould be to lose her.

He pulled her closer.

"My lady," Gilbert's mother continued, "please take this." She pressed a small, worn wooden box into Cristiane's hands. "'Tis a bone of St. Cuthbert. Been in my family a hundred years."

"Oh, but—"

"Please take it," she continued. "You are more deserving—"

"My lady!" Others added their voices, vying for Cristiane's attention. She was given gifts from all the women who were gathered—bits of ribbon, a newly sewn gown from Madam Williamson, food for their table at the castle. By the time Sir Elwin made his way through the crowd with their horses, both Cristiane's and Adam's arms were full.

Elwin took what he could carry as Adam lifted Cristiane atop his horse.

"Cristy!" Meg called, raising her arms to be lifted onto Cristiane's lap.

"Nay, Meg," Adam said. "You'll ride with Sir Elwin."

"I want Cristy!" the child insisted.

"Meggie!" Cristiane said from atop the horse. "Listen to me. If you ride with Sir Elwin, and I ride with your papa, we'll each have our own knight to protect us on the way home."

"But—"

"No 'but'," Cristiane said firmly. "Let Sir Elwin help you up."

Adam could hardly believe that Meg was arguing, and was further astonished when his daughter actually agreed to Cristiane's demand. He watched as Elwin lifted Meg into the saddle, then mounted behind her. Then Adam did the same, keeping Cristiane in front of him. Elwin led the way.

Adam would have prolonged the ride if he could. He put his arms 'round Cristiane's waist and pulled her back against him, relaxing to the sway of his horse's easy gait. The top of her head fit just under his chin, as if she were made for him.

And he had no doubt that she was.

Her hair was loose, and as they trotted up the path, it tickled his nose and chin. She smelled warm and feminine, and thoroughly enticing. He moved his hands to span the area below her breasts, gratified by her reaction.

She sighed.

'Twas all Adam could do to keep from leaving the path and finding a private place to further explore her reactions to him. If he could touch her this way, would she allow him to kiss her mouth, or her ear? He would give most anything to press his lips to the notch at the base of her throat, to spread his hands over the enticing softness of her breasts.

He knew these thoughts were untimely. He had no intention of acting precipitously, of frightening her. Besides, he had to consider his daughter. She would not appreciate arriving at the castle without her papa, *or* her new mama.

Adam contented himself for the moment with Cristiane's closeness, the softness of her body and the anticipation of pleasures to come.

Soon she would be his wife, and his efforts at wooing her would bring results they would both cherish.

Tomorrow, Cristiane would become Lady Bitterlee. The special permission had arrived from Alnwick only yesterday, and while she had been on pins and needles awaiting word from the bishop, Adam had been confident that it would arrive in time.

She had seen Sara Cole several times since the incident in town, but had spoken to her only once, to thank her for the use of her cottage. The other times, Sara had been coming or going to see Charles Penyngton, whose illness had again become worse.

Adam's relationship with Sara worried Cristiane. There could be little doubt that the townswoman was his mistress, and Cristiane wondered if that would continue after they were wed. She was too embarrassed to speak of it to Adam, even though she was desperate to understand the terms of their marriage.

He might mistake her concern for jealousy.

Still, she wished she knew what to expect of this union. 'Twas clear that Adam considered her a good nursemaid for his daughter. But he would soon want a male heir. Since Sara Cole was not of noble birth, she would not be a suitable mother for his son.

Which left Cristiane.

Sunlight filtered in through the solar windows, giving enough light for Agatha Williamson to work on the gown Cristiane would wear for her wedding. The seamstress fit the last bit of contrasting cloth into the bodice.

"'Tis too low," Cristiane complained.

"Aw now, you've got to give your bridegroom a tiny peek at your charms...."

Cristiane blushed. Adam had already seen her unclothed—and more than once. A bit of décolletage was naught compared to that, so Cristiane went along with Agatha, complaining no further until the woman pulled the laces at the back.

She sucked in a breath and said, "'Tis so tight, Madam Williamson!"

"To make the most of your other charms," the seamstress replied. "Believe me, your husband will have eyes only for you, my lady."

"Aye, because I'll be lying prostrate on the floor of the church for lack of air."

Agatha laughed but did not relent. "Nay, you'll be the most beautiful lady there."

Cristiane could only hope that would be true, at least upon the day she became Adam's wife.

* * *

"You look much better this morn, Charles," Adam said. 'Twas the morning of his wedding, and he'd wanted his old friend to attend. But even though Charles seemed improved, he was not well enough to make the ride to town and back.

"Aye," the seneschal replied. "I feel much better, too."

"Don't suppose I can persuade you to talk some sense into my fool nephew," Gerard said, leaning lazily against one wall of Charles's chamber.

"Regarding what?" Charles asked.

"Cease, Gerard," Adam said, more annoyed with his uncle than he'd ever been. "I've heard all your objections and they're unfounded."

"The Scotswoman knew a good thing when she saw it," Gerard said, sneering, "and she went after it."

Charles said, "Sir Gerard, I sincerely doubt—"

"Doubt what? That she did not intend to become mistress of the richest demesne in all Northumberland?"

"Exactly," Charles replied, though he barely got out the word before he went into a fit of coughing.

Adam did not like Gerard's accusations. They reminded him of Cristiane's plight—of being taken away from her home to be sent south to York, to family who could very well harbor hostility toward her, not only because of her Scottish blood, but also because of her mother's indiscretion.

Still, both he and Cristiane had been manipulated by Charles. He'd been encouraging Adam to take her to wife ever since her arrival on the isle. And he'd told Cristiane about her mother's unfortunate affair, with the hope that she would be less inclined to want to go to York because of it.

Well, all had worked according to Penyngton's plan,

though Adam's reasons for marrying Cristiane had naught to do with convenience, or with her suitability as a mother to his daughter.

His life had become full as it had never been before. Cristiane was exciting and adventuresome, willing to take a risk. Her beauty stole his breath away, and when he touched her…well, thus far, she had not shied away from him. That alone gave him hope that she would respond with enthusiasm—not abhorrence—when he finally made love to her.

Adam did not care whether or not Gerard was correct in his assumptions regarding Cristiane's desire to be mistress of Bitterlee. 'Twas the marriage he wanted, and he was certain he and Cristiane would fare well together. Besides, he could not have borne sending her to her uncle.

She belonged here on Bitterlee.

"*She* did not ask *me* to wed her, Gerard," Adam said.

"She did not need to," Gerard said. "She's teased you with her shapely arse and flaunted her—"

Adam slammed his uncle up against the wall, his forearm pinning the older man's throat so he was unable to speak.

"Another word, you bloody bastard," he said, his voice low. "One more word about my *wife* and you will no longer be welcome on Bitterlee soil. Is that clear?"

Gerard's eyes flamed angrily for a moment, then he capitulated. Adam let him loose after another moment, and Gerard stormed out of the chamber.

A long silence ensued as Adam remained standing in place, his heart pounding, his blood roaring in his ears. He would not tolerate any slurs against Cristiane. If there was anyone on the isle who was more pure of heart, and of body, then he did not know who it was.

"I don't suppose he'll be at the wedding," Charles finally remarked.

Adam said naught as he worked to control his anger. His uncle had been a difficult man ever since Adam's father had allowed him to come home years ago. But Gerard's bitterness had gone too far. Adam would not hesitate to boot him off the isle if he made one more insult, or gave the slightest offense to Cristiane.

He would not stand for it.

"What is the time?" Charles asked. "Should you be leaving for town?"

Adam relaxed his stance and went to the bedside. "Aye," he said. "I am sorry you will miss the ceremony, especially after all your work."

"My work?" Charles asked with feigned innocence.

Adam gave a knowing smile, patted Charles's hand and left the room.

Agatha Williamson dressed Cristiane for the marriage ceremony. All the men had been shooed out of the Williamson cottage, and the two women stood together, along with Meggie, who was also dressed in a new gown for the occasion.

Cristiane sneezed.

"You went and got yourself the ague, jumping into the river the other day," Agatha said. "Mind, I'm not complaining that you did it, but 'tis your wedding day, my lady, and you should not be ill when you meet your groom on the steps of the church."

"I'll be all right," Cristiane said. She blew her reddened nose. "I'm never ill."

"Well, you've got it now," Agatha said as she pulled tight the laces.

"Ooh! If I sneeze, I'll burst your seams," Cristiane complained.

"Not *my* seams," Agatha retorted. "They'll hold." She fussed a bit more over Cristiane's head rail, then stated, "You are beautiful, my lady."

Cristiane blushed at the compliment, so unexpected from one as brusque as Agatha Williamson.

"Are you ready, little love?" Agatha asked Meg.

"Aye," she replied.

"Then it's time to go."

Hand in hand, Cristiane and Meg walked to the church, Sir Elwin and Sir Raynauld flanking them. Townspeople followed almost reverently in procession as they made their way.

Adam stood waiting for his bride at the top of the stairs. He felt no nervousness at all, but distinctly different from the way he'd felt when he'd stood here waiting for Rosamund years before. He'd been young—too young—to marry, and to know how to deal with a wife.

This time, he had some ideas.

Cristiane looked radiant in a gown of deep green that emphasized her feminine attributes. Her hair was pleasingly arranged as a maiden's should be, combed to a high sheen and cascading down her back in luscious curls and waves. A flowery coronet adorned her head, and a short veil flowed from one point at the back.

Adam could hardly believe she was his.

She finally reached the church. Gathering up her skirts in one hand, she took Meg's hand in the other and climbed toward him, wearing an uncertain smile.

She was even more beautiful at close range.

"Papa!" Meg whispered.

Adam leaned down and kissed his daughter's cheek,

then turned to face the priest after giving her over to Sir Elwin.

Father Beaupré stood solemnly before the doors of the church and began the ceremony. "My Lord Bitterlee, are you of age to bind yourself in Holy Matrimony to this woman?"

"Yes, Father," Adam replied.

Beaupré turned slightly. "Lady Cristiane Mac Dhiubh, are you of age to bind yourself to Lord Bitterlee?"

"Aye, Father."

The questions continued, a mere formality in this case, since neither of them had parents to approve the match, and 'twas well known that there was no forbidden consanguinity between them. At the end of the interrogation, Adam handed Father Beaupré the document that gave the bishop's consent to the marriage without the usual three weeks wait.

Cristiane hardly heard the priest's words. Her attention was fully upon her groom, so handsome in his deep blue tunic, his shoulders broad, his narrow waist belted in silver. His dark hair was combed neatly back, his face freshly shaved, his scar raw upon his jaw.

He would have had an altogether forbidding appearance if not for his eyes, deeply gray, set off by thick black lashes. Cristiane saw promise in those stormy depths, of anticipated pleasures.

Blushing, she glanced down at the hand upon which her own rested so formally, and found herself craving a far more intimate touch.

Soon, she thought. She and her husband would share a bed tonight.

She had every hope that what transpired between them tonight would give Adam due cause to abandon Sara Cole, binding him to Cristiane for all time.

Chapter Twenty-One

Jongleurs entertained during the wedding feast. Jugglers and tumblers, musicians and tricksters delighted the company with their talents. Surprisingly, Meg ran off to play with Gemette and some of the other little girls. All of the children had been admonished to stay away from the river.

Cristiane held up very well through the meal, and then the dancing, but Adam could see that she was suffering. She was sniffling and sneezing, and her voice sounded thick and edgy, as if her throat was sore.

He had to get her home, to bed.

He was standing with Sara in front of her house on the hillside. "This will help clear Lady Cristiane's head," Sara said as she handed a stoppered crock to him. "And it will help her to sleep, too." Sara seemed on the verge of tears, though Adam did not know why, or how to react.

"Thank you, Sara," he replied as he embraced her. "What is it? What's wrong?"

"'Tis naught," she replied, pulling away.

"You are…" He took her arm. "Sara, you weep. What has happened?"

"'Tis not what has happened," she finally said, "but what will never be."

"I do not understand you."

One tear spilled from her eye and trailed down her cheek as she looked up at him. "Your marriage. I wish you well, Adam. You and Lady Cristiane suit each other well. 'Tis just that…I wish that…"

"What?"

"I grieve for what I can never have, for what will never be."

"You will not marry?" he asked. "Why? Is there no one who—"

She stopped him with a shake of her head. "Go to your bride, Adam. She awaits you. Besides, I must return to Sir Charles at the castle."

Adam had thought she was happy here. Content. Never had it occurred to him that she was pining for a husband of her own, and mayhap children. She'd never said anything about it, never once complained of her life here on Bitterlee.

He was reluctant to leave Sara in her troubled state. Nevertheless, he allowed her to persuade him to return to the wedding festivities, while she returned to the castle. He stepped away from her cottage and walked down the hill, preoccupied by her words.

With their father long dead, Adam should have become her protector. Yet he'd neglected her. So much had happened since her arrival on the isle. She'd been useful…mayhap *too* useful.

'Twas not too late to remedy the situation. Sara was not too old to wed, being several years younger than Adam. But who would be a suitable bridegroom? One of his knights? Surely she would not wed a man of lesser rank, even though she could not claim her noble blood.

Somehow, a solution would be found.

The sun had come out from behind a thick layer of clouds and the day had grown warm, but Cristiane felt chills. Her nose ran, her eyes were sensitive to the light and she could not keep herself from sneezing every couple of minutes. Besides all that, her gown was too tight. She was miserable.

In spite of it all, the marriage ceremony had been lovely, and Father Beaupreé's nuptial Mass uplifting. As Adam's wife, Cristiane felt truly welcomed into this close-knit community, whose women hugged her tearfully and whose men called out their well wishes.

Even Sara Cole had embraced her. ''Your husband is a good man,'' she'd said quietly in Cristiane's ear. ''Take care of him.''

Cristiane had been too astonished by her words to respond. Did they mean that Sara was giving him up, that she would no longer be his mistress?

''My lady,'' Agatha Williamson said, ''you are looking peaked. Come and sit, and drink this.''

Cristiane followed the woman to a table close to the church, where she sat down and drank the hot, spiced cider handed to her. 'Twas getting late. She looked around for Adam and caught sight of him on the hillside, outside of Sara Cole's cottage.

A wave of jealousy, as well as hopelessness, washed through her as he watched Adam hug Sara close.

He'd known the other woman so long.... There was no doubt in Cristiane's mind that he respected her skills, and probably loved her, too. How could Cristiane compete with that? How could she face the woman, knowing she would have been Adam's choice had she been well-born?

"Your husband ought to take you up to the castle, my lady," Agatha said, "before it gets any later, or colder."

"I—I think you're right," she stammered. Then she sneezed.

All was quiet at the castle when they arrived. Most everyone was still in town, feasting and celebrating the lord's marriage. The only ones who remained at the castle were Charles Penyngton and one old Bitterlee knight who was well past his fighting days, but who provided good company when called upon.

"Sara brought Meg home earlier," Adam said as they climbed the stairs to the east tower, "and she'll stay with Charles."

Cristiane was not comforted by the thought of Adam's lover spending this night—her wedding night—under the same roof. But there was naught she could say about it. Surely Sir Charles was in need of her medicines, and Cristiane did not begrudge him that. Besides, Sara had been kind enough to offer to bring Meg home, allowing Adam and Cristiane to ride together, alone.

Adam walked beside her until they stood in front of her chamber door. Then he reached up and smoothed a tendril of hair back from her face.

"Shall I help you to undress?" he asked quietly.

"I...I—"

"You are ill, Cristiane," he said, cupping her chin in his hand.

She shivered once, and Adam knew she burned with fever.

"Come," he said, opening the door and drawing her inside. After setting his saddle pack on the floor, he lit the fire that had been laid, then turned back to her. She had already removed the garland of flowers from her head.

"I can do it, my lord," she said, when he turned her around and untied the fastenings of her gown.

"Hush, Cristiane," he said from behind. "Allow me to help you."

He slid the bodice down her shoulders, then pushed her hair aside and kissed her neck. She shivered again, and this time Adam doubted it was from fever. Or rather, it was from a different kind of fever.

Emboldened by her reaction, he ran his hands down her arms, then circled her waist, pulling her back against his chest. "Be comfortable with my touch, Cristiane," he said. "When you are well again, I will make you my wife…and not a moment before."

She tipped her head, giving him better access to her neck, and he touched his lips to it, trailing small kisses from her ear to the end of her shoulder.

She trembled under his touch, but Adam was determined to be cautious, to go slowly with her, no matter that the effort was monumental. He had managed to control himself up until now, and he would continue to do so. He would not have Cristiane suffer an unsatisfactory first experience in their marriage bed, and learn to dread his touch.

Nay, when he made love to her, she would discover that 'twas not something to fear, but something to anticipate, and to savor.

He loosened the ties at her waist and let her skirts fall, then lifted her into his arms and carried her to the bed.

She looped her arms 'round his neck and let him carry her. 'Twas almost better that she was ill tonight, he thought. She did not have the energy to be embarrassed,

or to fight him. Circumstances made it possible for him
to see that she became accustomed to him before they
were truly intimate.

When he'd gotten her situated under the blanket, he
poured some of Sara's medicine into a cup and bade
Cristiane drink it. Then he unfastened his tunic and
pulled it over his head. His linen undertunic followed,
along with his shoes, then his chausses and braes.

"My lord?" Cristiane queried, her voice a mere
squeak, and her eyes widening with every item of clothes
that he removed.

"Rest easy, Cristiane," he said, climbing into the bed
with her. "'Tis only the first of many nights I intend to
sleep with my wife."

He turned to his side, pulled her close and cupped her
body with his own. Through the thin fabric of her chemise, he could feel her heat, her softness. And he questioned the prudence of spending the night with her, thus.

"Adam?" she asked.

He would be content only to lie with her, nuzzling
her neck, holding her. He allowed his fingers to creep
partway up to her breasts, caressing their lower fullness
through the thin fabric, but going no farther.

"I am sorry, Adam," she croaked.

"Hmm?"

"'Tis surely not the way you expected to spend your
wedding night."

"Nay, 'tis not," he replied. "Go to sleep, Cristiane."

Cristiane spent the first three days of her marriage in
bed. And most of that time was not with her husband.

Meg had come in to see her the first day, and she had
insisted upon remaining in the chamber, playing quietly
while Cristiane dozed. Sara had looked in on her, had

made her drink some bitter draught, and had conferred with Adam quietly before leaving.

Cristiane had seen her, and known that she was talking with Adam, but was unable to hear what was said.

Every night, Adam slept with her, holding her. And even through the haze of illness, Cristiane felt reassured that at least he was not with Sara Cole.

She awoke alone on the fourth day, feeling a great deal more healthy than she had only the night before. Her head had cleared, and her throat no longer felt swollen and as if it were on fire.

But she was hungry. Famished!

She pulled herself up and sat on the edge of bed, then had to wait out a wave of dizziness before moving any farther. When it passed, she got up and started to wash, only to be startled by Bea.

"Oh! My lady, you're out of bed!" she cried as she came through the door, carrying fresh bedding and dry towels.

"Aye," Cristiane said. "And feeling as if I'd fallen off a cliff."

"You look ever so much better today," Bea said. "We were all quite worried, what with you coming down with the ague, and all from jumping into the river to save Olive Raven's son. But Mistress Cole told us not to worry, and that it would take three days before you were well again."

The maid pulled the bedding off and occupied herself with spreading fresh linens over the ticking.

"Oh?" Cristiane said.

"And she was right, wasn't she?" Bea said, almost to herself. "Mistress Cole is never mistaken about these things."

Somehow, it did not please Cristiane to be one of Sara

Cole's predictions come true. "Where is Lord Bitterlee?" she asked as she returned to her ablutions.

"Your husband is in Sir Charles's chamber with Mistress Cole," she replied, tucking in the bottom edge of the blanket. "Sir Charles has not been well…"

She stopped and looked over at the maid. "Do you mean he's worse than he was?"

Bea nodded solemnly. "We've all added special prayers for him, and Father Beaupré has been offering Mass for him every day."

At once, Cristiane felt worse than small for her petty jealousy. What little energy she had, left her suddenly, and she sat down on a chair near the hearth. "Is there aught I can do for him?" she asked. "Any—"

"Mistress Cole said that you were to stay away from Sir Charles's chamber, for in his weakened state, he'd be in danger of catching your illness."

Cristiane did not know how 'twas possible to feel worse. Poor Charles lay ill, perhaps even dying, and because of it, Adam was spending time with the only woman whose presence was a threat to their marriage.

"And Meg?" Cristiane asked.

"Mathilde has full charge of her now," Bea said, scowling, "until you feel up to dealing with her. Lord Bitterlee did not want her bothering you, and since he's been so occupied with Sir Charles—"

"Aye," Cristiane said. Dismayed by this turn of events, she was more curt than she intended. "Bea, when you leave here, I'd like you to find Meg and have her brought to me."

"Yes, my lady," Bea replied. "Er, Mistress Cole said you'd be hungry. Shall I bring you something to eat?"

'Twas another full day before Cristiane had the strength to make her way downstairs. But even if she hadn't had the strength, she'd have managed somehow.

Adam had not come to her bed last night.

When she reached the great hall, she nearly turned around and went back upstairs when she saw Gerard sitting alone at his usual place at the long table. He was sipping from a cup of what Cristiane knew would be strong ale.

At least Meg was napping in her own chamber at the moment, and would not have to suffer her uncle's bitter tongue.

"Ah, so the mistress of Bitterlee approaches!" he said sarcastically.

Cristiane ignored him and spoke to a footman. "Is my husband here in the keep?"

"Aye—" he began, but Gerard interrupted.

"He is in Charles Penyngton's chamber," Gerard muttered, his voice slurred. "Why don't you sit down before you fall down? You look like a bloody codfish, all white and clammy."

Cristiane knew she was not yet at her best, but did not believe she looked as bad as that. Still, she went to the great hearth and sat down in one of the large, stuffed chairs before it.

Pointedly, she turned away from Gerard and spoke to the footman. "Would you please go to Lord Bitterlee and ask him to join me when he has a moment?"

"Aye, my lady," the man replied, as he left to do her bidding.

She had no real reason to summon Adam, only that she'd missed him the night before and needed the reassurance of his presence. Their married life had not started auspiciously, and she felt uncertain, vulnerable. If he had not bothered even to look in on her last night—

"Sara has been here night and day with Charles."

"'Tis good of her," Cristiane said to Gerard.

"She did the same when Adam's father sickened and died," he added, "and again, when she attended Rosamund in childbed." He took a long draught from his cup. "She even tended Adam when he returned from your bloody Falkirk."

Cristiane found herself unable to speak. She had not known that Sara had cared for Adam, though she should have realized it.

Why did Sara have to loom so heavily upon her mind now? Would she have to content herself with sharing her husband, as so many other noblewomen did?

Cristiane did not think that would be possible for her, even though her mother had prepared her for the practice that seemed to be so common among English lords. With very little provocation, she was consumed with envy over Sara's long relationship with Adam, and there was a very good chance that her feelings would only worsen.

If only she had the nerve to question Adam directly.

But alas, she did not. She was the new wife, a stranger to the isle, really, whose only distinction was her ability to handle wee Meg.

Gerard stood up and swayed for a moment, then picked up his cup and ambled over to the fireplace. He glared at Cristiane.

"So now you're a bloody heroine, I hear."

Refusing to be goaded, Cristiane did not answer him. She bit her tongue to keep from entering into an argument with him, then stood up and strode from the hall. She left the keep by way of the door near the chapel, and walked to the garden, replying to the greetings of everyone she passed.

She felt heartened by the people's reaction to her.

While still not entirely accepting, they were at least respectful now, and did not seem to despise her as they had before, when she'd first arrived on Bitterlee.

The day was overcast again and threatened rain, but Cristiane continued walking until she reached the bench on the far side of the pond. She hoped someone would tell Adam that she'd left the keep, but she had no doubt that he'd eventually find her here. After all, she was his wife now, and 'twas his duty to see to her, even if Sara Cole's company was preferable.

No one was in the great hall when Adam came looking for Cristiane.

"My lord, she was just here," a footman said from the hallway. "With your uncle."

Adam ran one hand across his mouth and jaw. He knew the kind of hurt his uncle was capable of inflicting with one word here, another there. The man was a master at disrupting the peace, and Adam did not know why he allowed Gerard to continue on Bitterlee.

It occurred to him that it might be wise to send his uncle elsewhere, as he had threatened.

"Mayhap she returned to her chamber?" the footman asked.

Adam doubted it. If he knew Cristiane at all, she would be outdoors somewhere. Considering her weakened state, she had likely gone no farther than the pond.

He headed out of the keep, taking the dogs and following the garden path to the water.

'Twas a relief to leave the confines of Penyngton's chamber. Bitterlee's seneschal—Adam's closest friend— was dying. And there was naught that he or Sara Cole could do about it.

Adam suspected that Sara had deeper feelings for

Charles than she'd previously let on, and he finally understood the sadness and futility she had expressed when they'd spoken after his wedding to Cristiane. There was a quiet desperation about the way Sara attended Charles now, and an underlying despair that she was not doing enough.

Adam well knew the feeling of futility. He'd neglected Cristiane and kept a vigil all night in Charles's room so that Sara could get some much-needed sleep. He had helped Charles through far too many violent coughing spells during the night. Yet there was naught he could do about the blood that his friend brought up each time.

Adam was weary, his emotions on edge. He'd been out of his mind with worry over Cristiane, and then Charles's condition had worsened. At least Meg was in good health and seemed content.

He arrived at the edge of the pond and saw Cristiane sitting on the bench on the far side. Circling the water, he saw that her complexion was still pale and drawn, and it startled him for an instant. He had no doubt she would recover fully, however. Sara had assured him of that, and he had complete faith in her knowledge of the healing arts.

Cristiane's attention was occupied by the ducklings, which had swum over to beg for food. Adam heard her make her apologies to them, saying that she'd come without bringing any bread.

They were unforgiving, and all seven of them stepped out of the water, waddling up to the bench to surround her. He smiled at the sight they made.

"'Tis sorry I am," she said, amidst all their quacking, "but surely you're old enough now to find your own food. Meggie and I—'' She suddenly heard him. ''Adam!''

'''Tis a treat to see you up and about, my lady wife,'' he said, taking her hand in his and kissing the back of it. More than a treat, 'twas pure relief to see her here in this natural setting. ''I was beginning to think you'd be abed forever.''

''Nay, Adam,'' she replied, as a bit of color came into her cheeks. ''I feel much better.''

''I'm glad to see it. Have you had food, drink?''

''Nay,'' she replied. ''I...I am not hungry.''

He sat down next to her, keeping her hand in his. One day—soon—she would welcome his touch, he promised himself. She was becoming accustomed to him. He'd been heartened by her response to him on their wedding night when he'd helped to undress her, and when he'd slept with her, holding her through the night while she was ill.

He'd missed that last night.

''Are you still feverish?'' he asked, touching her cheek and then her forehead with the palm of his hand.

Her eyelids lowered at his touch, and he felt her lean slightly toward him. He had the urge to pull her into his arms, but refrained. For now.

Instead, he let his thumb caress her cheek. ''You must take care for the next few days,'' he said. ''Sara said you would feel weak—''

Cristiane stood abruptly. ''Nay, I do not feel weak at all, my lord. I feel perfectly—''

''There is no shame in your illness, Cristiane,'' he said as he rose to his feet next to her. '''Twas likely caused by your heroic venture into the river the other day.''

She shrugged.

"Are you ready to return to the keep?"

"Aye," she said with a quick nod.

He did not understand what had come over her. The warmth she'd shown was gone now, and a chilly demeanor had taken its place.

Regardless, he took her hand and placed it in the crook of his elbow. Her changeable mood was likely a lingering effect of the illness, and no cause for worry.

"Meg has been playing in your room these last few days while you slept," he said. "She's been worried about you."

"*Meg,* my lord?" Cristiane asked, glancing up at him. "I thought she would always be Margaret to you."

"Your pet name suits her," he replied. "As does the way you treat her. She's grown so healthy, so much more...*normal* since you've come to Bitterlee."

"I'll come back here and feed the ducks with her later," she said.

"Do not overtax yourself, Cristiane," he countered, stopping in the path.

"'Twill not overtax me, my lord," Cristiane replied. "'Tis a short walk, and I want Meg to know I am all right. That everything is as it was. She worries..."

She seemed determined to do this, so Adam would not say her nay. But he would come along, and see that Cristiane suffered no untoward effect from her exertions.

Cristiane felt him watching her closely—for signs of infirmity. 'Twas frustrating to be laid so low, so soon after her marriage, and unable to establish herself as Adam's wife.

That was going to change. Tonight.

She was not quite sure what to do. She'd only been kissed once...well, twice, if she counted the fleeting touching of lips that had taken place at the church after Father Beaupré had declared them husband and wife.

But when Adam had touched her on their wedding night, kissing her shoulders, her neck, her ear, she had experienced exquisite pleasure. She had only to develop enough nerve to do the same to Adam, and she was certain he would have the same reaction she'd had.

Tonight, she was confident that all would go well. She would follow his lead, and touch him as he had touched her on their wedding night. She would kiss him the same way he'd kissed her the first time.

Cristiane quivered at the thought of the night ahead. She sensed that intimacy between them would solidify their marriage, and she was anxious for that. Besides, from the first time Cristiane had seen him, Adam was everything she'd ever imagined her husband should be— strong and powerful, yet gentle and kind. And Meggie was a sweet and loving daughter. The isle, with its waterfall, its intriguing coastline and all its birds was her idea of paradise.

It would have been perfect if not for Sara Cole.

"My lord!" a page called out as he approached them on the path.

"Yes, Jon?" Adam said.

"Mistress Cole needs you," the boy replied. "Sir Charles worsens…"

Adam raised one hand and cupped Cristiane's jaw. "I must go," he said.

"Adam, is there aught that I can do for Charles?"

"Nay, Sara has matters well in hand." He kissed her cheek. "Jon will see you back to the keep."

Chapter Twenty-Two

In spite of his limp, Adam trotted rather quickly back to the keep ahead of them, while Cristiane took Jon's arm and walked the rest of the way. She actually did feel rather fatigued, but she would never admit it to Adam—or Sara.

It bothered Cristiane to have such feelings of animosity toward the woman, for Sara had done a great deal of good in town, as well as for Charles, Cristiane's cousin. But 'twas difficult for her to feel charitable toward the woman who was competing for her husband's affections.

She felt useless. While Sara was well loved, and helpful, Cristiane could do naught for anyone. She'd been warned away from Charles, in case the miasma that had caused her illness should spread to him, so she could not even sit with him.

She had no idea how to assert herself as chatelaine here, or what such duties would entail.

Mayhap Sara would know, she thought sourly.

She reached the bailey and saw Gerard approaching, his expression sour and forbidding. Cristiane flinched inwardly when he flashed her a scathing look, but he turned away and headed down the path toward the waterfall.

Cristiane gave a short prayer of thanks that she had never run into him there, only to have the peace of the place disturbed by his forbidding presence. She just wished there was some way to avoid him in the keep.

She was truly tired by the time she reached the hall, so she decided to climb to her chamber and lie down for a while. It would not do for her to be overtired tonight, when Adam came to her.

Movement in the room woke her.

''I'm so sorry, my lady,'' Bea said, straightening up. The night was chill, and she had laid a fire to warm the chamber. ''I did not mean to wake you.''

'''Tis all right, Bea,'' Cristiane said, noting that it was completely dark except for the fire and one small lamp. ''I've slept too long already.''

''Are you hungry?'' the maid asked. ''I'll bring you some supper if—''

''Nay, I'll wait for Lord Bitterlee,'' Cristiane replied.

''Oh, my lady,'' Bea said, ''he has already dined. He sent me up to see how you fared, and to tell you that he is needed again with Sir Charles tonight.''

''Oh.'' Cristiane did not intend to sound so weak or so petulant, but she was unable to mask her feelings. Her husband was spending another night in Sara's company.

Cristiane chastised herself for being so petty. Poor Charles was in need of Sara's care, and Cristiane did not begrudge him that. Nor did she resent Charles's need for Adam. She'd seen with her own eyes what close friends the two men were.

''There's a young lady at the far end of the gallery

who could use your attention," Bea said. "That is, if you're up to it."

"Oh, yes," Cristiane replied, allowing herself to be distracted from her dismal thoughts. Her own trivial feelings of neglect were naught compared to what Meg must feel.

"I'll get her," Bea said, "and bring you some supper."

Within the hour, Cristiane was sitting before the fire with Meg, and the two were sharing a meal. Meg spoke little and kept her eyes downcast, but Cristiane was not going to allow her stepdaughter to withdraw again, just because she herself had been ill for a few days. She thought a bit of teasing might bring the lass out.

"'Twas too bad it rained so hard on my wedding day and spoiled the feast," she said to Meg.

The little girl frowned and looked up sharply. "Rain?"

"Aye. Buckets and buckets of the stuff," she said, slicing a piece of cheese and handing it to Meg. "I'd hoped for sunshine."

"Sunshine?" Her brows came together in a puzzled frown.

"Aye," Cristiane replied, refraining from laughing. "This isle must have a rain cloud hovering over it all—"

"But there *was* sunshine, Cristy!" Meg protested. "'Twas a beautiful day!"

"Are you sure, lass?" Cristiane teased. "I remember my gown getting soaked—"

"Nay," Meg said, coming 'round to put her hand on Cristiane's cheek. "That happened the day you went into the river to save Gilbert!"

"Oh, aye. I remember now," Cristiane said. "But I

wish we could have had music for dancing. I was so sorry the jongleurs from the castle could not—''

''They were there!'' Meg said. She suddenly caught on to the jest, and was giggling now, ready to argue every one of Cristiane's untruths, and to add some of her own. ''But 'twas too bad those eli-phaunts had to come and eat up all the food!''

Cristiane laughed and pulled Meg to her breast, hugging her tightly. ''Oh, Meggie lass...ye know I only had a wee touch of the ague, love. I willna leave ye,'' she promised, ''not ever, my wee sweet Meggie.''

Meg just held on.

Adam watched Sara take Charles's hand in her own. ''I'll be back in the morning,'' she said to him. ''You know I would not leave if Margery Smyth's babe were not breech.''

''Aye, Sara,'' Charles said weakly. ''Go and deliver the child. You're needed in town.''

Margery's nephew had come up to the castle to fetch her. There was no midwife in town, but over the years, the women had come to rely upon Sara for her help with difficult births.

'''Tis after dark, Sara,'' Adam said. ''I'll send one of my men with you, but you must still be careful on the path.''

''I will, my lord,'' she said, then turned back to Charles. ''I'll be back in the morning.''

She gave instructions to Adam, instructions that were unneeded, since Adam had seen everything that Sara had done over the last few days, and knew all the medicines that she had used for Charles. Not that any of them helped his condition.

Sara took her leave, and Adam sat in a chair near the

fire, turning it so he had a better view of his old friend. Charles had dozed off, which was a blessing, Adam supposed, for he was not coughing now, nor was his breathing quite so labored.

All was quiet for the moment, though Charles's situation was dire. He was burning up with fever again and had little awareness of his surroundings. His coughing spells were probably no worse than they'd been before, but in his weakened condition, they seemed to rattle him even more.

Adam closed his eyes and imagined Cristiane sleeping soundly in her chamber. He deeply regretted that he was not able to join her in her bed, but his responsibility as lord—and as Charles's friend—was clear. He could not leave Penyngton alone, no matter how much he wished he could go to his wife.

He dozed until Charles's coughing woke him, sometime during the night. He held him upright, supporting him so that he could catch his breath, then washed the flecks of blood from his mouth and chin. When Charles slept again, Adam returned to his chair, only to repeat these activities several times throughout the night.

"Adam..." A harsh whisper woke him once again.

Adam opened his eyes to the light of dawn and saw that Charles was awake. Adam sat up in his chair, rubbed his hand over his eyes and face, then went to him.

The patient's eyes were no longer bright with fever. Adam took his hand and sat down on the edge of the bed, looking at him intently. "How do you fare this morn?" he asked.

Charles's hand was cool, as was his face when Adam touched it.

"I...I think I'm somewhat better, my lord," Charles rasped.

Adam was afraid to count on it, but it did seem as if Charles had improved. His fever had broken once more, and he was no longer delirious. But the cough…

"Drink this," Adam said, holding a cup of water to Charles's lips. He grew even more hopeful. He was anxious for Sara to return and see the change in Charles. Even his color seemed better, and Adam did not think it was due to the rosy light of dawn.

Mayhap his friend would survive this consumption of the lung.

"Thank you for your concern, Mathilde," Cristiane said, "but I'll be taking Meg with me today. You are free to do with the day as you like."

Mathilde bristled at the dismissal, even though Cristiane tried to be kind and turn the situation to the woman's advantage. Cristiane would have thought Mathilde would appreciate having the day to herself.

"Come, Meg," Cristiane said, "and bring a wrap. 'Tis chilly outside today, and we've lots of places to explore."

"With Papa?" Meg replied, pulling on a woolen over-kirtle.

"Nay," Cristiane answered, keeping her voice light and unconcerned as she tied the kirtle in place. "He is with Sir Charles, who is not well. Get a cloak now, with a hood."

The child followed her directions and soon they were off, carrying a satchel with food for their noon meal. They left the keep and walked across the bailey to the castle wall without meeting anyone. Cristiane was especially glad not to have encountered Gerard, but she'd been braced for another nasty confrontation.

Pleasantly surprised that her preparation had not been necessary, she led the little girl out onto the path.

"Will we go to the waterfall, Cristy?"

"Not today," Cristiane replied. "There's a lovely place down by the sea."

"But—but you cannot go down to the sea here by the castle," Meg said. "There are cliffs all 'round."

"Ah, but you can," Cristiane said, "but only when you're with me or your papa."

She found the break in the rocks where 'twas possible to climb down, and carefully led Meg to the narrow sandy beach. There was a breeze down near the water, but they were adequately dressed, and it felt good to be outdoors.

They set their satchel of food and water on one of the big black rocks that jutted up from the sandy beach, and went exploring. Cristiane pointed out all the seabirds to Meg, the puffins and fulmars, and the great skua flying high overhead, then swooping to steal the catch of the smaller kittiwakes and herring gulls below.

They sat in the sun and laughed at the antics of the birds, and never heard Adam until he and the dogs were right upon them.

"My ladies," he said as the dogs ran ahead, darting in and out of the water to chase Cuddy ducks, "good morn to you."

Cristiane jumped up and Meg squealed with delight, wrapping her arms around her father's legs.

"Papa!"

He lifted her high in the air, then brought her down and kissed her. Then he took Cristiane's hand in his own and leaned over and kissed her cheek.

Cristiane blushed, and her heart pounded madly.

"How fares Sir Charles?" she asked.

"Much better today, I am pleased to say," Adam said as they resumed their walk along the beach together. He held Meg's hand and put one arm about Cristiane's waist.

Cristiane's insides were all aflutter at his touch and his news. Mayhap he would come to her tonight if Sir Charles was so improved. She could only hope he—

"Sara believes he might be over the worst," Adam added. "His fever broke this morn, and his cough is not so violent."

"That is good news, indeed," Cristiane said, though she could have done without mention of Sara Cole.

"Come," Adam said. "There is something I want to show you."

They walked on, until they reached a wide patch of sand and Adam bade them to stop. "Look out there," he said, pointing to a rocky island.

"'Tis another isle!" Meg cried. "Look, Papa!"

"Seals," Cristiane said excitedly. "They're sunning themselves, just like we were doing, Meg."

Delighted, they watched for a while as the seals dived into the water and swam, playing together, then returning to their warm places in the sun.

Adam stepped behind Cristiane and wrapped his arms around her waist, pulling her close. "I have missed you these last few nights, my lady wife," he said into her ear.

"As I have missed you, Adam," she replied, placing her hands over his. She pressed her back against him, relishing the solid wall of his chest behind her, oblivious to Meg's presence beside them.

"Tonight," he said, turning her in his arms. He dipped his head and touched his lips to hers.

She sighed and raised her arms so that they rested

upon the thick muscles of his upper arms. He gazed into her eyes for a moment, then dipped again, taking her mouth in a kiss that seared Cristiane to her toes.

Her heart fluttered as his tongue passed across her parted lips, then slipped inside. Heat built deep in her core as their mouths mated, and he slid his arms 'round her, pulling her body against his.

Suddenly, he made a quiet sound and pulled away, leaving Cristiane breathless and aching for more.

"Tonight," he repeated, then took her hand and continued up the beach.

"Pull the laces tighter, Bea," Cristiane said as Bea helped her with the gown she'd worn for her wedding. "I want it to be just as it was on my wedding day."

"Yes, my lady," Bea said, making it tighter. "'Tis a lovely gown, and the color suits you so. Madam Williamson outdid herself when she sewed this gown for you."

"Has Cook prepared all that I asked?"

"Yes, my lady," Bea replied. "'Twill be ready soon and—"

"What about wine?" Cristiane asked. "Did you find any?"

"Cook had some saved from a shipment Lord Adam brought in before he left for Scotland."

"Is it still good?"

"I'll tell Cook he's to taste it before he sends it up."

"Thank you, Bea," Cristiane said, turning to take the maid's hands in her own. She was nervous about the night ahead, and Bea had helped her with all her plans. "I don't know what I'd have done without you."

"'Twas my pleasure, my lady," Bea said, with a twinkle in her eye. "After all, you were robbed of your wedding night. 'Tis only right that you have it back...even if it is a few days late.''

Soon after it was fully dark, footmen arrived with platters of food and a bottle of wine, along with goblets and dishes. Bea quickly shooed them out of Cristiane's chamber, sending one of the men to go and ask Lord Bitterlee to attend his wife in her chamber. She and Cristiane arranged everything upon the table near the fireplace, then Bea took her leave.

It seemed to Cristiane that she checked her appearance in the small mirror a hundred times before she heard Adam's footsteps in the gallery outside her room. She very deliberately quit wringing her hands, and dropped them to her sides. At Adam's knock, she mustered all her nerve and replied calmly, ''Come in, Husband.''

Chapter Twenty-Three

Adam's eyes were fixed upon Cristiane. If he'd thought her beautiful at their wedding ceremony, she was doubly so now. The green gown enhanced the color of her eyes, which shone brightly against her fair skin. Her hair fell in soft curls to frame her face, dropping to her shoulders and down her back.

His hands itched to touch it.

"I—I've had a meal prepared for us, my lord," she said. She held herself stiffly, nervously. She bit one corner of her lower lip. "Are you h-hungry?"

His voice left him when he realized that she had recreated their wedding night.

He nodded and stepped over to the table, where plates had been set, along with a few platters of food. He spied a bottle of wine and had the truly inspired notion of getting Cristiane to drink some…and perhaps relax.

He cleared his throat, then uncorked the wine as he kept his eyes on his wife. "You are lovely in your wedding gown," he said. "Did I tell you that before?"

"Aye, my lord," she replied quietly. "Madam Williamson did a fine job—"

"She did," he interrupted, "but 'tis you who makes the gown so lovely."

He poured two goblets, then handed one to Cristiane. He lifted his cup and said, "I drink to you, my lady wife, and to many long years together."

Cristiane blushed and drank from her cup.

While they sat together on the settle and merely picked at their food, they spoke quietly of their wedding, of Meg and the isle, and of Cristiane's life in St. Oln. As Cristiane relaxed, Adam moved closer. His hands ached to touch her, but he did not want to move precipitously.

Casually, he lay one arm across the back of the settle and lightly ran his fingers over her shoulder.

"Our birds here on Bitterlee must be the same as the ones up in St. Oln," he said.

"Oh, aye," Cristiane replied, "but I've never seen a seal before."

"Meg never saw them before, either." He took a tendril of fiery hair between his fingers.

"I'm glad she was with us today, then," Cristiane said breathlessly. Her breasts rose and fell rapidly, and the pulse at the base of her throat fluttered like the wing of a tiny bird.

Desire raged through him, and he struggled to maintain control. Cristiane was sensitive to his touch, but moving too fast could be disastrous. Adam intended to have many years with her, enjoying every aspect of their marriage.

He touched the shell of her ear, then caressed her jaw. A shiver ran through her. Using one thumb, he feathered a soft touch across her lips.

"Adam…" She sighed.

He lowered his head and kissed the pulse at her throat.

"Adam." She turned slightly and lifted one hand to his shoulder. Her movements were shy and tentative, but encouraging.

He moved his lips to the edge of her jaw near her ear, breathing in her scent, tasting her. His hand slid from her shoulder to caress the upper curve of her breast. She made a small sound that caused him to think of one of the small birds on the beach.

He felt her hand on the back of his neck, stroking, teasing the hair with her fingers.

"Kiss me," she whispered. "Please, Adam, kiss me."

Adam was certain he'd misheard her. He raised his head and looked into her eyes, and found them shimmering with desire.

She wanted him.

With a groan, he slipped both arms around her and brought his lips to hers, kissing her fully, demanding as much as he gave. Her mouth was soft and sweet, and her body trembled, enticing him to seek more.

His tongue traced the seam of her lips and gained entry, her tongue shyly meeting his. He deepened the kiss, and his breath caught as her tongue grew bolder. He was unaware of having moved, but somehow she was beneath him on the settle. He pressed against her, nestling his hard body into the welcoming softness of hers.

Their heads moved and they changed angles, increasing the contact between them. His hands briefly rested upon her shoulders, then traced the outline of the delicate bones at her throat. A moment later, her breasts swelled beneath his palms, the tips beading against his fingers.

All at once, he stood and lifted Cristiane from the settle. He carried her to the bed, then set her on her feet next to it. Time stood still as he took her mouth again, caressing her shoulders and the curves of her breasts. He

located the ties that held her bodice together, and released them, then pulled the gown off her shoulders.

Cristiane quivered under his touch, though 'twas
clearly from arousal, and not from distaste.

He made quick work of his own clothes, pulling away
from Cristiane only long enough to drag his tunic over
his shoulders and head. 'Twas long enough for Cristiane
to feel embarrassed by her near nakedness, and attempt
to cover her breasts with her hands.

Adam covered her hands with his own, then raised
them to his chest, where she threaded her fingers through
the thick mat of hair. He closed his eyes for a moment
and relished the sensation of her fingers on his tight nip-
ples.

"Yes," he breathed.

He loosened the skirt of her gown and divested her of
it, then ran his hands up to her shoulders and down again
to cup the fullness of her breasts. As his thumbs teased
the taut peaks, Cristiane's head fell back.

Adam pressed his lips to the base of her throat, then
rained kisses down to her breasts, laving attention on
each one in turn, rejoicing in the arousal that made her
sigh with pleasure. He slid his hands back to her naked
hips, pulling her lower body close while Cristiane held
his head at her breast.

This was what she wanted. Adam's hands on her, his
lips touching her intimately. Naught in her past had prepared her for this, but she knew in her heart that it was
right. It was meant to be.

She felt him move slightly away from her, and knew
that, as he kissed and suckled her breasts, he was shov-
ing his chausses and braes down his legs and kicking
them away.

A second later, one hand was on her bottom, the other on her belly. He inched his fingers down until he was caressing her intimately, making her moan with the intensity of these new sensations. She'd never imagined that his touch would make her weaken and quiver so.

Heat spread everywhere he touched, its flames emanating from her core, licking her with fire all the way up her spine and down to her toes.

"Adam," she whispered.

He picked her up and eased her onto the bed, covering her with his body, one thigh between hers. He was solid and heavy, but his weight was welcome, exciting.

His eyes were dark in the flickering light of the fire and the candles. Cristiane opened to him and he breathed her name once…and again.

Adam took possession of her lips once more, kissing her as their tongues danced, mated. Cristiane shuddered and clung to him even as she welcomed him. He changed position slightly, and she felt his heated flesh at the entrance to her body.

He moaned and said, "You are moist, Cristiane… ready for me," he said, as if he could not believe it. Then he entered her, moving forward slowly, relentlessly.

Cristiane let out a tiny huff of breath, tilting to accommodate his size. His penetration was uncomfortable at first, burning and stretching her, but he stopped, giving her a moment to adjust to him.

Then he moved.

A flood of odd feelings swept through her, extraordinary sensations that propelled her forward at a dizzying speed. She had no control, and no desire for control. There was only a feeling of utter and complete freedom.

She arched against him as he moved, repeating the

motion again and again until she was consumed by a kind of pleasure that was so exquisite, so perfect, that she could not grasp its reality. 'Twas as if every sensation, every feeling and emotion she'd ever known culminated in this one wondrous moment with Adam.

His eyes were squeezed tight, his head thrown back, and all the muscles in his neck were taut. Cristiane knew he was experiencing the same kind of peak she'd known only a moment before. The thought of it was so arousing that it pushed her over the edge once more and she shattered again, even as Adam climaxed.

"Cristy!" His voice was strained, but 'twas clear he'd called her name.

They lay quietly entwined as their breathing returned to normal. Adam propped himself up on his elbows and looked down at her, then kissed the corner of her mouth. When he moved to leave her, Cristiane held on to him.

Boldly, she gazed into his eyes. "I would have you linger, m'lord," she said.

A moment passed, then Adam took her mouth again, kissing her deeply. A fierce shudder ran through him, and he was aroused again, filling her, moving with her, taking her to the same heights where she'd peaked with him only moments before.

Adam could not sleep. In awe, he watched Cristiane's lovely features as she dozed, and he marveled at the incredible hours he'd just spent with her.

Never in his wildest imaginings could he have known 'twould be like this. He'd been rendered profoundly speechless.

He had finally tucked Cristiane into the curve of his body and gently caressed her until she slept. He had no doubt she would have made love with him once again if he'd been so inclined.

He had been.

But he knew her body could not tolerate more. Not tonight, mayhap not tomorrow night. Yet now, as he lay next to his wife in her snug bed, listening to her even breaths and feeling the steady pulse in her chest, he felt hope. For the first time in years, he saw a future here on Bitterlee—for himself, for his daughter and his people.

All that they had endured over the past few years was about to change. They had a good crop in, the fishermen were successful and the livestock healthy. Even Charles looked better today than he had only yesterday.

Life was fine, indeed.

"And the ducklings can feed themselves now?" Meggie asked as she sat at Cristiane's feet near the pond.

"Aye," Cristiane replied. "They're old enough to make it on their own. But they'll still expect you to visit."

"Just like the fox at the waterfall?"

"Exactly," Cristiane said, laughing. She could not have been happier, or more content. She had awakened early that morn in Adam's arms, and had watched him sleep.

His whiskers were heavy and black in the morning, except for the thick, white line of scar along his jaw. He seemed almost boyish in sleep, without the worries and cares of his station, and Cristiane would always have him looking so untroubled, even though she knew 'twas not possible. Not for a lord who cared so much for the welfare of his people.

She felt an odd fluttering in her stomach when she thought of him, and of his kisses. She'd been embar-

rassed when he'd awakened to discover her gazing ador-
ingly at him, but he'd put her at ease with affectionate
touches and reassuring words.

He cared for her. He'd not said it exactly, but Cristiane did not know how 'twould be possible to share
such intimacy and not feel an intensity of emotion. She
was truly his wife now, and no matter what Sara Cole
had once been to him, that had surely changed.

Adam had not lingered in her chamber this morn, but
soon left to shave and dress in his own room. He had
gone to look in on Sir Charles before riding to town to
take care of some business. He had not said when he
would return, but Cristiane was unconcerned. Tonight
she would spend another glorious night in his arms.

"Will Papa come and find us here?" Meg asked.

"Aye, I hope he does," she replied, "if he returns
from town before we go back."

"He's gone to see Sara."

Meg's simple statement shattered Cristiane's new-
found confidence. She frowned, disbelieving, and shook
her head. "Nay, I donna think so, lass," she replied.

Meg laughed. "You sound so very different sometimes," she said.

But Cristiane hardly heard her. *Had* Adam gone to
see Sara? She did not like to consider that possibility,
but how could she be sure? 'Twas foolish and naive to
think that just because he'd spent the night in her bed,
his relationship with Sara was a thing of the past.

She swallowed and stilled the trembling in her hands.
How could she prepare herself to share her husband with
the townswoman?

"Cristy?" Meg asked, her face a mask of concern.
"Are you still ill?"

"N-nay, love," Cristiane stammered. "I just...thought of something, is all."

"Can we go to the waterfall now?" Meg asked. "And see if the little fox will come?"

Numbly, Cristiane allowed herself to be pulled to her feet. Meg grabbed her hand and drew her along the garden path and out the castle gate. 'Twas not until they were on the path to the waterfall that Cristiane was able to shake off her dismal thoughts.

Surely Adam had not gone to his lover the moment he'd left her bed. Meg's statement meant naught. The child had no real idea where her father had gone, but because he'd visited Sara in the past, Meg assumed he was visiting her now. Cristiane told herself she was worrying unnecessarily.

Adam returned from town and looked for his wife. She was not in her chamber, nor anywhere in the castle with Meg. Certain that they'd either be climbing the rocks on the beach or enticing the little fox down by the waterfall, he gave himself a few moments to visit with Charles. Rain threatened, and Cristiane would know it. She would soon return with Meg.

Adam greeted Sara quietly. He was more certain than ever that her feelings for Charles ran deep. She had spent the day with him, feeding him, giving him medicine and tending to his every need. 'Twas clear she could not accept the truth of his condition.

Charles looked as bad as he had two days ago. Though he'd lived through one crisis, anyone could see that there would be another. Soon. His color was gray, and he often had trouble catching his breath. Even more ominous, his cough was much weaker now.

Adam was grateful he had Cristiane to help him through this. When the end came, he would take comfort in her presence, her love. He had no doubt of her feelings for him, and at his first opportunity, he would tell her that he felt the same.

He did not know why he'd been reticent last night, except he'd been so stunned by her reaction to his lovemaking. Never in his wildest imaginings had he ever thought he'd have so sensual a wife, a woman whose appetite for him would equal his own.

"Sara..." he said when Charles dozed off. Adam drew her out of the chamber and stood in the shadowy gallery next to the hall. "Sara, you mus—"

"Please, my lord," she replied, "don't say it."

Adam hesitated, but knew he had to speak up. "It grieves me to say it, but it's time to prepare yourself. The fever may have abated, but you can see for yourself that he is not long for—"

She raised one hand and covered his lips as she burst into tears. Adam pulled her to him and held her.

"I know he cannot survive this, Adam," she said, her voice choked by her tears.

Adam ran one hand up and down her back, then smoothed a lock of hair back from her forehead. It hurt to see his sister so distressed, to know her anguish was caused by the imminent death of his closest friend.

"I've loved him ever since I came to Bitterlee," she said. "He was so kind to me, but he always said he was too old to take a wife, too old to sire the children he said I should have."

Adam did not know what to say, so he remained silent and let Sara whisper her secrets, her sorrows.

And he held her, offering what little comfort he could.

*   *   *

Dark clouds hovered low over the isle as Cristiane and Meg hurried up the path toward home. Cristiane wanted to be inside before the rain came. The white walls of the castle rose majestically ahead, and she was struck by the thought of this place as her home. This was where she belonged, where she would stay.

She was desperately in love with her husband and could only pray that he would soon come to love her. She vowed to do all in her power to be a good wife to him, so that he could not help but feel the same. She only needed to keep him from Sara for a time, and she would win his affections.

They entered the bailey through the gates and saw Gerard Sutton approaching on foot, a water skin slung over his arm, and a heavily laden satchel in his other hand. Cristiane's eyes darted around, looking for a route of escape, but found none. She had no choice but to walk past him.

"Tending the simpleton again, I see," he jeered.

Besides all the other emotions churning through her, anger boiled to the surface, and Cristiane decided she could no longer play the docile outcast. Adam had chosen her for his wife, even if his reason had been solely because of her talent with Meg. The child was her daughter now, and Cristiane would tolerate no more insults toward her.

"Meggie, love, run to the keep and go up to your chamber," she said. "Wait for me there."

The child did as she was told, and Cristiane turned to face the vile uncle of her husband. "You have berated my daughter once too many times, Sir Gerard," she said. "I'll not tolerate it again. Guard your tongue when you speak to her or—"

"Or what?" he scoffed. An evil light glittered in his eye as he spoke again. "You'll tell your husband? The man who has Sara Cole in his arms even now?"

The bottom fell out of Cristiane's stomach. She pressed her lips together to keep them from trembling, and braced herself against the wave of pain that threatened to overcome her. "You lie."

He laughed, then shrugged as if it were inconsequential. "See for yourself. They're hardly discreet—standing in the hall where anyone can see them."

Cristiane pulled her cloak about her and strode purposefully toward the keep, blocking the sound of Gerard's laughter from her ears. She entered through the door next to the chapel, just as Meg had done. Quietly, afraid of what she would see, yet certain that Gerard had lied only to hurt her, she walked down the gallery toward the great hall.

She stopped suddenly and felt the world shift under her feet. Gerard had not lied.

In the shadows across from her stood Adam and Sara, exactly as Gerard had described—locked in a tender embrace.

Pain hit hard, stealing her breath away. Tears welled in her eyes as the truth struck her, and Cristiane backed away from the sight of Adam holding his lover in his arms, caressing her, talking with her in low, intimate tones.

Cristiane found herself walking across the bailey again, hardly aware of her surroundings, propelled by some unconscious momentum. She stumbled out through the castle gate and continued on, half running along the path, oblivious to the darkening clouds or the increasing winds.

Eventually, she came to the break in the rocks, where

she climbed down the craggy cliff to the sea. With the wind whipping her clothes, she picked her way among the boulders, desperate to get as far from the castle as possible. She could not stay there. She had to get away and think!

Mayhap in time she could accustom herself to sharing her husband with the woman he loved, but today was not that day. Her emotions were raw after she'd spent a blissful night in his arms, only to discover it had meant naught to him.

She'd given all to Adam, her body as well as her heart. She had felt cherished and desired, and for the first time in ages, she'd felt as if she belonged.

She'd been wrong.

By the time she reached the water, big drops of rain had started to fall, but Cristiane did not care. She held her cloak around her and kept moving, farther than she'd gone before—losing herself in the wind and rain, heedless of the high waves and crashing surf. The storm pelted her now, soaking through her cloak, drenching her hair. She stumbled once and fell, scraping the heel of one hand on a rock.

She hardly noticed.

Awareness of her surroundings did not come until the wind was so strong that Cristiane could not catch her breath. She suddenly felt the chill through to her bones and realized that the heavy gusts might very well push her into the sea.

And she did not want to die. She wanted to make a life on Bitterlee with Adam and Meg. She was no coward. She had been a fool to run away from the challenge of winning her husband. Sara Cole might still have a hold on Adam's heart, but 'twas a tenuous one. It *had* to be.

With a resurgence of hope in her heart, Cristiane started back toward the cliff and began to look for shelter.

Rain battered the window of Cristiane's empty chamber. Adam had looked for her everywhere in the castle, but she was nowhere to be found.

He looked down at his daughter, whose eyes were bright with fear, and asked again, "She told you she would come to you here?"

"I-in my chamber, Papa."

"Let's look again, then," he said, though he had no real hope of finding her there. She had disappeared. Vanished.

And if he didn't find her, his heart would never be the same.

Holding Meg's hand, he returned to her chamber, where they both sat on the bed. Meg was distraught with the storm and the rumbles of thunder that were still far off in the distance. Adam wanted to shout questions at the child, but he knew he could not push her. "Tell me again, sweetheart," he said, controlling his anxiety, "what did Cristy say to you?"

"She said I was to r-run along to the keep, and wait in my chamber. A-and she would come to me here."

"How long ago?" he asked, though he doubted his daughter had any concept of time. "Was it this morn, after you broke your fast? Or—"

"'Twas not long ago, Papa," she cried, tears now streaming down her face. The sight of them wrenched Adam's heart, and he hugged her close. "We were at the p-pond, but it was going to rain, so we came back."

"But Cristy sent you ahead?"

"So she could t-talk to...to Sir G-Gerard."

Damnation! He should have known there was more to it. "What did Sir Gerard say?" Adam asked, keeping his voice level and controlled as he held her.

"He was cruel, Papa, and he m-made Cristy angry."

Adam moved away enough to be able to see his daughter's face. "And you have not seen her since?"

"No, Papa."

A kind of rage that Adam had not felt in years welled up in him, and he felt as if he would burst. If Gerard had done aught to endanger Cristiane, Adam would have no qualms about dispensing due punishment. "Come on," he said to Meg, taking her hand and helping her off the bed. He lifted her up and carried her out into the gallery and down the steps, quickly reaching the great hall.

He found Mathilde and put Meg in her care, with the admonishment that the child was not to be put on her knees for any reason. Then he suggested that the nurse-maid locate the children of the kitchen maids, and help to supervise all the children in play.

Grabbing a thick oilcloth cloak from a peg by the door, Adam whistled for his dogs. Ren and Gray jumped up from their places on the hearth and circled him excitedly. As soon as Adam opened the door, they bounded out of the keep ahead of him.

The clouds were thick and low, and the rain came down in torrents, but the worst of the storm had yet to reach the isle. Adam pulled up his hood, tucked his head down and made his way through the castle gate.

He paid no attention to the ache in his thigh, but followed the muddy path, considering only where Gerard might have taken Cristiane. And why.

He could not imagine Cristiane going willingly with his uncle...nor could he understand why Gerard would

take her away from the keep. It made no sense. Unless
Cristiane had run away from Gerard and had been unable
to get back to the castle.

That was the only explanation possible.

Adam reached the point where they would have left
the path to go down to the waterfall, but remembered
that was not one of Gerard's favored places. Nay, the
man had a cave far down the beach, where he liked to
go and drink himself into a stupor, and relive his past
glories in the army of King Edward.

Adam was certain that was where he would find him.

Chapter Twenty-Four

Cristiane watched as the storm came closer. Long daggers of lightning flashed close by, striking the water and setting off earsplitting crashes of thunder.

She felt minimally protected under an overhang of the cliff, but knew it would do her no good if the storm came closer and lightning struck. She wished she'd kept her wits about her when she'd run from the castle, but the shock of seeing Adam with Sara had overwhelmed her good sense.

Cristiane didn't realize how much she had counted on Adam breaking off with the townswoman, how much she needed his loyalty and devotion. She did not know how she was going to live here on Bitterlee as his wife, knowing that, in truth, she was no more than a nursemaid for his daughter.

She'd thought, after the previous night, that she was more to him…that perhaps he felt as she did, that there could be no one else, that—

A streak of lightning struck close, the shock of it knocking Cristiane to her knees. More frightened now, she could not decide whether to quickly move away from her little shelter, or stay and wait out the tempest.

Remembering what her father had taught her about storms, she decided to stay here, under cover of the over-hang.

She moved slightly, into a crouch, with her head down and her arms about her knees. The storm raged all around her, but Cristiane could not move. Fear of the violent weather and misery over Adam's duplicity paralyzed her. 'Twas foolish, she knew, to be so affected by Adam's actions, for her mother had prepared her for the likelihood of her husband keeping a mistress.

Yet, at their wedding, Adam had promised to love and honor her, to guard her and to forsake all others. Had he lied? Did all English husbands lie when they married?

Cristiane's brain hurt with all her ruminations. She'd gone from thinking that Adam *must* care for her as she did for him, to believing him capable of going to his mistress mere hours after sharing the most intimate of experiences with her.

She did not know what to think anymore.

After a time, it seemed that the lightning no longer struck so close, and the thunder was not as earth-shaking. Yet the rain continued to pour down, and the wind was still fierce. Somewhere in the distance, Cristiane thought she heard a different sound. She raised her head from her arms and listened.

Barking!

Adam's dogs were out in this tempest. Surely some-one would have brought them inside rather than allowing them to run free during a storm like this. They were suddenly upon her, barking and baying, as if they'd discovered the most delectable prey.

''Cristiane!''

Adam had never seen a more pitiful sight. She looked half-drowned and miserable. Gerard was nowhere in sight. "Are you all right?" he shouted over the combined noise of the dogs and the storm.

She began to speak, but then shook her head, as if unable to form the words to answer him.

"Where is Gerard?" he asked as he helped her to her feet.

He saw her shrug before he pulled her into his arms to hold her shivering body against him. They had to get out of this rain. He would not have her fall ill again.

"Come on," he said, taking her hand and leading her farther down the beach. "We have to get to shelter. This rain will last for hours."

They stayed close to the overhang, but the rain pelted them as they moved down the beach. Cristiane said naught, and Adam wondered what had happened to her. She had no visible injuries, but if Gerard had hurt her, Adam would not merely banish him from Bitterlee.

He would kill him.

Gerard's cave was not much farther. The dogs ran ahead, seemingly oblivious to the rain, while Adam strained his eyes, looking for the niche in the cliff where Gerard liked to go to brood. Adam put his arm around Cristiane and drew her close as they walked, but neither of them spoke.

"Up there!" he said when he saw the place. Let Gerard try to refuse them entry, he thought as he helped Cristiane up the rocks. He would haul his uncle's sorry arse to the sea and throw him in.

They clambered over loose rock to get to the entrance, but still Adam could see no sign of Gerard. "Just a few steps more, Cristiane," he urged.

They finally made it, and Adam drew her inside with him. 'Twas dark, but there was no indication of another occupant. He had not been here since he was a lad, and would have forgotten the place, except that Gerard had mentioned it once or twice in passing. Adam wondered where his uncle had gone.

"Come inside," he said. "'Tis safe here."

Still quiet, Cristiane followed him.

Adam knew Gerard would not spend so much time here without a few comforts. He allowed his eyes to adjust to the dark, then looked around to discover a lamp sitting on a table formed from rocks. He lit it, then turned back to Cristiane.

"I'll get a fire going and then you'll have to get out of those wet clothes," he said.

When she still did not speak, he said, "Cristy, what is it? What happened? Did Gerard bring you out here?"

"Nay, 'twas not your uncle," she replied.

"What then? Why are you out here in this tempest?"

"I..." She sniffed once and wiped the rain from her face.

"You what?"

She did not reply for a long time. Finally, she shook her head in a derisive manner. "I was just f-foolish, Adam," she said. "I thought...I believed that..." Crossing her arms, she rubbed them with her hands and turned away from him.

He took hold of one arm and turned her back. He would not let her withdraw from him. Whatever had happened could be redressed. "What? *What* did you think?"

"'Twas stupid really...."

"Cristy, tell me."

Her brows quivered and her nostrils flared as she forced back her tears. Adam looked into her eyes and saw pain there. He felt powerless. All he could do was run his hands up and down her arms.

"'Twas just as Gerard said when I came into the

k-keep and saw you with Sara,'' she said, her voice trembling as she strove to maintain control. ''I knew then that he was r-right. You l-love her, but only married me bec—''

''God's Cross, Cristy!'' Adam said, pulling her into his arms as understanding dawned. All the cruel remarks his uncle had made, all his outrageous insinuations…*''Never* listen to Gerard. He is a bitter old man who loves naught more than to stir up trouble.''

''But I saw y—''

''You saw me comforting my sister,'' he said as he leaned away to look at her. ''Sara is my father's bastard daughter. I should have told you before, but I… With Charles so ill, and you coming down with the fever, I just…''

Confusion clouded her eyes. Her chin trembled and she bit the corner of her lower lip.

''Sara cares deeply for Charles,'' Adam said. ''And it pains her to see him suffer.''

''Poor Sara!'' Cristiane cried. ''I never realized.… Oh, Adam, I feel terrible. Gerard's been saying things ever since I came here…about Sara, and how well suited she is to the isle. He intimated how much better a wife she would make you, so much better than a loathsome Scot. I tried not to heed him, but 'twas impossible. He seemed to always be there, ready to prey on all my—''

''—on all your uncertainties.'' Adam frowned. Gerard had deliberately worked to undermine Cristiane's confidence and comfort. If he'd been at it ever since her arrival on Bitterlee, 'twas no wonder she had believed the worst when she'd seen him with Sara. ''Cristy,'' he said, pulling her close, ''there is no other woman in my life. There is you, and only you.''

He lowered his head and kissed her while cupping her

face in his hands. There were fresh tears on her cheeks, and he rubbed them away with his thumbs. "Do not weep, love," he murmured, kissing her again and again. "'Twas only Gerard tormenting you. Naught that he said was real, or true."

She nodded and took a deep, quavering breath.

Reluctantly, he let her go. "Let me get a fire started," he said. "We must warm you and get you dry."

There were no spare clothes, nor any blankets in the cave. The oilcloth cloak had kept Adam reasonably dry, and so Cristiane lay wrapped up in it next to him, on a primitive pallet that Gerard had set up deep inside the cave. A fire, made from driftwood that Gerard must have dragged in, burned near the mouth of the cave, and the dogs lay nearby, guarding the entrance. Cristiane's clothes were draped over some rocks near the fire in the hope that they would dry.

She doubted they would. The rain was still coming down in sheets, and showed no sign of letting up.

Not that she cared. She was content to stay here, safe and warm in the arms of her husband, with all her worries about him—and his lover—untrue.

"Why did you not talk to me about Sara?" Adam asked. He held her close, caressing her back as they lay together.

"I was embarrassed," she said, lowering her eyelids so she would not have to look at him. "I...thought if I...if you..." She shook her head and frowned, still uncomfortable speaking of it. "Was I to ask you outright about your lover?"

"Cristy..." he said, tipping her chin up and forcing her to look at him. "I love you." He kissed her deeply, slipping his hands inside the oilcloth, caressing the bare flesh beneath. "There could be no one else for me."

"Oh, Adam," she whispered, "I love you, too. I could not bear it, thinking you cared for Sara, and I did not know what to do. I ran from the castle without thinking."

"Promise me you'll never run away again," he said huskily. His hand slipped down to trace tantalizing patterns over her buttocks. "Come to me if aught troubles you, Cristy. We must talk to one another...."

"Aye, in future, I will," she whispered as goose bumps rose on her skin.

Then Adam's hand stilled. He was silent, pensive for a moment. "I wonder if Gerard drove Rosamund to her death with his insinuations."

"Drove her?" Cristiane asked.

"She caused her own death," he said grimly, "by jumping from one of the castle parapets."

Cristiane took in a sharp breath. "Oh, Adam," she said. "I am so sorry. I cannot imagine what you went through."

"She died a week before I was carried back to the isle from the battle at Falkirk," he continued. "If he taunted and goaded her with untruths just as he's done to you..."

Cristiane felt sickened, and covered her mouth with one hand. Gerard had succeeded in manipulating her to a point near utter despair. 'Twas not difficult to believe that he'd done the same to Rosamund.

"Sir Gerard's tenure on the isle is finished. When I see him next, I intend to banish him," Adam said, tucking Cristiane firmly against him once again. "He can return to King Edward's court or fend for himself elsewhere. I'll not have him disrupting my family."

Cristiane swallowed the lump in her throat. Her fears were for naught, and Adam would see to it that Gerard caused neither her nor Meg any problems in the future.

She could ask for no more.

"Oh! *Meg!*" Cristiane cried. "I told her to wait for me in her chamber and—"

"She is fine," Adam said. He began to nuzzle Cristiane's neck. "Playing with the servants' children."

"Oh," she replied, relieved. "Ooh…" She closed her eyes, and her breath came quick and fast as Adam's lips moved lower, his hands spreading the oilcloth apart. His mouth sought the hard peaks of her breasts, then he teased each one with his tongue and teeth as his hands slid down her body.

"Teach me, Adam," Cristiane said, boldly unfastening his belt. "I want to please you."

"Ah, Cristy," Adam replied, already exquisitely aroused. "To please me, you have naught to do but touch me, love me. Hunger for my touch."

She moved his chausses and braes aside and grazed his most sensitive flesh with her hands. "I do, m'lord," she breathed. "I do."

Epilogue

Castle Bitterlee
Autumn, 1303

Bitterlee's two noble swans paddled regally across the pond, their small brood following faithfully. How they'd happened to come to Bitterlee was a mystery to all on the isle, but no one questioned it overmuch. The beautiful fowl seemed to exemplify the recent growth and prosperity of the isle.

Music played all around, and the castle grounds were teeming with townspeople, here to celebrate the harvest and the renaming of the isle. There had already been games and dancing, and soon the feasting would begin.

Adam stood behind the bench where Cristiane sat holding their tiny son, Thomas, and rubbed her shoulders. While Thomas slept, she tipped her head, first to one side, then to the other, to afford Adam better access. Her muscles were tired after the long day, and his attentions were appreciated, but Cristiane always cherished Adam's touch.

"Ah…that feels heavenly, Adam," she said.

He leaned down, touching his lips to her ear. "'Tis naught compared to what I have in mind for later, love," he said quietly. Shivers of delight ran though her with his promising words.

"Oh?" she asked, smiling. "And what might that be?"

"*Mama,*" Meg called out, "Charles will not hold my hand near the water!"

Adam sighed. "I'll handle this," he said, straightening. "Your son is a feisty lad."

"*My* son?" she said, displaying a distinctly innocent face.

Adam tossed back a smile at her as he went to deal with little Charles, who had been a trial to his sister ever since he'd learned to walk.

Naturally the children had a nurse, but Cristiane would never wholly entrust their care to her, not after seeing the damage that a mediocre nurse could do to a child. Though Mathilde had done only what she'd thought best, she had nearly succeeded in making Meggie as timid and fearful as she'd made Rosamund.

"The lad knows his own mind, m'lord," Sir Raynauld remarked. He had become Adam's seneschal soon after Charles Penyngton's death, and was proving to be an apt manager.

Cristiane knew that Adam missed Charles, just as he missed Sara, who had left Bitterlee more than a year before.

Their lives were full, though, and life was good on the isle. So good that Adam had decided that their home had been called the Isle of Bitter Life long enough. 'Twas time to change its name to reflect the prosperity and joy of its inhabitants. And he'd petitioned the king for permission to do just that.

Cristiane's heart beat a little faster as she watched her husband lift his small, giggling son to his shoulders. Those big hands that she'd always admired were so gentle and loving, with her and with their children.

Little Charles ruffled his fingers though his father's hair, making a delightful mess of it.

"He is stubborn is all," Meg said in true sisterly fashion. "He could fall into the pond, and then what?"

"Why, you would have to reach in and save him," Adam said.

"Any young maid who swims as well as you should have no trouble," Raynauld added.

But Meg's annoyance with her little brother was clear, as was her opinion of her father's and Raynauld's teasing. She lifted her chin in a truly superior manner, turned and walked away with great dignity, until she saw some of her friends running down the path. Then she quickly shrugged off her regal air and joined them.

Cristiane repositioned Thomas and stood up. His birth in midsummer had been an easy one, and she felt as fit as ever. Adam returned to her with Charles still on his shoulders, and put one arm around her waist.

"My lord," Raynauld said, "they're signaling for you to come and begin the feast."

Taking their leave of the pond, they started down the path, back to the bailey, where trestle tables had been set up out-of-doors, and were now laden with platters of food and pitchers of ale.

"Have you decided whether to give your speech before or after the meal, my lord?" Raynauld asked.

"Before," Adam replied. "If I wait until later, they'll all be too far into their cups to hear my brilliant remarks."

The children's young nurse met them near the keep

and took the baby and Charles away. Adam placed Cristiane's hand upon his own and accompanied her, with great formality, to the dais.

Adam gained everyone's attention and began his speech, talking of their great harvest, and the season's tremendous fishing successes. He spoke with pride of his growing family, of the traditions of the isle and of his hopes for the future.

"Which is why I've asked the king to allow me to call our isle home by another name. A new name...a more fitting name. Raise your cups," he called out, even as he raised his own. Cristiane came to her feet next to him and he put his arm around her. "Drink to the Isle of Hope!"

There was silence for a moment while they drank, then the cups hit the tables, and the shouts and applause were deafening. The music resumed and Adam looked down at Cristiane. She had brought love and good fortune to him. She had given him the hope he now felt in his heart.

When she looked up at him, her eyes were bright with pride and happiness.

"You know you are queen of the Isle of Hope," he said, taking her in his arms.

"Only if you are king, my lord," she replied.

"Do not mention that to King Edward," he jested. Then he tipped his head down, while she raised hers, and their lips met somewhere in between. Adam pulled her close and kissed her deeply, as she slipped her arms around his shoulders, then up to his neck.

Their actions did not go unnoticed. The crowd clapped and cheered noisily at their lord and lady's amorous activity.

Adam was breathless when he finally broke the kiss,

but he kept his wife in his embrace. "You are my life and my hope, Cristiane," he said fervently. "I love you."

She reached up and touched his face. "Oh Adam," she replied. "My life could not be fuller, or happier. I love you, too. With all my heart and my soul."

Hand in hand, they joined the crowd, enjoying the frolics of the inhabitants of Hope.

* * * * *

My Lady's Pleasure

The intoxicating new Regency from

Julia Justiss

bestselling author of
My Lady's Trust

New to the passion galloping in
her veins, Lady Valeria Arnold
was shocked by the wanton
impulses that drew her to
Teagan Fitzwilliams. The
dashing rake was nothing more
than a wastrel with the devil's
own luck at cards—surely not
the kind of man that a woman
could trust her heart to. Or
was all that about to change...?

"Justiss is a promising
new talent..."
—*Publishers Weekly*

MY LADY'S PLEASURE
Available in bookstores June 2002

Harlequin Historicals®
Historical Romantic Adventure!

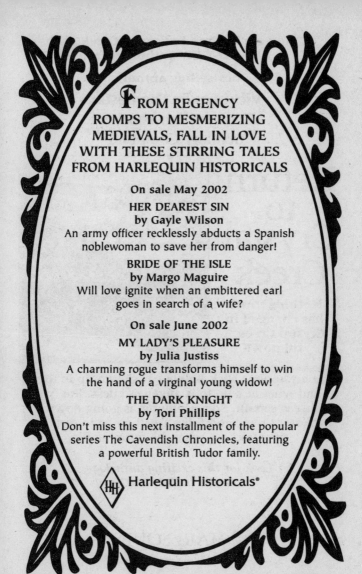

C'mon back home to Crystal Creek with a BRAND-NEW anthology from

bestselling authors

Vicki Lewis Thompson
Cathy Gillen Thacker
Bethany Campbell

Return to Crystal Creek

Nothing much has changed in Crystal Creek... till now!

The mysterious Nick Belyle has shown up in town, and what he's up to is anyone's guess. But one thing is certain. Something big is going down in Crystal Creek, and folks aren't going to rest till they find out what the future holds.

*Look for this exciting anthology,
on-sale in July 2002.*

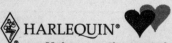

If you enjoyed what you just read,
then we've got an offer you can't resist!

Take 2 bestselling
love stories FREE!
Plus get a FREE surprise gift!